EX LIBRIS

VINTAGE CLASSICS

A BURNT-OUT CASE

Graham Greene was born in 1904. On coming down from Balliol College, Oxford, he worked for four years as sub-editor on *The Times*. He established his reputation with his fourth novel, *Stamboul Train*. In 1935 he made a journey across Liberia, described in *Journey Without Maps*, and on his return was appointed film critic of the *Spectator*. In 1926 he was received into the Roman Catholic Church and visited Mexico in 1938 to report on the religious persecution there. As a result he wrote *The Lawless Roads* and, later, his famous novel *The Power and the Glory*. *Brighton Rock* was published in 1938 and in 1940 he became literary editor of the *Spectator*. The next year he undertook work for the Foreign Office and was stationed in Sierra Leone from 1941 to 1943. This later produced the novel, *The Heart of the Matter*, set in West Africa.

As well as his many novels, Graham Greene wrote several collections of short stories, four travel books, six plays, three books of autobiography – *A Sort of Life*, *Ways of Escape* and *A World of My Own* (published posthumously) – two of biography and four books for children. He also wrote hundreds of essays, and film and book reviews, some of which appear in the collections *Reflections* and *Mornings in the Dark*. Many of his novels and short stories have been filmed and *The Third Man* was written as a film treatment. Graham Greene was a member of the Order of Merit and a Companion of Honour. He died in 1991.

ALSO BY GRAHAM GREENE

Novels

The Man Within
It's a Battlefield
A Gun for Sale
The Confidential Agent
The Ministry of Fear
The Third Man
The End of the Affair
The Quiet American
Travels with my Aunt
Dr Fischer of Geneva or
The Bomb Party
The Human Factor
The Tenth Man
Stamboul Train
England Made Me
Brighton Rock
The Power and the Glory
The Heart of the Matter
The Fallen Idol
Loser Takes All
Our Man in Havana
The Comedians
The Honorary Consul
Monsignor Quixote
The Captain and the Enemy

Short Stories

Collected Stories
The Last Word and Other Stories
May We Borrow You Husband?
Twenty-One Stories

Travel

Journey Without Maps
The Lawless Roads
In Search of a Character
Getting to Know the General

Essays

Yours etc.
Reflections
Mornings in the Dark
Collected Essays

Plays

Collected Plays

Autobiography

A Sort of Life
Ways of Escape
Fragments of an Autobiography
A World of my Own

Biography

Lord Rochester's Monkey
An Impossible Woman

Children's Books

The Little Train
The Little Horse-Bus
The Little Steamroller
The Little Fire Engine

GRAHAM GREENE

A Burnt-out Case

WITH AN INTRODUCTION BY
Giles Foden

VINTAGE BOOKS
London

Published by Vintage 2004

5 7 9 10 8 6

Copyright © Graham Greene 1960

Introduction copyright © Giles Foden 2004

First published in Great Britain by William Heinemann 1960

First published by Vintage in 2001

Vintage
Random House, 20 Vauxhall Bridge Road,
London SW1V 2SA

www.vintage-classics.info

Addresses for companies within The Random House Group Limited
can be found at: www.randomhouse.co.uk/offices.htm

The Random House Group Limited Reg. No. 954009

A CIP catalogue record for this book
is available from the British Library

ISBN 9780099478430

The Random House Group Limited supports The Forest Stewardship
Council (FSC), the leading international forest certification organisation.
All our titles that are printed on Greenpeace approved FSC certified
paper carry the FSC logo. Our paper procurement policy can be
found at www.rbooks.co.uk/environment

Set in Sabon by Palimpsest Book Production Ltd
Grangemouth, Stirlingshire

Printed and bound in Great Britain by
CPI Cox & Wyman, Reading, RG1 8EX

Introduction

In some ways this was a perfect book for me – even though its themes and concerns are very much in the realm of imperfection. I first read it as a young Catholic growing up in Africa, at a time when leper colonies were still common. I can remember visiting one with my mother. It was run by nuns at Ntakataka on Lake Malawi. I was horrified by the sheer smoothness of the attenuated limbs that the former lepers proferred, just as happens in the novel: 'Deo Gratias was knocking on the door. Querry heard the scrape of his stump as it attempted to raise the latch. A pail of water hung on his wrist like a coat on a cloakroom knob.'

For me the book's power was amplified by the fact that five or six years before I read *A Burnt-out Case* my father had lost most of one of his arms in a car accident in the bush. It left him with a rounded stump like those of the men and women I had seen in the leprosarium. He had an artificial arm with a socket for the stump and a hand that grabbed, but they were too hot to wear very often in the tropics. He had a hook that clipped into the arm, too, but we just kept that in a drawer.

At the time I was struggling, as do young and old, and not just in Africa, with the exigencies of a faith that seemed to be of no help whatsoever in a place beset with disease and death. So Greene's story of Querry, the celebrated architect who comes to the Congo simply to escape and finds the world and, perhaps, God catching up with him, held my interest.

Yet I had come to *A Burnt-out Case* (published in 1960) after reading *The Heart of the Matter* (1948), and initially found the earlier book more enjoyable. The story of Scobie's fall seemed to offer so much more incident and excitement. At the level of novelistic satisfaction, if not psychological impact, I felt something was lacking from *A Burnt-out Case*. Later I realised that was exactly the point. The thrust of the novel is, somewhat paradoxically, to express a sense of 'lack'; to make you feel that something you had expected is missing.

Greene goes into the issue of what a reader might expect from a novel in *A Burnt-out Case* in some depth. 'A writer doesn't write for his readers, does he?' says Querry at one point, adding that he has to take 'elementary precautions all the same to make them comfortable'. Querry tells Rycker – the factory manager who spreads news of the architect's arrival – that he dramatises too much. Can we interpret this as Greene's self-reproach about *The Heart of the Matter* and his still more reader-friendly 'entertainments'? In his memoir, *Ways of Escape*, he describes *The Heart of the Matter* as 'a success in the great vulgar sense of that term', adding that there 'must have been something corrupt there, for the book appealed too often to weak elements in its readers'.

In *A Burnt-out Case*, the corrupting presence is the yellow-press journalist Montagu Parkinson, who comes in search of Querry: 'There is a strong allurement in corruption and there was no doubt of Parkinson's; he carried it on the surface of his skin like phosphorus, impossible to mistake.' Like Rycker, Parkinson alters the truth to hype things up. This theme in the novel – the sense that both Rycker and Parkinson appeal to the market, to the fallen world – is one of the reasons for the continuing relevance of *A Burnt-out Case*. The novel skirts the market-driven values of the adventure tale or romance with some distaste, integrating those worries into the piece in the characters of Rycker and Parkinson.

It is not a friendly book, and, as he mentions in *Ways of Escape*, Greene himself found it difficult to write. 'I went to the Belgian Congo in January 1959 with a new novel already beginning to form in my head by way of a situation – a stranger who turns up in a remote leper settlement for no apparent reason . . . Never had a novel proved more recalcitrant or more depressing. The reader had only to endure the company of the burnt-out character called in the novel Querry for a few hours' reading, but the author had to live with him and in him for eighteen months.'

Reading A Burnt-out Case again, I am struck by a strong sense of how it stands in relation to the colonial literature that preceded it. The Bishop's boat, in which Querry travels up the river, that 'resembled a small battered Mississippi paddle-steamer with a high nineteenth-century forestructure', is powerfully reminiscent of the 'tin-pot steamer' in Conrad's Heart of Darkness. One can draw many parallels between Querry and Marlow. Both have a strong sense of moral disgust, even if Marlow does not share Querry's degree of (self-proclaimed) inner desolation. As an author, too, Conrad shared Greene's complex relation with genre fiction; both used adventure tropes in a semi-parodic fashion.

We know Greene read a lot of Conrad. He quotes Conrad's Congo diary in his travel book Journey without Maps (1936) to show what he calls the 'unexplained brutality' of Africa. Immediately afterwards comes a reference to Céline's Voyage au Bout de la Nuit. Used to describe the sense of despair so often associated with the continent, it is reminiscent of passages in A Burnt-out Case: 'Hidden away in all this flowering forest of twisted vegetation, a few decimated tribes of natives squatted among fleas and flies, crushed by taboos and eating nothing all the time but rotten tapioca.'

Perhaps the most powerful literary figure whose legacy Querry inherits is that of Heyst in another novel by Conrad, namely Victory. Like Querry, Heyst says he believes in 'nothing', and wants 'nothing' – nothing except to be left alone, which is why he retreats to his island, a paradise that is bound to be disturbed. Querry retreats instead to a kind of hell (the leprosarium), and finds a sort of peace there. But the lifebuoy thrown him by fate is only a temporary one, just as Heyst's idyll with Lena in Victory is temporary. Respite must come to an end like everything else.

Greene is consumed with this idea of ending, in particular

with the paradox of what is left after something has gone. This idea of the residual is symbolically rendered by the lepers' truncated arms and legs. When does a limb stop being a limb? Querry, in describing how he is finished with architecture and womanising as well as religion, is constantly using such phrases as 'I have come to an end of all that'; but every time he says such things it is as if he is emphasising their persistence. A cognate of the word for 'end' in Céline's title, *bout*, seems useful here: Querry is always at the 'butt' of faith, but it never quite burns down.

In some ways the novel can be read as an investigation of post-Christian faith, an attempt to see what can be raised from the ashes of a century notable for its cruelty. Yet it is dangerous to see *A Burnt-out Case* in such totalising terms. Its appeal to or against ending feels closer to Matthew Arnold's poem about ebbing Christian faith, 'Dover Beach', than to works written in response to the Holocaust. Some further remarks in Greene's *Ways of Escape* appear to recognise the way in which Arnold's poem acts as a 'nineteenth-century forestructure' for the novel:

This account may seem cynical and unfeeling, but in the years between *The Heart of the Matter* and *The End of the Affair* I felt myself used and exhausted by the victims of religion. The vision of faith as untroubled sea was lost for ever; faith was more like a tempest in which the lucky were engulfed and lost, and the unfortunate survived to be flung battered and bleeding on the shore. A better man could have found a life's work on the margin of that cruel sea, but my own course of life gave me no confidence in any aid I might proffer. I had no apostolic mission, and the cries for spiritual assistance maddened me because of my impotence. What was the Church for but to aid these sufferers? What was the priesthood for? I was like a man without medical knowledge in a village struck with plague. It was in those years, I think, that Querry was born, and Father Thomas too.

But Arnold is far too well-adjusted and Anglican to be a father figure for Greene. His greatest intellectual debt is to the bastardised Jansenism of François Mauriac, with his fascination for *le dieu caché*, the absent God of negative theology. There is something of this in the Superior's sermon in the course of the story: 'Bad things are not there – they are nothing. Hate means no love. Envy means no justice. They are just empty spaces where Yezu ought to be.'

This kind of reverse feedback effect works through *A Burnt-out Case* at the level of individual psychology as well as at the high pitch of the cosmogonic. Just as la Pharisienne in Greene's 1945 essay on Mauriac, 'under her layer of destructive egotism and false pity is disclosed sympathetically to the religious core,' so too Querry must show himself faithful, even if it is through gritted teeth. In this way revelation of character becomes akin to divine revelation: the process of insight is the 'reverse of the obvious' as Greene puts it earlier in the essay.

For all that, the obvious is very much with us. Nowhere is it more so than in Africa, where brutality and despair show man's fallen state – show our imperfections, our lack of wholeness – so very plainly. History, human time, is the operative ground for this. Yet although such recent moral outrages as the Sharpeville massacre are referenced in the novel, Greene's response is a theological one to the human condition in general rather than to the particular cruelties of the age. Indeed the whole notion of 'the age' (and all ages) is brought into question, as the imponderable notion of what might lie beyond human time – beyond the sheer, sublunary idea of time itself – is considered.

For it is not just a question of Querry himself becoming a burnt-out case, like a leper whose disease has run its course. Finality bestrides the novel like a stone colossus. When the cuckolded Greek trader whose story Doctor Colin remembers drives his car into his shop-front, the vehicle comes 'to the final halt of all time' against the cash-register. The lepers themselves, progressing towards 'the limit of mutilation', stand in for all humanity – for the sense that we are all 'amputees of space', as the one-armed Swiss poet Blaise Cendrars once memorably put it.

God knows, you do not have to be suffering from leprosy

or have lost an arm to feel that something is missing from life. Cut off from divinity, these days, coming to our dusty end, any day soon, what hope can there be? Doctor Colin raises the possibility that evolution might save us, but Querry dismisses this as the 'old song of progress' (another Conradian reference), pointing out that it is 'every bit as superstitious as what the fathers believe'.

Colin, in turn, dismisses Querry's dismissal, saying that one has to gamble on one's superstitions. In a sense this is what Querry does, placing his faith in the mysterious utterance made by his African 'servant' and fellow burnt-out case Deo Gratias. 'Pendélé,' the word the man keeps repeating when Querry finds him half dead in a swamp, does not yield an exact meaning, but Colin hazards a guess that it 'means something the same as *Bunkasi* – and that meant pride, arrogance, perhaps a kind of dignity and independence'.

Querry thinks otherwise. 'I am certain he meant a place – somewhere in the forest, somewhere near water, where something of great importance was happening to him.' He uses the word 'strangled' to describe how Deo Gratias felt in the leprosarium, and this may be the clue to the meaning of 'Pendélé.' According to David Ward in his critical book on literature set in Africa, *Chronicles of Darkness* (1989), the word seems to occupy a multiple, 'variable space in which psychological, cultural, political, religious, even mystical interpretations of independence, dignity, pride, may be entertained . . . It has something to do with the constricting relationship between Deo Gratias and the world of *dependence* which the well-meaning missionary Fathers have set up in the interior.'

But the puzzle may not be so easily enfolded in the colonial context that Ward gives it. 'Pendélé' seems French, or possibly creolised French, rather than African: otherwise why the accents? Through the root French verb *pendre*, to hang, it has many connotations besides dependence. There is a glancing reference to hanging in the novel at one point, but the true suggestion of 'Pendélé' may be something closer to 'suspension' or 'support'. When Querry finds Deo Gratias it is beneath a rotten bridge made of tree trunks, and the reader immediately thinks of an earlier, extremely plangent passage:

In the deep bush trees grew unnoticeably old through centuries and here and there one presently died, lying half collapsed for a while in the ropy arms of the lianas until sooner or later they gently lowered the corpse into the only space large enough to receive it, and that was the road, narrow like a coffin or a grave.

Talking to Deo Gratias about the incident later, Querry manages to wheedle out of him that the water associated with the putative place 'Pendélé' 'fell from the sky'; and it also seems reasonably clear that the African 'was a child in those days on your mother's back'. The only certainty is that in the time of 'Pendélé' – '*nous étions heureux*,' as Deo Gratias puts it. We were happy.

The suspension that was there in those paradisal days has gone, but the accumulative power of all these vague gestures towards the idea of suspension is considerable. They seem to me to link to the idea of the God-shaped hole that Greene inherited from Mauriac. To have been suspended at all, one needs a kind of sky-hook. Even if we have fallen, the hook was once there. Just as the amputee or leper can sense his phantom limb, so something – or Someone – once held it up.

Maybe this 'irreducible grain of faith', as Philip Stratford (one of Greene's editors) has called it, is the best we can hope for. It is a laughable idea of course, but there it is. And anyway, laughter may be what cures Querry, along with that curious form of self-suspension which involves helping others. As Doctor Colin puts it: 'He'd learned to serve other people, you see, and to laugh. An odd laugh, but it was a laugh all the same.'

Giles Foden, 2004

To Docteur Michel Lechat

Dear Michel,

I hope you will accept the dedication of this novel which owes any merit it may have to your kindness and patience; the faults, failures and inaccuracies are the author's alone. Dr Colin has borrowed from you his experience of leprosy and nothing else. Dr Colin's leproserie is not your leproserie – which now, I fear, has probably ceased to exist. Even geographically it is placed in a region far from Yonda. Every leproserie, of course, has features in common, and from Yonda and other leproseries which I visited in the Congo and the Cameroons I may have taken superficial characteristics. From the fathers of your Mission I have stolen the Superior's cheroots – that is all, and from your Bishop the boat that he was so generous as to lend me for a journey up the Ruki. It would be a waste of time for anyone to try to identify Querry, the Ryckers, Parkinson, Father Thomas – they are formed from the flotsam of thirty years as a novelist. This is not a *roman à clef*, but an attempt to give dramatic expression to various types of belief, half-belief, and non-belief, in the kind of setting, removed from world-politics and household-preoccupations, where such differences are felt acutely and find expression. This Congo is a region of the mind, and the reader will find no place called Luc on any map, nor did its Governor and Bishop exist in any regional capital.

You, if anyone, will know how far I have failed in what I attempted. A doctor is not immune from 'the long despair of doing nothing well', the *cafard* that hangs around a writer's life. I only wish I had dedicated to you a better book in return for the limitless generosity I was shown at Yonda by you and the fathers of the Mission.

Affectionately yours,
Graham Greene

A BURNT-OUT CASE

PART ONE

CHAPTER 1

I

The cabin-passenger wrote in his diary a parody of Descartes: 'I feel discomfort, therefore I am alive,' then sat pen in hand with no more to record. The captain in a white soutane stood by the open windows of the saloon reading his breviary. There was not enough air to stir the fringes of his beard. The two of them had been alone together on the river for ten days – alone, that is to say, except for the six members of the African crew and the dozen or so deck-passengers who changed, almost indistinguishably, at each village where they stopped. The boat, which was the property of the Bishop, resembled a small battered Mississippi paddle-steamer with a high nineteenth-century forestructure, the white paint badly in need of renewal. From the saloon windows they could see the river before them unwind, and below them on the pontoons the passengers sat and dressed their hair among the logs of wood for the engine.

If no change means peace, this certainly was peace, to be found like a nut at the centre of the hard shell of discomfort – the heat that engulfed them where the river narrowed to a mere hundred metres: the shower that was always hot from the ship's engine: in the evening the mosquitoes, and in the day the tsetse flies with wings raked back like tiny jet-fighters (a board above the bank at the last village had warned them in three languages: 'Zone of sleeping sickness. Be careful of the tsetse flies'). The captain read his breviary with a fly-whisk in his hand, and whenever he made a kill he held up the tiny corpse for the passenger's inspection, saying 'tsetse' – it was nearly the limit of their communication, for neither spoke the other's language with ease or accuracy.

This was somewhat the way in which the days passed. The passenger would be woken at four in the morning by the tinkling sound of the sanctus bell in the saloon, and presently from the window of the Bishop's cabin, which he shared with a crucifix, a chair, a table, a cupboard where cockroaches lurked, and one picture – the nostalgic photograph of some church in Europe covered in a soutane of heavy snow – he would see the congregation going home across the gang-plank. He would watch them as they climbed the steep bank and disappeared into the bush, swinging lanterns like the carol singers he had once seen during his stay in a New England village. By five the boat was on the move again, and at six as the sun rose he would eat his breakfast with the captain. The next three hours, before the great heat had begun, were for both men the best of the day, and the passenger found that he could watch, with a kind of inert content, the thick, rapid, khaki-coloured stream against which the small boat fought its way at about three knots, the engine, somewhere below the altar and the Holy Family, groaning like an exhausted animal and the big wheel churning away at the stern. A lot of effort it seemed for so slow a progress. Every few hours a fishing village came into sight, the houses standing high on stilts to guard them against the big rains and the rats. At times a member of the crew called up to the captain, and the captain would take his gun and shoot at some small sign of life that only he and the sailor had eyes to detect among the green and blue shadows of the forest: a baby crocodile sunning on a fallen log, or a fishing eagle which waited motionless among the leaves. At nine the heat had really begun, and the captain, having finished reading his breviary, would oil his gun or kill a few more tsetse flies, and sometimes, sitting down at the dining-table with a box of beads, he would set himself the task of manufacturing cheap rosaries.

After the midday meal both men retired to their cabins as the forests sauntered by under the exhausting sun. Even when the passenger was naked it was difficult for him to sleep, and he was never finally able to decide between letting a little draught pass through his cabin or keeping the hot air out.

The boat possessed no fan, and so he woke always with a soiled mouth, and while the warm water in the shower cleaned his body it could not refresh it.

There yet remained another hour or two of peace towards the end of the day, when he sat below on a pontoon while the Africans prepared their chop in the early dark. The vampire bats creaked over the forest and candles flickered, reminding him of the Benedictions of his youth. The laughter of the cooks went back and forth from one pontoon to the other, and it was never long before someone sang, but he couldn't understand the words.

At dinner they had to close the windows of the saloon and draw the curtains to, so that the steersman might see his way between the banks and snags, and then the pressure-lamp gave out too great a heat for so small a room. To delay the hour of bed they played *quatre cent vingt et un* wordlessly like a ritual mime, and the captain invariably won as though the god he believed in, who was said to control the winds and waves, controlled the dice too in favour of his priest.

This was the moment for talk in garbled French or garbled Flemish if they were going to talk, but they never talked much. Once the passenger asked, 'What are they singing, father? What kind of song? A love song?'

'No,' the captain said, 'not a love song. They sing only about what has happened during the day, how at the last village they bought some fine cooking-pots which they will sell for a good profit farther up the river, and of course they sing of you and me. They call me the great fetishist,' he added with a smile and nodded at the Holy Family and the pull-out altar over the cupboard where he kept the cartridges for his gun and his fishing-tackle. He killed a mosquito with a slap on his naked arm and said, 'There's a motto in the Mongo language, "The mosquito has no pity for the thin man."'

'What do they sing about me?'

'They are singing now, I think.' He put the dice and counters away and listened. 'Shall I translate for you? It is not altogether complimentary.'

'Yes, if you please.'

3

'"Here is a white man who is neither a father nor a doctor. He has no beard. He comes from a long way away – we do not know from where – and he tells no one to what place he is going nor why. He is a rich man, for he drinks whisky every evening and he smokes all the time. Yet he offers no man a cigarette."'

'That had never occurred to me.'

'Of course,' the captain said, 'I know where you are going, but you have never told me why.'

'The road was closed by floods. This was the only route.'

'That wasn't what I meant.'

About nine in the evening they usually, if the river had not widened and thus made navigation easy, pulled into the bank. Sometimes they would find there a rotting upturned boat which served as shelter when it rained for unlikely passengers. Twice the captain disembarked his ancient bicycle and bounced off into the dark interior to try to obtain some cargo from a *colon* living miles away and save it from the hands of the Otraco company, the great monopolist of the river and the tributaries, and there were times, if they were not too late in tying up, when they received unexpected visitors. On one occasion a man, a woman, and a child, with sickly albino skins that came from years of heat and humidity, emerged from the thick rain-forest in an old station wagon; the man drank a glass or two of whisky, while he and the priest complained of the price that Otraco charged for fuelling wood and spoke of the riots hundreds of miles away in the capital, while the woman sat silent holding the child's hand and stared at the Holy Family. When there were no European visitors there were always the old women, their heads tied up in dusters, their bodies wrapped in mammy-cloths, the once bright colours so faded that you could scarcely detect the printed designs of match-boxes, soda-water siphons, telephones, or other gimmicks of the white man. They shuffled into the saloon on their knees and patiently waited under the roaring pressure-lamp until they were noticed. Then, with an apology to his passenger, the captain would send him to his cabin, for these were confessions that he had to hear in secret. It was the end of one more day.

II

For several mornings they were pursued by yellow butterflies which were a welcome change from the tsetses. The butterflies came tacking into the saloon as soon as it was light, while the river still lay under a layer of mist like steam on a vat. When the mist cleared they could see one bank lined with white nenuphars which from a hundred yards away resembled a regiment of swans. The colour of the water in this wider reach was pewter, except where the wheel churned the wake to chocolate, and the green reflection of the woods was not mirrored on the surface but seemed to shine up from underneath the paper-thin transparent pewter. Two men who stood in a pirogue had their legs extended by their shadows so that they appeared to be wading knee-deep in the water. The passenger said, 'Look, father, over there. Doesn't that suggest to you an explanation of how Christ was thought to be walking on the water?' but the captain, who was taking aim at a heron standing behind the rank of nenuphars, did not bother to answer. He had a passion for slaughtering any living thing, as though only man had the right to a natural death.

After six days they came to an African seminary standing like an ugly red-brick university at the top of the clay bank. At this seminary the captain had once taught Greek, and so they stopped here for the night, partly for old times' sake and partly to enable them to buy wood at a cheaper price than Otraco charged. The loading began immediately – the young black seminarists were standing ready, before the ship's bell rang twice, to carry the wood on to the pontoons so that the boat might be cast off again at the first hint of light. After their dinner the priests gathered in the common-room. The captain was the only one to wear a soutane. One father, with a trim pointed beard, dressed in an open khaki shirt, reminded the passenger of a young officer of the Foreign Legion he had once known in the East whose recklessness and ill-discipline had led to an heroic and wasteful death; another of the fathers might have been taken for a professor of economics, a third for a lawyer, a fourth for a doctor, but the too easy laughter, the exaggerated excitement over some simple game of cards with matches for stakes had the innocence and immaturity of isolation – the innocence of explorers marooned on an ice-cap or of men imprisoned by a war which has long passed out of hearing. They turned the radio on for the evening news, but this was just habit, the imitation of an act performed years ago for a motive they no longer remembered clearly; they were not interested in the tensions and changing cabinets of Europe, they were barely interested in the riots a few hundred miles away on the other side of the river, and the passenger became aware of his own safety among them – they would ask no intrusive questions. He was again reminded of the Foreign Legion. If he had been a murderer escaping from justice, not one would have had the curiosity to probe his secret wound.

And yet – he could not tell why – their laughter irritated him, like a noisy child or a disc of jazz. He was vexed by the pleasure which they took in small things – even in the bottle of whisky he had brought for them from the boat. Those who marry God, he thought, can become domesticated too – it's just as hum-drum a marriage as all the others. The word 'Love' means a formal touch of the lips as in the ceremony of the Mass, and 'Ave Maria' like 'dearest' is a phrase to open a letter. This marriage like the world's marriages was held together by habits and tastes shared in common between God and themselves – it was God's taste to be worshipped and their taste to worship, but only at stated hours like a subur-ban embrace on a Saturday night.

The laughter rose higher. The captain had been caught cheating, and now each priest in turn tried to outdo his neigh-bour by stealing matches, making surreptitious discards, call-ing the wrong suit – the game, like so many children's games, was about to reach an end in chaos, and would there be tears before bed? The passenger got impatiently up and walked away from them around the dreary common-room. The face of the new Pope, looking like an eccentric headmaster, stared at him from the wall. On top of a chocolate-coloured dresser lay a few *romans policiers* and a stock of missionary journals. He opened one: it reminded him of a school magazine. There was an account of a football match at a place called Oboko and an old boy was writing the first instalment of an essay called 'A Holiday in Europe'. A wall-calendar bore the photograph of another mission: there was the same kind of hideous church built of unsuitable brick beside a priest's verandahed house. Perhaps it was a rival school. Grouped in front of the buildings were the fathers: they were laughing too. The passenger wondered when it was that he had first begun to detest laughter like a bad smell.

He walked out into the moonlit dark. Even at night the air was so humid that it broke upon the cheek like tiny beads of rain. Some candles still burned on the pontoons and a torch moved along the upper deck, showing him where the boat was moored. He left the river and found a rough track which started behind the classrooms and led towards what geographers might have called the centre of Africa. He followed it a short way, for no reason that he knew, guided by the light of moon and stars; ahead of him he could hear a kind of music. The track brought him into a village and out the other side. The inhabitants were awake, perhaps because the moon was full: if so they had marked its exact state better than his diary. Men were beating on old tins they had salvaged from the mission, tins of sardines and Heinz beans and plum jam, and someone was playing a kind of home-made harp. Faces peered at him from behind small fires. An old woman danced awkwardly, cracking her hips under a piece of sacking, and again he felt taunted by the innocence of the laughter. They were not laughing at him, they were laughing with each other, and he was abandoned, as he had been in the living-room of the seminary, to his own region where laughter was like the unknown syllables of an enemy tongue. It was a very poor village: the thatch of the clay huts had been gnawed away a long time since by rats and rain, and the women wore only

CHAPTER 2

I

Doctor Colin examined the record of the man's tests – for six months now the search for the leprosy bacilli in smears taken from the skin had shown a negative result. The African who stood before him with a staff under his shoulder had lost all his toes and fingers. Doctor Colin said, 'Excellent. You are cured.'

The man took a step or two nearer to the doctor's desk. His toeless feet looked like rods and when he walked it was as though he were engaged in pounding the path flat. He said with apprehension, 'Must I go away from here?'

Doctor Colin looked at the stump the man held out like a piece of wood which had been roughly carved into the beginnings of a human hand. There was a rule that the leproserie should take contagious cases only: the cured had to return to their villages or, if it were possible, continue what treatment was necessary as out-patients in the hospital at Luc, the provincial capital. But Luc was many days away whether by road or river. Colin said, 'It would be hard for you to find work outside. I will see what can be done for you. Go and speak to the sisters.' The stump seemed useless, but it was extraordinary what a mutilated hand could be taught to do; there was one man in the leproserie without fingers who had been taught to knit as well as any sister. But even success could be saddening, for it showed the value of the material they had so often to discard. For fifteen years the doctor had dreamt of a day when he would have funds available for constructing special tools to fit each mutilation, but now he hadn't money enough even to provide decent mattresses in the hospital.

'What's your name?' he asked.

9

'Deo Gratias.'

Impatiently the doctor called out the next number.

It was a young woman with palsied fingers – a claw-hand. The doctor tried to flex her fingers, but she winced with the stab of the nerves, though she continued to smile with a kind of brave coquetry as though she thought in that way she might induce him to spare her further pain. She had made up her mouth with a mauve lipstick which went badly with the black skin, and her right breast was exposed, for she had been feeding her baby on the dispensary step. Her arm was scarred for half its length where the doctor had made an incision to release the ulnar nerve which had been strangled by its sheath. Now the girl was able with an effort to move her fingers a further degree. The doctor wrote on her card, for the sisters' attention, 'Paraffin wax', and turned to the next patient.

In fifteen years Doctor Colin had only known two days hotter than this one. Even the Africans were feeling the heat, and half the usual number of patients had come to the dispensary. There was no fan, and Doctor Colin worked below a make-shift awning on the veranda: a table, a hard wooden chair, and behind him the little office that he dreaded to enter because of the insufficient ventilation. His filing cabinets were there, and the steel was hot to the touch.

Patient after patient exposed his body to him; in all the years he had never become quite accustomed to the sweet gangrenous smell of certain leprous skins, and it had become to him the smell of Africa. He ran his fingers over the diseased surface and made his notes almost mechanically. The notes had small value, but his fingers, he knew, gave the patients comfort: they realized that they were not untouchable. Now that a cure had been found for the physical disease, he had always to remember that leprosy remained a psychological problem.

From the river Doctor Colin heard the sound of a ship's bell. The Superior passed by the dispensary on his bicycle, riding towards the beach. He waved, and the doctor raised his hand in answer. It was probably the day for the Otraco boat which was long overdue. It was supposed to call once a fortnight with mail, but they could never depend on it, for it was delayed more often than not by unexpected cargo or by a faulty pipe.

A baby began to cry and immediately like dogs all the babies around the dispensary started to howl together. 'Henri,' Doctor Colin called; his young African dispenser rapped out a phrase in his native tongue – 'Babies to the breast' and instantaneously peace returned. At twelve-thirty the doctor broke off for the day. In the little hot office he wiped his hands with spirit.

He walked down towards the beach. He had been expecting a book to be sent him from Europe: a Japanese Atlas of Leprosy, and perhaps it had come with the mail. The long street of the leper village led towards the river: small two-roomed houses built of brick with mud huts in the yards behind. When he had arrived fifteen years ago there had been only the mud huts – now they served as kitchens, and yet still when anyone was about to die, he would retire into the yard. He couldn't die peacefully in a room furnished with a radio-set and a picture of the latest Pope; he was prepared to die only where his ancestors had died, in the darkness surrounded by the smell of dry mud and leaves. In the third yard on the left an old man was dying now, sitting in a battered deck-chair, inside the shadow of the kitchen door.

Beyond the village, just before the river came into sight, the ground was being cleared for what would one day be the new hospital block. A gang of lepers was pounding the last square yards supervised by Father Joseph, who worked beside them, beating away himself at the ground in his old khaki pants and a soft hat which looked as though it had been washed up on the beach many years ago.

'Otraco?' Doctor Colin called out to him.

'No, the Bishop's boat,' Father Joseph replied, and he paced away, feeling the ground with his feet. He had long ago caught the African habit of speaking as he moved, with his back turned, and his voice had the high African inflexion. 'They say there's a passenger on board.'

'A passenger?'

Doctor Colin came into sight of the funnel where it stuck up between the long avenue of logs that had been cut ready for fuel. A man was walking up the avenue towards him. He raised his hat, a man of his own age, in the late fifties with a grizzled morning stubble, wearing a crumpled tropical suit. 'My name is Querry,' he introduced himself, speaking in an accent which Colin could not quite place as French or Flemish any more than he could immediately identify the nationality of the name.

'Doctor Colin,' he said. 'Are you stopping here?'

'The boat goes no farther,' the man answered, as if that were indeed the only explanation.

II

Once a month Doctor Colin and the Superior went into a confidential huddle over figures. The support of the leproserie was the responsibility of the Order; the doctor's salary and the cost of medicine were paid by the State. The State was the richer and the more unwilling partner, and the doctor made every effort to shift what burden he could from the Order. In the struggle with the common enemy the two of them had become close friends – Doctor Colin was even known occasionally to attend Mass, though he had long ago, before he had come to this continent of misery and heat, lost faith in any god that a priest would have recognized. The only trouble the Superior ever caused him was with the cheroot which the priest was never without, except when saying Mass and in sleep; the cheroots were strong and Doctor Colin's quarters cramped, and the ash always found a way between his pamphlets and reports. Now he had to shake the ash off the accounts he had prepared for the chief medical officer in Luc; in them he had deftly and unobtrusively transferred to the State the price of a new clock and three mosquito-nets for the mission.

'I am sorry,' the Superior apologized, dropping yet more ash on to an open page of the Atlas of Leprosy. The thick bright colours and the swirling designs resembled the reproduction of a Van Gogh landscape, and the doctor had been turning the pages with a purely aesthetic pleasure before the Superior joined him. 'Really I am impossible,' the Superior said, brushing at the page. 'Worse than usual, but then I've had a visit from M. Rycker. The man upsets me.'

'What did he want?'

'Oh, he wanted to find out about our visitor. And of course he was very ready to drink our visitor's whisky.'

'Was it worth three days' journey?'

'Well, at least he got the whisky. He said the road had been impossible for four weeks and he had been starved of intellectual conversation.'

'How is his wife – and the plantation?'

'Rycker seeks information. He never gives it. And he was anxious to discuss his spiritual problems.'

'I would never have guessed he had any.'

'When a man has nothing else to be proud of,' the Superior said, 'he is proud of his spiritual problems. After two whiskies he began to talk to me about Grace.'

'What did you do?'

'I lent him a book. He won't read it, of course. He knows all the answers – six years wasted in a seminary can do a lot of harm. What he really wanted was to discover who Querry might be, where he came from, and how long he was going to stay. I would have been tempted to tell him if I had known the answer myself. Luckily Rycker is afraid of lepers, and Querry's boy happened to come in. Why did you give Querry Deo Gratias?'

'He's cured, but he's a burnt-out case, and I don't want to send him away. He can sweep a floor and make a bed without fingers or toes.'

'Our visitors are sometimes fastidious.'

'I assure you Querry doesn't mind. In fact he asked for him. Deo Gratias was the first leper whom he saw when he came off the boat. Of course I told him the man was cured.'

'Deo Gratias brought me a note. I don't think Rycker liked me touching it. I noticed that he didn't shake hands with me when he said good-bye. What strange ideas people have about leprosy, doctor.'

'They learn it from the Bible. Like sex.'

'It's a pity people pick and choose what they learn from the Bible,' the Superior said, trying to knock the end of his cheroot into the ashtray. But he was always doomed to miss.

'What do you think of Querry, father? Why do you think he's here?'

'I'm too busy to pry into a man's motives. I've given him a room and a bed. One more mouth to feed is not an embarrassment. And to do him justice he seemed very ready to help – if there were any help that he was capable of giving. Perhaps he is only looking for somewhere quiet to rest in.'

'Few people would choose a leproserie as a holiday resort. When he asked me for Deo Gratias I was afraid for a moment that we might have a leprophil on our hands.'

'A leprophil? Am I a leprophil?'

'No, father. You are here under obedience. But you know very well that leprophils exist, though I daresay they are more often women than men. Schweitzer seems to attract ·them. They would rather wash the feet with their hair like the woman in the gospel than clean them with something more antiseptic. Sometimes I wonder whether Damien was a leprophil. There was no need for him to become a leper in order to serve them well. A few elementary precautions – I wouldn't be a better doctor without my fingers, would I?'

'I don't find it very rewarding looking for motives. Querry does no harm.'

'The second day he was here, I took him to the hospital. I wanted to test his reactions. They were quite normal ones – nausea not attraction. I had to give him a whiff of ether.'

'I'm not as suspicious of leprophils as you are, doctor. There are people who love and embrace poverty. Is that so bad? Do we have to invent a word ending in phil for them?'

'The leprophil makes a bad nurse and ends by joining the patients.'

'But all the same, doctor, you've said it yourself, leprosy is a psychological problem. It may be very valuable for the leper to feel loved.'

'A patient can always detect whether he is loved or whether it is only his leprosy which is loved. I don't want leprosy loved. I want it eliminated. There are fifteen million cases in the world. We don't want to waste time with neurotics, father.'

'I wish you had a little time to waste. You work too hard.'

But Doctor Colin was not listening. He said, 'You remember that little leproserie in the bush that the nuns ran. When D.D.S. was discovered to be a cure, they were soon reduced to half a dozen patients. Do you know what one of the nuns said to me? "It's terrible, doctor. Soon we'll have no lepers at all." There surely was a leprophil.'

'Poor woman,' the Superior said. 'You don't see the other side.'

'What other side?'

'An old maid, without imagination, anxious to do good, to be of use. There aren't so many places in the world for people like that. And the practice of her vocation is being taken away from her by the weekly doses of D.D.S. tablets.'

'I thought you didn't look for motives.'

'Oh, mine's a very superficial reading like your own diagnosis, doctor. But it would be a good thing for all of us if we were even more superficial. There's no real harm in a superficial judgement, but if I begin to probe into what lies behind that desire to be of use, oh well, I might find some terrible things, and we are all tempted to stop when we reach that point. Yet if we dug farther, who knows? – the terrible too might be only a few skins deep. Anyway it's safer to make superficial judgements. They can always be shrugged off. Even by the victims.'

'And Querry? What of him? Superficially speaking, of course.'

PART TWO

CHAPTER I

I

In an unfamiliar region it is always necessary for the stranger
to begin at once to construct the familiar, with a photograph
perhaps or a row of books if they are all that he has brought
with him from the past. Querry had no photographs and no
books except his diary. The first morning when he was woken
at six by the sound of prayers from the chapel next door, he
felt the panic of complete abandonment. He lay on his back
listening to the pious chant, and if there had been some magic
power in his signet ring, he would have twisted it and asked
whatever djinn answered him to be transferred again to that
place which for want of a better name he called his home.
But magic, if such a thing existed at all, was more likely to
lie in the rhythmical and incomprehensible chant next door.
It reminded him, like the smell of a medicine, of an illness
from which he had long recovered. He blamed himself for
not realizing that the area of leprosy was also the area of this
other sickness. He had expected doctors and nurses: he had
forgotten that he would find priests and nuns.

Deo Gratias was knocking on the door. Querry heard the
scrape of his stump as it attempted to raise the latch. A pail
of water hung on his wrist like a coat on a cloakroom-knob.
Querry had asked Doctor Colin before engaging him whether
he suffered pain, and the doctor had reassured him, answering that mutilation was the alternative to pain. It was the
palsied with their stiffened fingers and strangled nerves who
suffered – suffered almost beyond bearing (you heard them
sometimes crying in the night), but the suffering was in some
sort a protection against mutilation. Querry did not suffer,
lying on his back in bed, flexing his fingers.

And so from the first morning he set himself to build a routine, the familiar within the unfamiliar. It was the condition of survival. Every morning at seven he breakfasted with the fathers. They drifted into their common-room from whatever task they had been engaged on for the last hour, since the chanting had ceased. Father Paul with Brother Philippe was in charge of the dynamo which supplied electricity to the Mission and the leper village; Father Jean had been saying Mass at the nuns' house; Father Joseph had already started the labourers to work on clearing the ground for the new hospital; Father Thomas, with eyes sunk like stones in the pale clay of his face, swallowed his coffee in a hurry, like a nauseating medicine, and was off to superintend the two schools. Brother Philippe sat silent, taking no part in any conversation: he was older than the fathers, he could speak nothing but Flemish and he had the kind of face which seems worn away by weather and patience. As the faces began to develop features as negatives do in a hypo-bath, Querry separated himself all the more from their company. He was afraid of the questions they might ask, until he began to realize that, like the priests in the seminary on the river, they were going to ask none of any importance. Even the questions they found necessary were phrased like statements – 'On Sundays a bus calls here at six-thirty if you wish to go to Mass' – and Querry was not required to answer that he had given up attending Mass more than twenty years before. His absence was never remarked.

After breakfast he would take a book he had borrowed from the doctor's small library and go down to the bank of the river. It had widened out in this reach and was nearly a mile across. An old tin barge, rusty with long disuse, enabled him to avoid the ants; and he sat there until the sun, soon after nine, became too high for comfort. Sometimes he read, sometimes he simply watched the steady khaki flow of the stream, which carried little islands of grass and water jacinth endlessly down at the pace of crawling taxis, out of the heart of Africa, towards the far-off sea.

On the other shore the great trees, with roots above the ground like the ribs of a half-built ship, stood out over the green jungle wall, brown at the top like stale cauliflowers. The cold grey trunks, unbroken by branches, curved a little this way and a little that, giving them a kind of reptilian life. Porcelain-white birds stood on the backs of coffee-coloured cows, and once for a whole hour he watched a family who sat in a pirogue by the bank doing nothing; the mother wore a bright yellow dress, the man, wrinkled like bark, sat bent over a paddle he never used, and a girl with a baby on her lap smiled and smiled like an open piano. When it was too hot to sit any longer in the sunlight he joined the doctor at the hospital or the dispensary, and when that was over half the day had safely gone. He no longer felt nausea from anything he saw, and the bottle of ether was not required. After a month he spoke to the doctor.

'You are very short-handed, aren't you, for dealing with eight hundred people?'

'Yes.'

'If I could be of any use to you – I know I am not trained . . .'

'You will be leaving soon, won't you?'

'I have no plans.'

'Have you any knowledge of electro-therapy?'

'No.'

'You could be trained, if you were interested. Six months in Europe.'

'I don't want to return to Europe,' Querry said.

'Never?'

'Never. I am afraid to return.' The phrase sounded in his own ears melodramatic and he tried to withdraw it. 'I don't mean afraid. Just for this reason and that.'

The doctor ran his fingers over the patches on a child's back. To the unpractised eye the child looked perfectly healthy. 'This is going to be a bad case,' Doctor Colin said. 'Feel this.'

Querry's hesitation was no more perceptible than the leprosy. At first his fingers detected nothing, but then they stumbled on places where the child's skin seemed to have grown an extra layer. 'Have you no kind of electrical knowledge?'

'I'm sorry.'

'Because I'm expecting some apparatus from Europe. It's long overdue. With it I will be able to take the temperature of the skin simultaneously in twenty places. You can't detect it with your fingers, but this nodule here is warmer than the skin around it. I hope one day to be able to forestall a patch. They are trying that in India now.'

'You are suggesting things too complicated for me,' Querry said. 'I'm a man of one trade, one talent.'

'What trade is that?' the doctor asked. 'We are a city in miniature here, and there are few trades for which we could not find a place.' He looked at Querry with sudden suspicion. 'You are not a writer, are you? There's no room for a writer here. We want to work in peace. We don't want the press of the world discovering us as they discovered Schweitzer.'

'I'm not a writer.'

'Or a photographer? The lepers here are not going to be exhibits in any horror museum.'

'I'm not a photographer. Believe me I want peace as much as you do. If the boat had gone any farther, I would not have landed here.'

'Then tell me what your trade is, and we will fit you in.'

'I have abandoned it,' Querry said. A sister passed on a bicycle busy about something. 'Is there nothing simple I can do to earn my keep?' he asked. 'Bandaging? I've had no training there either, but it can't be difficult to learn. Surely there has to be someone who washes the bandages. I could release a more valuable worker.'

'That is the sisters' province. My life here would not be worth living if I interfered with their arrangements. Are you feeling restless? Perhaps next time the boat calls you could go back to the capital. There are plenty of opportunities in Luc.'

'I am never going to return,' Querry said.

'In that case you had better warn the fathers,' the doctor said with irony. He called to the dispenser, 'That's enough. No more this morning.' While he washed his hands in spirits he took a look at Querry over his shoulder. The dispenser was shepherding the lepers out and they were alone. He said, 'Are you wanted by the police? You needn't be afraid of telling me – or any of us. You'll find a leproserie just as safe as the Foreign Legion.'

'No. I've committed no crime. I assure you there's nothing of interest in my case. I have retired, that's all. If the fathers don't want me here, I can always go on.'

'You've said it yourself – the boat goes no farther.'

'There's the road.'

'Yes. In one direction. The way you came. It's not often open though. This is the season of rains.'

'There are always my feet,' Querry said.

Colin looked for a smile, but there was none on Querry's face. He said, 'If you really want to help me and you don't mind a rough journey you might take the second truck to Luc. The boat may not be back for weeks. My new apparatus should have arrived by now in the town. It will take you about eight days there and back – if you are lucky. Will you go? It will mean sleeping in the bush, and if the ferries are not working you'll have to return. You can hardly call it a road,' he went on; he was determined that the Superior should not accuse him of persuading Querry to go. 'It's only if you want to help . . . you can see how impossible it is for any of us. We can't be spared.'

'Of course. I'll start right away.'

It occurred to the doctor that perhaps here too was a man under obedience, but not to any divine or civil authority, only to whatever wind might blow. He said, 'You could pick up some frozen vegetables too and some steak. The fathers and I could do with a change of diet. There's a cold storage at Luc. Tell Deo Gratias to fetch a camp-bed from my place. If you put a bicycle in the back you could spend the first night at the Perrins', but you can't reach them by truck. They are down by the river. Then there are the Chantins about eight hours farther on – unless they've gone home, I can't remember. And last of all there's always Rycker at the second ferry, about six hours from Luc. You'd get a warm welcome from him, I'm sure of that.'

'I'd rather sleep in the lorry,' Querry said. 'I'm not a sociable man.'

'I warn you, it's not an easy journey. And we could always wait for the boat.'

He paused a while for Querry to answer, but all that Querry

found to say was, 'I shall be glad to be of use.' The distrust between them deadened intercourse; it seemed to the doctor that the only sentences he could find to speak with any safety had been preserved for a long time in a jar in the dispensary and smelt of formaldehyde.

II

The river drew a great bow through the bush, and generations of administrators, who had tried to cut across the arc with a road from the regional capital of Luc, had been defeated by the forest and the rain. The rain formed quagmires and swelled the tributary streams until the ferries were unusable, while at long intervals, spaced like a layer of geological time, the forest dropped trees across the way. In the deep bush trees grew unnoticeably old through centuries and here and there one presently died, lying half collapsed for a while in the ropy arms of the lianas until sooner or later they gently lowered the corpse into the only space large enough to receive it, and that was the road, narrow like a coffin or a grave. There were no hearses to drag the corpse away; if it was to be removed at all it could only be by fire.

During the rains no one ever tried to use the road; a few *colons* in the forest would then be completely isolated unless, by bicycle, they could reach the river and camp there in a fisherman's village until a boat came. Then, when the rains were over, weeks had still to pass before the local government could spare the men to build the necessary fires and clear the road. After a few years of complete neglect the road would have dis-appeared completely and forever. The forest would soon convert it to a surface crawl, like the first scratches on a wall of early man, and there would remain then reptiles, insects, a few birds and primates, and perhaps the pygmoids – the only human beings in the forest who had the capacity to survive without a road.

The first night Querry stopped the truck at a turn in the road where a track led off towards the Perrins' plantation. He opened a tin of soup and a tin of Frankfurters, while Deo Gratias put up a bed for him in the back of the truck and lit the paraffin cooker. He offered to share his food with Deo

Gratias, but the man had some mess of his own ready prepared in a pot wrapped in an old rag, and the two of them sat in silence with the truck between them as though they were in separate rooms. When the meal was over Querry moved round the bonnet with the intention of saying something to Deo Gratias, but the 'boy' by rising to his feet made the occasion as formal as though Querry had entered his hut in the village, and the words, whatever they were, died before they had been spoken. If the boy had possessed an ordinary name, Pierre, Jean, Marc, it might have been possible to begin some simple sentence in French, but Deo Gratias – the absurd name stuck on Querry's tongue.

He walked a little way from the truck, because he knew how far he was from sleep, up the path which led eventually to the river or to the Perrins, and he heard the thud of Deo Gratias's feet behind him. Perhaps he had followed with the idea of protecting him or perhaps because he feared to be left alone in the dark beside the truck. Querry turned with impatience because he had no wish for company, and there the man stood on his two rounded toeless feet, supported on his staff, like something which had grown on that spot ages ago and to which people on one special day made offerings.

'Is this the path to the Perrins?'

The man said yes, but Querry guessed it was what Africans always replied to a question couched like that. He went back to the truck and lay down on the camp-bed. He could hear Deo Gratias settling himself for the night under the belly of the truck, and he lay on his back, staring up at where the stars ought to have been visible, but the gauze of the mosquito-net obscured them. As usual there was no silence. Silence belonged to cities. He dreamt of a girl whom he had once known and thought he loved. She came to him in tears because she had broken a vase which she valued, and she became angry with him because he didn't share her suffering. She struck him in the face, but he felt the blow no more than a dab of butter against his cheek. He said, 'I am sorry, I am too far gone, I can't feel at all, I am a leper.' As he explained his sickness to her he awoke.

This was a specimen of his days and nights. He had no

trouble beyond the boredom of the bush. The ferries worked; the rivers were not in flood, in spite of the rain which came torrentially down on their last night. Deo Gratias made a tent over the back of the truck with a ground-sheet and lay down himself as he had done every night in the shelter of the chassis. Then the sun was out again and the track became a road a few miles out of Luc.

III

They searched a long time for the doctor's apparatus before they found a clue. The cargo department of Otraco knew nothing of it and suggested the customs, which was no more than a wooden hut by a jetty in the tiny river port, where bat-eared dogs yapped and ran. The customs were uninterested and uncooperative, so that Querry had to dig out the European controller who was having an after-lunch siesta in a block of blue and pink modern flats by a little public garden where no one sat on the hot cement benches. The door of the apartment was opened by an African woman, tousled and sleepy, who looked as though she had been sharing the controller's siesta. The controller was an elderly Fleming who spoke very little French. The pouches under his eyes were like purses that contained the smuggled memories of a disappointing life. Querry had already become so accustomed to the bush-life that this man seemed to belong to another age and race than his own. The commercial calendar on the wall with a coloured reproduction of a painting by Vermeer, the triptych of wife and children on the locked piano, and a portrait of the man himself in a uniform of antique cut belonging to an antique war were like the deposits of a dead culture. They could be dated accurately, but no research would disclose the emotions that had once been attached to them.

The controller was very cordial and confused, as though he were anxious to hide with hospitality some secret of his siesta; he had forgotten to do up his flies. He invited Querry to sit down and take a glass, but when he heard that Querry had come from the leproserie he became restless and anxious, eyeing the chair on which Querry sat. Perhaps he expected to see the bacilli of leprosy burrowing into the upholstery. He knew nothing, he said, of any apparatus and suggested that it might be at the cathedral. When Querry stopped on the landing outside he could hear the tap running in the bathroom. The controller was obviously disinfecting his hands.

True enough the apparatus some time ago had been lodged at the cathedral, although the priest in charge, who had assumed the crates contained a holy statue or books for the fathers' library, at first denied all knowledge. They had gone off by the last Otraco boat and were somewhere stuck on the river. Querry drove to the cold storage. The hour of siesta was over, and he had to queue for string-beans.

The high vexed colonial voices, each angry about something different, rose around him, competing for attention. It seemed to him for a moment that he was back in Europe, and his shoulders instinctively hunched through fear of recognition. In the crowded store he realized how on the river and in the streets of the leproserie there had been a measure of peace. 'But you simply must have potatoes,' a woman's voice was saying. 'How dare you deny it? They came in on yesterday's plane. The pilot told me.' She was obviously playing her last card, when she appealed to the European manager. 'I'm expecting the Governor to dinner.' Surreptitiously the potatoes emerged, ready wrapped in cellophane.

A voice said, 'You are Querry, aren't you?'

He turned. The man who spoke to him was tall, stooping, and overgrown. He was like the kind of plant people put in bathrooms, reared on humidity, shooting too high. He had a small black moustache like a smear of city soot and his face was narrow and flat and endless, like an illustration of the law that two parallel lines never meet. He put a hot restless hand on Querry's arm. 'My name is Rycker. I missed you the other day when I called at the leproserie. How did you get over here? Is a boat in?'

'I came by truck.'

'You were fortunate to get through. You must stay a night at my place on your way home.'

'I have to get back to the leproserie.'

'They can do without you. They'll have to do without you. After last night's rain there'll be too much water for the ferry. Why are you waiting here?'

'I only wanted some *haricots verts* and some . . .'

'Boy! Some *haricots verts* for this master. You know you have to shout at them a little. They understand nothing else. The only alternative to staying with us is to remain here till the water goes down, and I can assure you, you won't like the hotel. This is a very provincial town. Nothing here to interest a man like you. You are *the* Querry, aren't you?' and Rycker's mouth shut trapwise, while his eyes gleamed roguishly like a detective's.

'I don't know what you mean.'

'We don't all live quite out of the world like the fathers and our dubious friend the doctor. Of course this is a bit of a desert, but all the same one manages – somehow – to keep in touch. Two dozen lagers, boy, and make it quick. Of course I shall respect your incognito. I will say nothing. You can trust me not to betray a guest. You'll be far safer at my place than at the hotel. Only myself and my wife. As a matter of fact it was my wife who said to me, "Do you suppose he can possibly be *the* Querry?"'

'You've made a mistake.'

'Oh no, I haven't. I can show you a photograph when you come to my house – in one of the papers that lie around in case they may prove useful. Useful! This one certainly has, hasn't it, because otherwise we would have thought you were only a relation of Querry's or that the name was pure coincidence, for who would expect to find *the* Querry holed up in a leproserie in the bush? I have to admit I am somewhat curious. But you can trust me, trust me all the way. I have serious enough problems of my own, so I can sympathize with those of another man. I've buried myself too. We'd better go outside, for in a little town like this even the walls have ears.'

'I'm afraid . . . they are expecting me to return . . .'

'God rules the weather. I assure you, M. Querry, you have no choice.'

CHAPTER 2

House and factory overlooked the ferry; no situation could have been better chosen for a man with Rycker's devouring curiosity. It was impossible for anyone to use the road that led from the town to the interior without passing the two wide windows which were like the lenses of a pair of binoculars trained on the river. They drove under the deep blue shadows of the palm trees towards the river; Rycker's chauffeur and Deo Gratias followed in Querry's lorry.

'You see, M. Querry, how it is. The river's far too high. Not a chance to pass tonight. Who knows whether even tomorrow . . . ? So we have time for some interesting talks, you and I.'

As they drove through the yard of the factory, among the huge boilers abandoned to rust, a smell like stale margarine lay heavily around them. A blast of hot air struck from an open doorway, and the reflection of a furnace billowed into the waning light. 'To you, of course,' Rycker said, 'accustomed to the factories of the West, this must appear a bit ramshackle. Though I can't remember whether you ever were closely concerned with any factories.'

'No.'

'There were so many spheres in which *the* Querry led the way.'

He recurred again and again to the word 'the' as though it were a title of nobility.

'The place functions,' he said as the car bumped among the boilers, 'it functions in its ugly way. We waste nothing. When we finish with the nut there's nothing left. Nothing. We've crushed out the oil,' he said with relish rolling the r, 'and as for the husk – into the furnace with it. We don't need any other fuel to keep the furnaces alive.'

They left the two cars in the yard and walked over to the house. 'Marie, Marie,' Rycker called, scraping the mud off his shoes, stamping across the veranda. 'Marie.'

A girl in blue jeans with a pretty unformed face came quickly round the corner in answer to his call. Querry was on the point of asking 'Your daughter?' when Rycker forestalled him. 'My wife,' he said. 'And here, *chérie*, is *the* Querry. He tried to deny it, but I told him we had a photograph.'

'I am very glad to meet you,' she said. 'We will try to make you comfortable.' Querry had the impression that she had learnt such occasional speeches by heart from her governess or from a book of etiquette. Now she had said her piece she disappeared as suddenly as she had come; perhaps the school-bell had rung for class.

'Sit down,' Rycker said. 'Marie is fixing the drinks. You can see I've trained her to know what a man needs.'

'Have you been married long?'

'Two years. I brought her out after my last leave. In a post like this it's necessary to have a companion. You married?'

'Yes – that is to say I have been married.'

'Of course I know you are thinking that she is very young for me. But I look ahead. If you believe in marriage you have to look to the future. I've still got twenty years of – let's call it active life ahead of me, and what would a woman of thirty be like in twenty years? A man keeps better in the tropics. Don't you agree?'

'I've never thought about it. And I don't yet know the tropics.'

'There are enough problems without sex I can assure you. St Paul wrote, didn't he, that it was better to marry than burn. Marie will stay young long enough to save me from the furnace.' He added quickly, 'Of course I'm only joking. We have to joke, don't we, about serious things. At the bottom of my heart I believe very profoundly in love.' He made the claim as some men might claim to believe in fairies.

The steward came along the veranda carrying a tray and Mme Rycker followed him. Querry took a glass and Mme Rycker stood at his elbow while the steward poised the syphon – a division of duties. 'Will you tell me how much soda?' Mme Rycker asked.

'And now, my dear, you'll change into a proper dress,' Rycker said.

Over the whisky he turned again to what he called 'Your case.' He had now less the manner of a detective than of a counsel who by the nature of his profession is an accomplice after the fact. 'Why are you here, Querry?'

'One must be somewhere.'

'All the same, as I said this morning, no one would expect to find you working in a leproserie.'

'I am not working.'

'When I drove over some weeks ago, the fathers said that you were at the hospital.'

'I was watching the doctor work. I stand around, that's all. There's nothing I can do.'

'It seems a waste of talent.'

'I have no talent.'

Rycker said, 'You mustn't despise us poor provincials.'

When they had gone into dinner, and after Rycker had said a short grace, Querry's hostess spoke again. She said, 'I hope you will be comfortable,' and, 'Do you care for salad?' Her fair hair was streaked and darkened with sweat and he saw her eyes widen with apprehension when a black-and-white moth, with the wing-spread of a bat, swooped across the table. 'You must make yourself at home here,' she said, her gaze following the moth as it settled like a piece of lichen on the wall. He wondered whether she had ever felt at home herself. She said, 'We don't have many visitors,' and he was reminded of a child forced to entertain a caller until her mother returns. She had changed, between the whisky and the dinner, into a cotton frock covered with a pattern of autumnal leaves which was like a memory of Europe.

'Not a visitor like *the* Querry anyway,' Rycker interrupted her. It was as though he had turned off a knob on a radio-set which had been tuned in to a lesson in deportment after he had listened enough. The sound of the voice was shut off the air, but still, behind the shy and wary eyes, the phrases were going on for no one to hear. 'The weather has been a little hot lately, hasn't it? I hope you had a good flight from Europe.'

Querry said, 'Do you like the life here?' The question startled her; perhaps the answer wasn't in her phrase-book. 'Oh yes,' she said, 'yes. It's very interesting,' staring over his shoulder through the window to where the boilers stood like modern statues in the floodlit yard; then she shifted her eyes back to the moth on the wall and the gecko pointing at his prey.

'Fetch that photograph, dear,' Rycker said.

'What photograph?'

'The photograph of our guest.'

She trailed reluctantly out, making a detour to avoid the wall where the moth rested and the lizard pointed, and returned soon with an ancient copy of *Time*. Querry remembered the ten years younger face upon the cover (the issue had coincided with his first visit to New York). The artist, drawing from a photograph, had romanticized his features. It wasn't the face he saw when he shaved, but a kind of distant cousin. It reflected emotions, thoughts, hopes, profundities that he had certainly expressed to no reporter. The background of the portrait was a building of glass and steel which might have been taken for a concert-hall, or perhaps even for an *orangerie*, if a great cross planted outside the door had not indicated it was a church.

'So you see,' Rycker said, 'we know all.'

'I don't remember that the article was very accurate.'

'I suppose the Government – or the Church – have commissioned you to do something out here?'

'No. I've retired.'

'I thought a man of your kind never retired.'

'Oh, one comes to an end, just as soldiers do and bank managers.'

When the dinner was over the girl left, like a child after the dessert. 'I expect she's gone to write up her journal,' Rycker said. 'This is a red-letter day for her, meeting *the* Querry. She'll have plenty to put down in it.'

'Does she find much to write?'

'I wouldn't know. At the beginning I used to take a quiet

look, but she discovered that, and now she locks it up. I expect I teased her a little too much. I remember one entry: "Letter from mother. Poor Maxime has had five puppies." It was the day I was decorated by the Governor, but she forgot to put anything about the ceremony.'

'It must be a lonely life at her age.'

'Oh, I don't know. There are a lot of household duties even in the bush. To be quite frank, I think it's a good deal more lonely for me. She's hardly – you can see it for yourself – an intellectual companion. That's one of the disadvantages of marrying a young wife. If I want to talk about things which really interest me, I have to drive over to the fathers. A long way to go for a conversation. Living in the way I do, one has a lot of time to think things over. I'm a good Catholic, I hope, but that doesn't prevent me from having spiritual problems. A lot of people take their religion lightly, but I had six years when I was a young man with the Jesuits. If a novice master had been less unfair you wouldn't have found me here. I gathered from that article in *Time* that you are a Catholic too.'

'I've retired,' Querry said for the second time.

'Oh come now, one hardly retires from *that*.'

The gecko on the wall leapt at the moth, missed and lay motionless again, the tiny paws spread on the wall like ferns.

'To tell you the truth,' Rycker said, 'I find those fathers at the leproserie an unsatisfactory lot. They are more interested in electricity and building than in questions of faith. Ever since I heard you were here I've looked forward to a conversation with an intellectual Catholic.'

'I wouldn't call myself that.'

'In the long years I've been out here I've been thrown back on my own thoughts. Some men can manage, I suppose, with clock-golf. I can't. I've read a great deal on the subject of love.'

'Love?'

'The love of God. Agape not Eros.'

'I'm not qualified to talk about that.'

'You underrate yourself,' Rycker replied. He went to the sideboard and fetched a tray of liqueurs, disturbing the gecko who disappeared behind a reproduction of some primitive *Flight into Egypt*. 'A glass of Cointreau,' Rycker said, 'or would you prefer a Van Der Hum?' Beyond the veranda Querry saw a thin figure in a gold-leafed dress move towards the river. Perhaps out of doors the moths had lost their terror.

'In the seminary I formed the habit of thinking more than most men,' Rycker said. 'A faith like ours, when profoundly understood, sets us many problems. For instance – no, it's not a mere instance, I'm jumping to the heart of what really troubles me, I don't believe my wife understands the true nature of Christian marriage.'

Out in the darkness there was a plop-plop-plop. She must be throwing small pieces of wood into the river.

'It sometimes seems to me,' Rycker said, 'that she's ignorant of almost everything. I find myself wondering whether the nuns taught her at all. You saw for yourself – she doesn't even cross herself at meals when I say grace. Ignorance, you know, beyond a certain point might even invalidate a marriage in canon law. That's one of the matters I have tried in vain to discuss with the fathers. They would much prefer to talk about turbines. Now you are here . . .'

'I'm not competent to discuss it,' Querry said. In the moments of silence he could hear the river flooding down.

'At least you listen. The fathers would already have started talking about the new well they propose to dig. A well, Querry, a well against a human soul.' He drank down his Van Der Hum and poured himself another. 'They don't realize . . . just suppose that we weren't properly married, she could leave me at any time, Querry.'

'It's easy to leave what you call a proper marriage, too.'

'No, no. It's much more difficult. There are social pressures – particularly here.'

'If she loves you . . .'

'That's no protection. We are men of the world, Querry, you and I. A love like that doesn't last. I tried to teach her the importance of loving God. Because if she loved Him, she wouldn't want to offend Him, would she? And that would be some security. I have tried to get her to pray, but I don't think she knows any prayers except the *Pater Noster* and the *Ave Maria*. What prayers do you use, Querry?'

'None – except occasionally, from habit, in a moment of danger.' He added sadly, 'Then I pray for a brown teddy bear.'

'You are joking, I know that, but this is very serious. Have another Cointreau?'

'What's really worrying you, Rycker? A man?'

The girl came back into the light of the lamp which hung at the corner of the veranda. She was carrying a *roman policier* in the *Série Noire*. She gave a whistle that was scarcely audible, but Rycker heard it. 'That damn puppy,' he said. 'She loves her puppy more than she loves me – or God.' Perhaps the Van Der Hum affected the logic of his transitions. He said, 'I'm not jealous. It's not a man I worry about. She hasn't enough feeling for that. Sometimes she even refuses her duties.'

'What duties?'

'Her duties to me. Her married duties.'

'I've never thought of those as duties.'

'You know very well the Church does. No one has any right to abstain except by mutual consent.'

'I suppose there may be times when she doesn't want you.'

'Then what am I supposed to do? Have I given up the priesthood for nothing at all?'

'I wouldn't talk to her too much, if I were you, about loving God,' Querry said with reluctance. 'She mightn't see a parallel between that and your bed.'

'There's a close parallel for a Catholic,' Rycker said rapidly. He put up his hand as though he were answering a question before his fellow novices. The bristles of hair between the knuckles were like a row of little moustaches.

'You seem to be very well up in the subject,' Querry said.

'At the seminary I always came out well in moral theology.'

'I don't fancy you need me then – or the fathers either. You have obviously thought everything out satisfactorily yourself.'

'That goes without saying. But sometimes one needs confirmation and encouragement. You can't imagine, Querry, what a relief it is to go over these problems with an educated Catholic.'

'I don't know that I would call myself a Catholic.'

Rycker laughed. 'What? *The* Querry? You can't fool me. You are being too modest. I wonder they haven't made you a count of the Holy Roman Empire – like that Irish singer, what was his name?'

'I don't know. I am not musical.'

'You should read what they say about you in *Time*.'

'On matters like that *Time* isn't necessarily well informed. Would you mind if I went to bed? I'll have to be up early in the morning if I'm to reach the next ferry before dark.'

'Of course. Though I doubt if you'll be able to cross the river tomorrow.'

Rycker followed him along the veranda to his room. The darkness was noisy with frogs, and for a long while after his host had said good night and gone, they seemed to croak with Rycker's hollow phrases: grace: sacrament: duty: love, love, love.

CHAPTER 3

I

'You want to be of use, don't you?' the doctor asked sharply. 'You don't want menial jobs just for the sake of menial jobs? You aren't either a masochist or a saint.'

'Rycker promised me that he would tell no one.'

'He kept his word for nearly a month. That's quite an achievement for Rycker. When he came here the other day he only told the Superior in confidence.'

'What did the Superior say?'

'That he would listen to nothing in confidence outside the confessional.'

The doctor continued to unpack the crate of heavy electrical apparatus which had arrived at last by the Otraco boat. The lock on the dispensary door was too insecure for him to trust the apparatus there, so he unpacked it on the floor of his living-room. One could never be certain of the African's reaction to anything unfamiliar. In Leopoldville six months before, when the first riots broke out, the attack had been directed at the new glass-and-steel hospital intended for African patients. The most monstrous rumours were easily planted and often believed. It was a land where Messiahs died in prison and rose again from the dead: where walls were said to fall at the touch of fingernails sanctified by a little holy dust. A man whom the doctor had cured of leprosy wrote him a threatening letter once a month; he really believed that he had been turned out of the leproserie, not because he was cured, but because the doctor had personal designs on the half acre of ground on which he used to grow bananas. It only needed someone, in malice or ignorance, to suggest that the new machines were intended to torture the patients and some fools would break into the dispensary and destroy them. Yet in our century you could hardly call them fools. Hola Camp, Sharpeville, and Algiers had justified all possible belief in European cruelty.

So it was better, the doctor explained, to keep the machines out of sight at home until the new hospital was finished. The floor of his sitting-room was covered with straw from the crates.

'The position of the power-plugs will have to be decided now.' The doctor asked, 'Do you know what this is?'

'No.'

'I've wanted it for so long,' the doctor said, touching the metal shape tenderly as a man might stroke the female flank of one of Rodin's bronzes. 'Sometimes I despaired. The papers I have had to fill in, the lies I've told. And here at last it *is*.'

'What does it do?'

'It measures to one twenty-thousandth of a second the reaction of the nerves. One day we are going to be proud of this leproserie. Of you too and the part you will have played.'

'I told you I've retired.'

'One never retires from a vocation.'

'Oh yes, make no mistake, one does. One comes to an end.'

'What are you here for then? To make love to a black woman?'

'No. One comes to an end of that too. Possibly sex and a vocation are born and die together. Let me roll bandages or carry buckets. All I want is to pass the time.'

'I thought you wanted to be of use.'

'Listen,' Querry said and then fell silent.

'I *am* listening.'

'I don't deny my profession once meant a lot to me. So have women. But the use of what I made was never important to me. I wasn't a builder of council houses or factories. When I made something I made it for my own pleasure.'

'Is that the way you loved women?' the doctor asked, but Querry hardly heard him. He was talking as a hungry man eats.

'Your vocation is quite a different one, doctor. You are

concerned with people. I wasn't concerned with the people who occupied my space – only with the space.'

'I wouldn't have trusted your plumbing then.'

'A writer doesn't write for his readers, does he? Yet he has to take elementary precautions all the same to make them comfortable. My interest was in space, light, proportion. New materials interested me only in the effect they might have on those three. Wood, brick, steel, concrete, glass – space seems to alter with what you use to enclose it. Materials are the architect's plot. They are not his motive for work. Only the space and the light and the proportion. The subject of a novel is not the plot. Who remembers what happened to Lucien de Rubempré in the end?'

'Two of your churches are famous. Didn't you care what happened inside them – to people?'

'The acoustics had to be good of course. The high altar had to be visible to all. But people hated them. They said they weren't designed for prayer. They meant that they were not Roman or Gothic or Byzantine. And in a year they had cluttered them up with their cheap plaster saints; they took out my plain windows and put in stained glass dedicated to dead pork-packers who had contributed to diocesan funds, and when they had destroyed my space and my light, they were able to pray again, and they even became proud of what they had spoilt. I became what they called a great Catholic architect, but I built no more churches, doctor.'

'I am not a religious man, I don't know much about these things, but I suppose they had a right to believe their prayers were more important than a work of art.'

'Men have prayed in prison, men have prayed in slums and concentration camps. It's only the middle-classes who demand to pray in suitable surroundings. Sometimes I feel sickened by the word prayer. Rycker used it a great deal. Do you pray, doctor?'

'I think the last time I prayed was before my final medical exam. And you?'

'I gave it up a long time ago. Even in the days when I believed, I seldom prayed. It would have got in the way of work. Before I went to sleep, even if I was with a woman, the last thing I had always to think about was work. Problems which seemed insoluble would often solve themselves in sleep. I had my bedroom next to my office, so that I could spend two minutes in front of the drawing-board the last thing of all. The bed, the bidet, the drawing-board, and then sleep.'

'It sounds a little hard on the woman.'

'Self-expression is a hard and selfish thing. It eats everything, even the self. At the end you find you haven't even got a self to express. I have no interest in anything any more, doctor. I don't want to sleep with a woman nor design a building.'

'Have you no children?'

'I once had, but they disappeared into the world a long time ago. We haven't kept in touch. Self-expression eats the father in you too.'

'So you thought you could just come and die here?'

'Yes. That *was* in my mind. But chiefly I wanted to be in an empty place, where no new building or woman would remind me that there was a time when I was alive, with a vocation and a capacity to love – if it was love. The palsied suffer, their nerves feel, but I am one of the mutilated, doctor.'

'Twenty years ago we might have been able to offer you your death, but now we deal only in cures. D.D.S. costs three shillings a year. It's much cheaper than a coffin.'

'Can you cure me?'

'Perhaps your mutilations haven't gone far enough yet. When a man comes here too late the disease has to burn itself out.' The doctor laid a cloth tenderly over his machine. 'The other patients are waiting. Do you want to come or would you like to sit here thinking of your own case? It's often the way with the mutilated – they want to retire too, out of sight.'

The air in the hospital lay heavily and sweetly upon them: it was never moved by a fan or a breeze. Querry was conscious of the squalor of the bedding – cleanliness was not important to the leper, only to the healthy. The patients brought their own mattresses which they had probably possessed for a lifetime – rough sacking from which the straw had escaped.

The bandaged feet lay in the straw like ill-wrapped packages of meat. On the veranda the walking cases sat out of the sun – if you could call a walking case a man who, when he moved, had to support his huge swollen testicles with both hands. A woman with palsied eyelids who could not close her eyes or even blink sat in a patch of shade out of the merciless light. A man without fingers nursed a baby on his knee, and another man lay flat on the veranda with one breast long and drooping and teated like a woman's. There was little the doctor could do for any of these; the man with elephantiasis had too weak a heart for an operation, and though he could have sewn up the woman's eyelids, she had refused to have it done from fear, and as for the baby it would be a leper too in time. Nor could he help those in the first ward who were dying of tuberculosis or the woman who dragged herself between the beds, her legs withered with polio. It had always seemed to the doctor unfair that leprosy did not preclude all other diseases (leprosy was enough for one human being to bear), and yet it was from the other diseases that most of his patients died. He passed on and Querry tagged at his heels, saying nothing.

In the mud kitchen at the back of one of the lepers' houses an old man sat in the dark on an ancient deck-chair. He made an effort to rise when the doctor crossed the yard, but his legs wouldn't support him and he made a gesture of courteous apology. 'High blood pressure,' the doctor said softly. 'No hope. He has come to his kitchen to die.' His legs were as thin as a child's and he wore a clout like a baby's napkin round the waist for decency. Querry had seen where his clothes had been left neatly folded in the new brick cottage under the Pope's portrait. A holy medal lay in the hollow of his breast among the scarce grey hairs. He had a face of great kindness and dignity, a face that must have always accepted life without complaint, the face of a saint. Now he inquired after the doctor's health as though it were the doctor who was sick, not he.

'Is there anything that I can fetch you?' the doctor asked, and no, the old man replied, he had everything he needed. He wanted to know whether the doctor had heard recently from his family and he made inquiries after the health of the doctor's mother.

'She has been in Switzerland, in the mountains. A holiday in the snow.'

'Snow?'

'I forgot. You have never seen snow. It is frozen vapour, frozen mist. The air is so cold that it never melts and it lies on the ground white and soft like the feathers of a *pique-bœuf*, and the lakes are covered with ice.'

'I know what ice is,' the old man said proudly. 'I have seen ice in a refrigerator. Is your mother old like me?'

'Older.'

'Then she ought not to travel far away from her home. One should die in one's own village if it is possible.' He looked sadly at his own thin legs. 'They will not carry me or I should walk to mine.'

'I would arrange for a lorry to take you,' the doctor said, 'but I don't think you would stand the journey.'

'It would be too much trouble for you,' the old man said, 'and in any case there is no time because I am going to die tomorrow.'

'I will tell the Superior to come and see you as soon as he can.'

'I do not wish to be any trouble to him. He has many duties. I will not be dead till the evening.'

By the old deck-chair stood a bottle with a Johnny Walker label. It contained a brown liquid and some withered plants tied together with a loop of beads. 'What has he got there,' Querry asked after they left him, 'in the bottle?'

'Medicine. Magic. An appeal to his God Nzambi.'

'I thought he was a Catholic.'

'If I sign a form I call myself a Catholic too. So does he. I believe in nothing most of the time. He half believes in Christ and half believes in Nzambi. There's not much difference between us as far as Catholicism is concerned. I only wish I were as good a man.'

'Will he really die tomorrow?'

'I think so. They have a wonderful knack of knowing.'

In the dispensary a leper with bandaged feet stood waiting with a small boy in her arms. Every rib in the child's body showed. It was like a cage over which a dark cloth has been flung at night to keep a bird asleep, and like a bird his breath moved under the cloth. It was not leprosy that would kill him, the doctor said, but sicklaemia, an incurable disease of the blood. There was no hope. The child would not live long enough to become a leper, but there was no point in telling the mother that. He touched the little hollow chest with his finger, and the child winced away. The doctor began to abuse the woman in her own language, and she argued unconvincingly back, clutching the boy against her hip. The boy stared passively over the doctor's shoulder with sad frog-like eyes as though nothing that anyone said would ever concern him seriously again. When the woman had gone, Doctor Colin said, 'She promises it won't happen any more. But how can I tell?'

'What won't happen?'

'Didn't you see the little scar on his breast? They have been cutting a pocket in his skin to put their native medicines in. She says it was the grandmother who did it. Poor child. They won't let him die in peace without pain. I told her that if it happened again, I would cease treating her for leprosy, but I daresay they won't let me see the boy a second time. In that state he's as easy to hide as a needle.'

'Can't you put him in the hospital?'

'You've seen what sort of a hospital I've got. Would you want a boy of yours to die there? Next,' he called angrily, 'next,' and the next was a child too, a boy of six. His father accompanied him, and his fingerless fist rested on the boy's shoulder to give him comfort. The doctor turned the child round and ran his hand over the young skin.

'Well,' he said, 'you should be noticing things by this time. What do you think of this case?'

'One of his toes has gone already.'

'That's not important. He's had jiggers and they've neglected them. It happens often in the bush. No – here's the first patch. The leprosy has just begun.'

'Is there no way to protect the children?'

'In Brazil they take them away at birth, and thirty per cent of the babies die. I prefer a leper to a dead child. We'll cure him in a couple of years.' He looked up quickly at Querry and away again. 'One day – in the new hospital – I'll have a special children's ward and dispensary. I'll anticipate the patch. I'll live to see leprosy in retreat. Do you know there are some areas, a few hundred miles from here, where one in five of the people are lepers? I dream of movable prefabricated hospitals. War has changed. In 1914 generals organized battles from country houses, but in 1944 Rommel and Montgomery fought from moving caravans. How can I convey what I want to Father Joseph? I can't draw. I can't even design one room to the best advantage. I'll only be able to tell him what's wrong after the hospital is built. He's not even a builder. He's a good bricklayer. He's putting one brick on another for the love of God as they used to build monasteries. So you see I need you,' Doctor Colin said. The boy's four toes wriggled impatiently on the cement floor, waiting for the meaningless conversation between the white men to reach a conclusion.

II

Querry wrote in his journal: 'I haven't enough feeling left for human beings to do anything for them out of pity.' He carefully recalled the scar on the immature breast and the four toes, but he was unmoved; an accumulation of pinpricks cannot amount to the sensation of pain. A storm was on the way, and the flying ants swarmed into the room, striking against the light until he shut the window. Then they fell on the cement floor and lost their wings and ran this way and that as though they were confused at finding themselves so suddenly creatures of earth not air. With the window closed the wet heat increased and he had to put blotting paper under his wrist to catch the sweat.

He wrote, in an attempt to make clear his motives to Doctor Colin:

A vocation is an act of love: it is not a professional career. When desire is dead one cannot continue to make love. I've come to the end of desire and to the end of a vocation. Don't try to bind me in a loveless marriage and to make me imitate what I used to perform with passion. And don't talk to me like a priest about my duty. A talent – we used to learn that lesson as children in scripture lessons – should not be buried when it still has purchasing power, but when the currency has changed and the image has been superseded and no value is left in the coin but the weight of a wafer of silver, a man has every right to hide it. Obsolete coins, like corn, have always been found in graves.

The notes were rough and disjointed: he had no talent to organize his thought in words. He ended:

What I have built, I have always built for myself, not for the glory of God or the pleasure of a purchaser. Don't talk to me of human beings. Human beings are not my country. And haven't I offered anyway to wash their filthy bandages?

He tore the pages out and sent them by Deo Gratias to Doctor Colin. At the end a half-sentence had been thrust out into the void – 'I will do anything for you in reason, but don't ask me to try to revive . . .' like a plank from a ship's deck off which a victim has been thrust.

Doctor Colin came to his room later and tossed the letter, crumpled into a paper ball, on to his table. 'Scruples,' the doctor said impatiently. 'Just scruples.'

'I tried to explain . . .'

'Who cares?' the doctor said, and that question 'Who cares?' went echoing obsessively on in Querry's brain like a line of verse learnt in adolescence.

He had a dream that night from which he woke in terror. He was walking down a long railway-track, in the dark, in a cold country. He was hurrying because he had to reach a priest and explain to him that, in spite of the clothes he was wearing, he was a priest also and he must make his confession and obtain wine with which to celebrate Mass. He was under orders of some kind from a superior. He had to say his

Mass now that night. Tomorrow would be too late. He would lose his chance forever. He came to a village and left the rail-way-track (the small station was shuttered and deserted: perhaps the whole branch line had been closed long since by the authorities) and presently found himself outside the priest's door, heavy and medieval, studded with great nails the size of Roman coins. He rang and was admitted. A lot of chattering pious women surrounded the priest, but he was friendly and accessible in spite of them. Querry said, 'I must see you at once, alone. There is something I have to tell you,' and already he began to feel the enormous relief and security of his confession. He was nearly home again. The priest took him aside into a little room where a decanter of wine stood on a table, but before he had time to speak the holy women came billowing in through the curtain after them, full of little pious jests and whimsicalities. 'But we must be alone,' Querry cried, 'I have to speak to you,' and the priest pushed the women back through the curtain, and they swayed for a moment to and fro like clothes on hangers in a cupboard. All the same the two of them were sufficiently alone now for him to speak, and with his eyes on the wine he was able at last really to begin. 'Father . . .' but at that moment, when he was about to lose the burden of his fear and responsibility, a second priest entered the room and taking the father on one side began to explain to him how he had run short of wine and had come to borrow his, and still talking he picked up the decanter from the table. Then Querry broke down. It was as though he had had an appointment with hope at this turn of the road and had arrived just too late. He let out a cry like that of an animal in pain and woke. It was raining hard on all the tin roofs, and when the lightning flashed he could see the small white cell that his mosquito-net made, the size of a coffin, and in one of the leper-houses near by a quarrel had begun between a man and a woman. He thought, 'I was too late,' and an obsessional phrase bobbed up again, like a cork attached to some invisible fishing-net below the water, 'Who cares?' 'Who cares?'

When the morning came at last he went to the carpenter

CHAPTER 4

I

After two months a measure of natural confidence had grown between Querry and Deo Gratias. At first it was based only on the man's disabilities. Querry was not angry with him when he spilt water; he kept his temper when one of his drawings was smeared by ink from a broken bottle. It takes a long time to learn even the simplest tasks without fingers and toes, and in any case a man who cares for nothing finds it difficult – or absurd – to be angry. There was one occasion when the crucifix which the fathers had left hanging on Querry's wall was broken by some maladroitness on the part of the mutilated man and he expected Querry to react as he might have reacted himself if a fetish of his own had been carelessly or heartlessly destroyed. It was easy for him to mistake indifference for sympathy.

One night when the moon was full Querry became aware of the man's absence as one might become aware of some hitherto unnoticed object missing from a mantelpiece in a temporary home. His ewer had not been filled and the mosquito-net had not been drawn down, and later, as he was on his way to the doctor's house, where he had to discuss a possible cut in the cost of building, he met Deo Gratias stumbling with his staff down the central road of the leproserie as quickly as he was able on toeless feet. The man's face was wet with sweat and when Querry spoke to him he swerved away into someone's backyard. When Querry returned half an hour later he stood there still, like a tree-stump that the owner had not bothered to move. The sweat looked like traces of the night's rain on the bark and he appeared to be listening to something a long way off. Querry listened too, but he could hear nothing except the rattle of the crickets and the swelling diapason of the frogs. In the morning Deo Gratias had not returned, and Querry felt an unimportant disappointment that the servant had not spoken a word to him before he left. He told the doctor that the boy had gone. 'If he doesn't come back tomorrow will you find me another?'

'I don't understand,' Doctor Colin said. 'I only gave him the job so that he might stay in the leproserie. He had no wish to go.' Later that day a leper picked up the man's staff from a path that led into the thickest bush, and brought it to Querry's room where he was at work, taking advantage of the last light.

'But how do you know that the staff is his? All the mutilated lepers have them,' Querry asked and the man simply repeated that it belonged to Deo Gratias – no argument, no reason, just one more of the things they knew that he knew nothing about.

'You think some accident has happened to him?'

Something, the man said in his poor French, had happened, and Querry got the impression that an accident was what the man feared least of all.

'Why don't you go and look for him then?' Querry asked.

There was not enough light left, the man said, under the trees. They would have to wait till morning.

'But he's been gone already nearly twenty-four hours. If there has been an accident we have waited long enough. You can take my torch.'

The morning would be better, the man repeated, and Querry saw that he was scared.

'If I go with you, will you come?'

The man shook his head, so Querry went alone.

He could not blame these people for their fears: a man had to believe in nothing if he was not to be afraid of the big bush at night. There was little in the forest to appeal to the romantic. It was completely empty. It had never been humanized, like the woods of Europe, with witches and charcoal-burners and cottages of marzipan; no one had ever walked under these trees lamenting lost love, nor had anyone listened to the silence and communed like a lake-poet with his heart. For there was no silence; if a man here wished to be heard at night he had to raise his voice to counter the continuous chatter of the insects as in some monstrous factory where thousands of sewing-machines were being driven against time by myriads of needy seamstresses. Only for an hour or so, in the midday heat, silence fell, the siesta of the insect.

But if, like these Africans, one believed in some kind of divine being, wasn't it just as possible for a god to exist in this empty region as in the empty spaces of the sky where men had once located him? These woody spaces would remain unexplored, it seemed likely now, for longer than the planets. The craters of the moon were already better known than the forest at the door that one could enter any day on foot. The sharp sour smell of chlorophyl from rotting vegetation and swamp-water fell like a dentist's mask over Querry's face.

It was a stupid errand. He was no hunter. He had been bred in a city. He couldn't possibly hope to discover a human track even in daylight, and he had accepted too easily the evidence of the staff. Shining his torch on this side and that he elicited only stray gleams and flashes among the foliage which might have been the reflection of eyes, but were more probably little pools of rainwater caught in the curls of the leaves. He must have been walking now for half an hour, and he had probably covered a mile along the narrow path. Once his finger slipped on the trigger of the torch and in the moment of darkness he walked off the twisting path slap into the forest-wall. He thought: I have no reason to believe that my battery will see me home. He continued to digest the thought as he walked farther in. He had said to Doctor Colin to explain the reason for his stay, 'the boat goes no farther', but it is always possible to go a little deeper on one's own feet. He called 'Deo Gratias! Deo Gratias!' above the noise of the insects, but the absurd name which sounded like an invocation in a church received no response.

His own presence here was hardly more explicable than that of Deo Gratias. The thought of his servant lying injured in the forest waiting for the call or footstep of any human being would perhaps at an earlier time have vexed him all night until he was forced into making a token gesture. But now that he cared for nothing, perhaps he was being driven only by a vestige of intellectual curiosity. What had brought Deo Gratias here out of the safety and familiarity of the leproserie? The path, of course, might be leading somewhere – to a village perhaps where Deo Gratias had relations – but he had already learned enough of Africa to know that it was more likely to peter out – to be the relic of a track made by men who had come searching for caterpillars to fry, it might well mark the farthest limit of human penetration. What was the meaning of the sweat he had seen pouring down the man's face? It might have been caused by fear or anxiety or even, in the heavy river-heat, by the pressure of thought. Interest began to move painfully in him like a nerve that has been frozen. He had lived with inertia so long that he examined his 'interest' with clinical detachment.

He must have been walking now, he told himself, over an hour. How had Deo Gratias come so far without his staff on mutilated feet? He felt more than ever doubtful whether the battery would last him home. None the less, he went on. He realized how foolish he had been not to tell the doctor or one of the fathers where he was going in case of accident, but wasn't an accident perhaps exactly what he was seeking? In any case he went on, while the mosquitoes droned to the attack. There was no point in waving them away. He trained himself to submit.

Fifty yards further he was startled by a harsh animal sound – the kind of grunt he could imagine a wild boar giving. He stopped and moved his waning light in a circle round him. He saw that many years ago this path must have been intended to lead somewhere, for in front of him were the remains of a bridge made from the trunks of trees that had long ago rotted. Two more steps and he would have fallen down the gap, not a great fall, a matter of feet only, into a shallow overgrown marsh, but for a man mutilated in hands and feet far enough: the light shone on the body of Deo Gratias, half in the water, half out. He could see the tracks made in the

wet and slippery ground by hands like boxing gloves which
had tried to catch hold. Then the body grunted again, and
Querry climbed down beside it.

Querry couldn't tell whether Deo Gratias was conscious or
not. His body was too heavy to lift, and he made no effort
to cooperate. He was warm and wet like a hummock of soil;
he felt like part of the bridge that had fallen in many years
ago. After ten minutes of struggle Querry managed to drag
his limbs out of the water – it was all he could do. The obvious thing now, if his torch would last long enough, was to
fetch help. Even if the Africans refused to return with him
two of the fathers would certainly aid him. He made to climb
up on to the bridge and Deo Gratias howled, as a dog or a
baby might howl. He raised a stump and howled, and Querry
realized that he was crippled with fear. The fingerless hand
fell on Querry's arm like a hammer and held him there.

There was nothing to be done but wait for the morning.
The man might die of fear, but neither of them would die
from damp or mosquito-bites. He settled himself down as
comfortably as he could by the boy and by the last light of
the torch examined the rocky feet. As far as he could tell an
ankle was broken – that seemed to be all. Soon the light was
so dim that Querry could see the shape of the filament in the
dark, like a phosphorescent worm; then it went out altogether.
He took Deo Gratias's hand to reassure him, or rather laid
his own hand down beside it; you cannot take a fingerless
hand. Deo Gratias grunted twice, and then uttered a word.
It sounded like 'Pendélé'. In the darkness the knuckles felt as
a rock might that has been eroded for years by the weather.

II

'We both had a lot of time to think,' Querry said to Doctor
Colin. 'It wasn't light enough to leave him till about six. I
suppose it was about six – I had forgotten to wind my watch.'

'It must have been a long bad night.'

'One has had worse alone.' He seemed to be searching his
memory for an example. 'Nights when things end. Those are

the interminable nights. In a way you know this seemed a
night when things begin. I've never much minded physical
discomfort. And after about an hour when I tried to move
my hand, he wouldn't let it go. His fist lay on it like a paper-
weight. I had an odd feeling that he needed me.'

'Why odd?' Doctor Colin asked.

'Odd to me. I've needed people often enough in my life. You
might accuse me of having used people more than I have ever
loved them. But to be needed is a different sensation, a tran-
quillizer, not an excitement. Do you know what the word
"Pendélé" means? Because after I moved my hand he began to
talk. I had never properly listened to an African talking before.
You know how one listens with half an ear, as one does to children. It wasn't easy to follow the mixture of French and whatever language it is that Deo Gratias speaks. And this word
"Pendélé" continually cropped up. What does it mean, doctor?'

'I've an idea that it means something the same as *Bunkasi*
– and that means pride, arrogance, perhaps a kind of dignity
and independence if you look at the good side of the word.'

'It's not what he meant. I am certain he meant a place –
somewhere in the forest, near water, where something of great
importance to him was happening. He had felt strangled his
last day in the leproserie; of course he didn't use the word
"strangled", he told me there wasn't enough air, he wanted
to dance and shout and run and sing. But, poor fellow, he
couldn't run or dance, and the fathers would have taken a
poor view of the kind of songs he wanted to sing. So he set
out to find this place beside the water. He had been taken
there once by his mother when he was a child, and he could
remember how there had been singing and dancing and games
and prayers.'

'But Deo Gratias comes from hundreds of miles away.'

'Perhaps there is more than one "Pendélé" in the world.'

'A lot of people left the leproserie three nights ago. They've
most of them come back. I expect they had some kind of
witchcraft going on. He started too late and he couldn't catch
up with them.'

'I asked him what prayers. He said they prayed to Yezu

Klisto and someone called Simon. Is that the same as Simon Peter?'

'No, not quite the same. The fathers could tell you about Simon. He died in gaol nearly twenty years ago. They think he'll rise again. It's a strange Christianity we have here, but I wonder whether the Apostles would find it as difficult to understand as the collected works of Thomas Aquinas. If Peter could have understood those, it would have been a greater miracle than Pentecost, don't you think? Even the Nicaean Creed – it has the flavour of higher mathematics to me.'

'That word "Pendélé" runs in my head.'

'We always connect hope with youth,' Doctor Colin said, 'but sometimes it can be one of the diseases of age. The cancerous growth you find unexpectedly in the dying after a deep operation. These people here are all dying – oh, I don't mean of leprosy, I mean of us. And their last disease is hope.'

'Then you'll know where to look for me,' Querry said, 'if I should be missing.' An unexpected sound made the doctor look up; Querry's face was twisted into the rictus of a laugh. The doctor realized with astonishment that Querry had perpetrated a joke.

PART THREE

CHAPTER I

I

Rycker and his wife drove into town for cocktails with the Governor. In a village by the road stood a great wooden cage on stilts where once a year at a festival a man danced above the flames lit below: in the bush thirty kilometres before they had passed something sitting in a chair constructed out of a palm-nut and woven fibres into the rough and monstrous appearance of a human being. Inexplicable objects were the fingerprints of Africa. Naked women smeared white with grave-clay fled up the banks as the car passed, hiding their faces.

Rycker said, 'When Mme Guelle asks you what you will drink, say a glass of Perrier.'

'Not an *orange pressée*?'

'Not unless you can see a jug of it on the sideboard. We mustn't inconvenience her.'

Marie Rycker took in the advice seriously and then turned her eyes from her husband and stared away at the dull forest wall. The only path that led inside was closed with fibre-mats for a ceremony no white man must see.

'You heard what I said, darling?'

'Yes. I will remember.'

'And the *canapés*. Don't eat too many of them like you did last time. We haven't come to the Residence to take a meal. It creates a bad impression.'

'I won't touch a thing.'

'That would be just as bad. It would look as though you had noticed they were stale. They usually are.'

The little medal of St Christopher jingle-jangled like a fetish below the windscreen.

'I am frightened,' the girl said. 'It is all so complicated and Mme Guelle does not like me.'

'It isn't that she doesn't like you,' Rycker explained kindly. 'It is only that last time, you remember, you began to leave before the wife of the Commissioner. Of course, we are not bound by these absurd colonial rules, but we don't want to seem pushing and it is generally understood that as leading *commerçants* we come after the Public Works. Watch for Mme Cassin to leave.'

'I never remember any of their names.'

'The very fat one. You can't possibly miss her. By the way if Querry should be there don't be shy of inviting him for the night. In a place like this one longs for intelligent conversation. For the sake of Querry I would even put up with that atheist Doctor Colin. We could make up another bed on the veranda.'

But neither Querry nor Colin was there.

'A Perrier if you are sure it's no trouble,' Marie Rycker said. Everybody had been driven in from the garden, for it was the hour when the D.D.T. truck cannoned a stinging hygienic fog over the town.

Mme Guelle graciously brought the Perrier with her own hands. 'You are the only people,' she said, 'who seem to have met M. Querry. The mayor would have liked him to sign the Golden Book, but he seems to spend all his time in that sad place out there. Now you perhaps could pry him out for all our sakes.'

'We don't really know him,' Marie Rycker said. 'He spent the night with us when the river was in flood, that's all. He wouldn't have stayed otherwise. I don't think he wants to see people. My husband promised not to tell . . .'

'Your husband was quite right to tell *us*. We should have looked such fools, having *the* Querry in our own territory without being aware of it. How did he strike you, dear?'

'I hardly spoke to him.'

'His reputation in certain ways is very bad they tell me. Have you read the article in *Time*? Oh yes, of course, your husband showed it to us. Not of course that they write of *that*. It's only what they say in Europe. One has to remember though that some of the great saints of the Church passed through a certain period of – how shall I put it?'

'Do I hear you talking of saints, Mme Guelle?' Rycker asked. 'What excellent whisky you always have.'

'Not exactly saints. We were discussing M. Querry.'

'In my opinion,' Rycker said, raising his voice a little like a monitor in a noisy classroom, 'he may well be the greatest thing to happen in Africa since Schweitzer, and Schweitzer after all is a Protestant. I found him a most interesting companion when he stayed with us. And have you heard the latest story?' Rycker asked the room at large, shaking the ice in his glass like a hand-bell. 'He went out into the bush two weeks ago, they say, to find a leper who had run away. He spent the whole night with him in the forest, arguing and praying, and he persuaded the man to return and complete his treatment. It rained in the night and the man was sick with fever, so he covered him with his body.'

'What an unconventional thing to do,' Mme Guelle said. 'He's not, is he . . . ?'

The Governor was a very small man with a short-sight which gave him an appearance of moral intensity; physically he had the air of looking to his wife for protection, but like a small nation, proud of its culture, he was an unwilling satellite. He said, 'There are more saints in the world than the Church recognizes.' This remark stamped with official approval what might otherwise have been regarded as an eccentric or even an ambiguous action.

'Who is this man Querry?' the Director of Public Works asked the Manager of Otraco.

'They say he's a world-famous architect. You should know. He comes into your province.'

'He's not here officially, is he?'

'He's helping with the new hospital at the leproserie.'

'But I passed those plans months ago. They don't need an architect. It's a simple building job.'

'The hospital,' Rycker said, interrupting them and drawing them within his circle, 'you can take it from me, is only a first step. He is designing a modern African church. He hinted at that to me himself. He's a man of great vision. What he builds lasts. A prayer in stone. There's Monseigneur coming in. Now we shall learn what the Church thinks of Querry.'

The Bishop was a tall rakish figure with a neatly trimmed beard and the roving eye of an old-fashioned cavalier of the boulevards. He generously avoided putting out his hand to the men so that they might escape a genuflection. Women however liked to kiss his ring (it was a form of innocent flirtation), and he readily allowed it.

'So we have a saint among us, Monseigneur,' Mme Guelle said.

'You honour me too much. And how is the Governor? I don't see him here.'

'He's gone to unlock some more whisky. To tell the truth, Monseigneur, I was not referring to you. I'd be sorry to see you become a saint – for the time being, that is.'

'An Augustinian thought,' the Bishop said obscurely.

'We were talking about Querry, *the* Querry,' Rycker explained. 'A man in that position burying himself in a leproserie, spending a night praying with a leper in the bush – you must admit, Monseigneur, that self-sacrifices like that are rare. What do you think?'

'I am wondering, does he play bridge?' Just as the Governor's comment had given administrative approval to Querry's conduct, so the Bishop's question was taken to mean that the Church in her wise and traditional fashion reserved her opinion.

The Bishop accepted a glass of orange juice. Marie Rycker looked at it sadly. She had parked her Perrier and didn't know what to do with her hands. The Bishop said to her kindly, 'You should learn bridge, Mme Rycker. We have too few players round here now.'

'I am frightened of cards, Monseigneur.'

'I will bless the pack and teach you myself.' Marie Rycker was uncertain whether the Bishop was joking; she tried out an unnoticeable kind of smile.

Rycker said, 'I can't imagine how a man of Querry's calibre can work with that atheist Colin. That's a man, you can take it from me, who doesn't know the meaning of the word charity. Do you remember last year when I tried to organize a Lepers' Day? He would have nothing to do with it. He said he couldn't afford to accept charity. Four hundred dresses and suits had been accumulated and he refused to distribute them, just because there weren't enough to go round. He said he would have had to buy the rest out of his own pocket to avoid jealousy – why should a leper be jealous? You should talk to him one day, Monseigneur, on the nature of charity.'

But Monseigneur had moved on, his hand under Marie Rycker's elbow.

'Your husband seems very taken up with this man Querry,' he said.

'He thinks he may be somebody he can talk to.'

'Are you so silent?' the Bishop asked, teasing her gently as though he had indeed picked her up outside a café on the boulevards.

'I can't talk about his subjects.'

'What subjects?'

'Free Will and Grace and – Love.'

'Come now – love . . . you know about that, don't you?'

'Not that kind of love,' Marie Rycker said.

II

By the time the Ryckers came to go – they had to wait a long time for Mme Cassin – Rycker had drunk to the margin of what was dangerous; he had passed from excessive amiability to dissatisfaction, the kind of cosmic dissatisfaction which, after probing faults in others' characters, went on to the examination of his own. Marie Rycker knew that if he could be induced at this stage to take a sleeping-pill all might yet be well; he would probably reach unconsciousness before he reached religion which, like the open doorway in a red-lamp district, led invariably to sex.

'There are times,' Rycker said, 'when I wish we had a more spiritual bishop.'

'He was kind to me,' Marie Rycker said.

'I suppose he talked to you of cards.'

'He offered to teach me bridge.'

'I suppose he knew that I had forbidden you to play.'

'He couldn't. I've told no one.'

'I will not have my wife turned into a typical *colon*.'

'I think I am one already.' She added in a low voice, 'I don't want to be different.'

He said sharply. 'Spending all their time in small talk . . .'

'I wish I could. How I wish I could. If anyone could only teach me that . . .'

It was always the same. She drank nothing but Perrier, and yet the alcohol on his breath would make her talk as though the whisky had entered her own blood, and what she said then was always too close to the truth. Truth, which someone had once written made us free, irritated Rycker as much as one of his own hang-nails. He said, 'What nonsense. Don't talk like that for effect. There are times when you remind me of Mme Guelle.' The night sang discordantly at them from either side of the road, and the noises from the forest were louder than the engine. She had a longing for all the shops which climbed uphill along the rue de Namur: she tried to look through the lighted dashboard into a window full of shoes. She stretched out her foot beside the brake and said in a whisper, 'I take size six.'

'What did you say?'

'Nothing.'

In the light of the headlamp she saw the cage strutting by the road like a Martian.

'You are getting into a bad habit of talking to yourself.'

She said nothing. She couldn't tell him, 'There is no one else to speak to,' about the *pâtisserie* at the corner, the day when Sister Thérèse broke her ankle, the *plage* in August with her parents.

'A lot of it is my own fault,' Rycker said, reaching his second stage. 'I realize that. I have failed to teach you the real values as I see them. What can you expect from the manager of a palm-oil factory? I was not meant for this life.

I should have thought even you could have seen that.' His vain yellow face hung like a mask between her and Africa. He said, 'When I was young I wanted to be a priest.' He must have told her this, after drinks, at least once a month since they married, and every time he spoke she remembered their first night in the hotel at Antwerp, when he had lifted his body off her like a half-filled sack and dumped it at her side, and she, feeling some tenderness because she thought that in some way she had failed him, touched his shoulder (which was hard and round like a swede in the sack), and he asked her roughly, 'Aren't you satisfied? A man can't go on and on.' Then he had turned on his side away from her: the holy medal that he always wore had got twisted by their embrace and now lay in the small of his back, facing her like a reproach. She wanted to defend herself, 'It was you who married me. I know about chastity too – the nuns taught me.' But the chastity she had been taught was something which she connected with clean white garments and light and gentleness, while his was like old sackcloth in a desert.

'What did you say?'

'Nothing.'

'You are not even interested when I tell you my deepest feelings.'

She said miserably, 'Perhaps it was a mistake.'

'Mistake?'

'Marrying me. I was too young.'

'You mean I am too old to give you satisfaction.'

'No – no. I didn't mean . . .'

'You know only one kind of love, don't you? Do you suppose that's the kind of love the saints feel?'

'I don't know any saints,' she said desperately.

'You don't believe I am capable in my small way of going through the Dark Night of the Soul? I am only your husband who shares your bed . . .'

She whispered. 'I don't understand. Please, I don't understand.'

'What don't you understand?'

'I thought that love was supposed to make you happy.'

'Is that what they taught you in the convent?'

'Yes.'

He made a grimace at her, breathing heavily, and the coupé was filled momentarily with the scent of Vat 69. They passed beside the grim constructed figure in the chair; they were nearly home.

'What are you thinking?' he asked.

She had been back in the shop in the rue de Namur watching an elderly man who was gently, so gently, easing her foot into a stiletto-heeled shoe. So she said, 'Nothing.'

Rycker said in a voice suddenly kind, 'That is the opportunity for prayer.'

'Prayer?' She knew, but without relief, that the quarrel was over, for from experience she knew too that, after the rain had swept by, the lightning always came nearer.

'When I have nothing else to think of, I mean that I *have* to think of, I always say a *Pater Noster*, an *Ave Maria*, or even an Act of Contrition.'

'Contrition?'

'That I have been unjustly angry with a dear child whom I love.' His hand fell on her thigh and his fingers kneaded gently the silk of her skirt, as though they were seeking some muscle to fasten on. Outside the rusting abandoned cylinders showed they were approaching the house; they would see the lights of the bedrooms when they turned.

She wanted to go straight to her room, the small hot uninviting room where he sometimes allowed her to be alone during her monthly or unsafe periods, but he stopped her with a touch; she hadn't really expected to get away with it. He said, 'You aren't angry with me, Mawie?' He always lisped her name childishly at the moments when he felt least childish.

'No. It's only – it wouldn't be safe.' Her hope of escape was that he feared a child.

'Oh come. I looked up the calendar before I came out.'

'I've been so irregular the last two months.' Once she had bought a douche, but he had found it and thrown it away and afterwards he had lectured her on the enormity and unnaturalness of her act, speaking so long and emotionally on the subject of Christian marriage that the lecture had ended on the bed.

He put his hand below her waist and propelled her gently in the direction he required. 'Tonight,' he said, 'we'll take a risk.'

'But it's the worst time. I promise . . .'

'The Church doesn't intend us to avoid all risk. The safe period mustn't be abused, Mawie.'

She implored him, 'Let me go to my room for a moment. I've left my things there,' for she hated undressing in front of his scrutinizing gaze. 'I won't be long. I promise I won't be long.'

'I'll be waiting for you,' Rycker promised.

She undressed as slowly as she dared and took a pyjama jacket from under her pillow. There was no room here for anything but a small iron bed, a chair, a wardrobe, a chest-of-drawers. On the chest was a photograph of her parents – two happy elderly people who had married late and had one child. There was a picture postcard of Bruges sent by a cousin, and an old copy of *Time*. Underneath the chest she had hidden a key and now she unlocked the bottom drawer. Inside the drawer was her secret museum: a too-clean missal which she had been given at the time of her first communion, a sea-shell, the programme of a concert in Brussels. André Lejeune's *History of Europe* in one volume for the use of schools, and an exercise book containing an essay which she had written during her last term (she had received the maximum marks) on the Wars of Religion. Now she added to her collection the old copy of *Time*. Querry's face covered Lejeune's *History*: it lay, a discord, among the relics of childhood. She remembered Mme Guelle's words exactly: 'His reputation in certain ways is very bad.' She locked the drawer and hid the key – it was unsafe to delay any further. Then she walked along the veranda to *their* room, where Rycker was stretched naked inside the mosquito tent of the double-bed under the wooden body on the cross. He looked like a drowned man fished up in a net – hair lay like seaweed on his belly and legs; but at her entrance he came immediately to life, lifting the side of the tent. 'Come, Mawie,' he said. A Christian marriage, how often she had been told it by her religious instructors, symbolized the marriage of Christ and His Church.

CHAPTER 2

The Superior with old-fashioned politeness ground out his cheroot, but Mme Rycker was no sooner seated than absent-mindedly he lit another. His desk was littered with hardware catalogues and scraps of paper on which he had made elaborate calculations that always came out differently, for he was a bad mathematician – multiplication with him was an elaborate form of addition and a series of subtractions would take the place of long division. One page of a catalogue was open at the picture of a bidet which the Superior had mistaken for a new kind of foot-bath. When Mme Rycker entered he was trying to calculate whether he could afford to buy three dozen of these for the leproserie: they were just the thing for washing leprous feet.

'Why, Mme Rycker, you are an unexpected visitor. Is your husband . . .'

'No.'

'It's a long way to come alone.'

'I had company as far as the Perrins'. I spent the night there. My husband asked me to bring you two drums of oil.'

'How very kind of him.'

'I am afraid we do too little for the leproserie.'

It occurred to the Superior that he might ask the Ryckers to supply a few of the novel foot-baths, but he was uncertain how many they could afford. To a man without possessions any man with money appears rich – should he ask for one foot-bath or the whole three dozen? He began to turn the photographs towards Marie Rycker, cautiously, so that it might look as though he were only fiddling with his papers. It would be so much easier for him to speak if she were to exclaim, 'What an interesting new foot-bath,' so that he could follow up by saying –

Instead of that she confused him by changing the subject. 'How are the plans for the new church, father?'

61

'New church?'

'My husband told me you were building a wonderful new church as big as a cathedral, in an African style.'

'What an extraordinary idea. If I had the money for that' – not with all his scraps of paper could he calculate the cost of a 'church like a cathedral' – 'why, we could build a hundred houses, each with a foot-bath.' He turned the catalogue a little more towards her. 'Doctor Colin would never forgive me for wasting money on a church.'

'I wonder why my husband . . . ?'

Was it possibly a hint, the Superior wondered, that the Ryckers were prepared to finance . . . He could hardly believe that the manager of a palm-oil factory had made himself sufficiently rich, but Mme Rycker of course might have been left a fortune. Her inheritance would certainly be the talk of Luc, but he only made the journey to the town once a year. He said, 'The old church, you know, will serve us a long time yet. Only half our people are Catholics. Anyway it's no use having a great church if the people still live in mud huts. Now our friend Querry sees a way of cutting the cost of a cottage by a quarter. We were such amateurs here until he came.'

'My husband has told everyone that M. Querry is building a church.'

'Oh no, we have better uses for him than that. The new hospital too is a long way from being finished. Any money we can beg or steal must go to equipping it. I've just been looking at these catalogues . . .'

'Where is M. Qerry now?'

'Oh, I expect he's working in his room, unless he's with the doctor.'

'Everybody was talking about him at the Governor's two weeks ago.'

'Poor M. Querry.'

A small black child hardly more than two feet high walked into the room without knocking, coming in like a scrap of shadow from the noonday glare outside. He was quite naked and his little tassel hung like a bean-pod below the pot-belly.

He opened a drawer in the Superior's desk and pulled out a sweet. Then he walked out again.

'They were being quite complimentary,' Mme Rycker said. 'Is it true – about his boy getting lost . . . ?'

'Something of the sort happened. I don't know what *they* are saying.'

'That he stayed all night and prayed . . .'

'M. Querry is hardly a praying man.'

'My husband thinks a lot of him. There are so few people my husband can talk to. He asked me to come here and invite . . .'

'We are very grateful for the two drums of oil. What you have saved with those, we can spend . . .' He turned the photograph of the bidet a little farther towards Mme Rycker.

'Do you think I could speak to him?'

'The trouble is, Mme Rycker, this is his hour for work.'

She said imploringly, 'I only want to be able to tell my husband that I've asked him,' but her small toneless voice contained no obvious appeal and the Superior was looking elsewhere, at a feature of the foot-bath which he did not fully understand. 'What do you think of that?' he asked.

'What?'

'This foot-bath. I want to get three dozen for the hospital.'

He looked up because of her silence and was surprised to see her blushing. It occurred to him that she was a very pretty child. He said, 'Do you think . . . ?'

She was confused, remembering the ambiguous jokes of her more dashing companions at the convent. 'It's not really a foot-bath, father.'

'What else could it be for then?'

She said with the beginnings of humour, 'You'd better ask the doctor – or M. Querry.' She moved a little in her chair, and the Superior took it for a sign of departure.

'It's a long ride back to the Perrins', my dear. Can I offer you a cup of coffee, or a glass of beer?'

'No. No thank you.'

'Or a little whisky?' In all the long years of his abstinence the Superior had never learnt that whisky was too strong for the midday sun.

'No thank you. Please, father, I know you are busy. I don't want to be a nuisance, but if I could just see M. Querry and ask him . . .'

'I will give him your message, my dear. I promise I won't forget. See, I am writing it down.' He hesitated which sum to disfigure with the memo – 'Querry–Rycker'. It was impossible for him to tell her that he had given his promise to Querry to leave him undisturbed, 'particularly by that pious imbecile, Rycker'.

'It won't do, father. It won't do. I promised I'd see him myself. He won't believe I've tried.' She broke off and the Superior thought later, 'I really believe she was going to ask me for a note, the kind of note children take to school, saying that they have been genuinely ill.'

'I'm not even sure where he is,' the Superior said, emphasizing the word 'sure' to avoid a lie.

'If I could just look for him.'

'We can't have you wandering around in this sun. What would your husband say?'

'That's what I am afraid of. He'll never believe that I did my best.' She was obviously close to tears and this made her look younger, so that it was easy to discount the tears as the facile meaningless grief of childhood.

'I tell you what,' the Superior said, 'I will get him to telephone – when the line is in order.'

'I know that he doesn't like my husband,' she said with sad frankness.

'My dear child, it's all in your imagination.' He was at his wit's end. He said, 'Querry's a strange fellow. None of us really know him. Perhaps he likes none of us.'

'He stays with you. He doesn't avoid you.'

The Superior felt a stab of anger against Querry. These people had sent him two drums of oil. Surely they deserved in return a little civility. He said, 'Stay here. I'll see if Querry's in his room. We can't have you looking all over the leproserie . . .'

He left his study and turning the corner of the veranda

made for Querry's room. He passed the rooms of Father Thomas and Father Paul which were distinguished from each other by nothing more personal than an individual choice of crucifix and a differing degree of untidiness: then the chapel: then Querry's room. It was the only one in the place completely bare of symbols, bare indeed of almost everything. No photographs of a community or a parent. The room struck the Superior even in the heat of the day as cold and hard, like a grave without a cross. Querry was sitting at his table, a letter before him, when the Superior entered. He didn't look up.

'I'm sorry to disturb you,' the Superior said.

'Sit down, father. Just a moment while I finish this.' He turned the page and said, 'How do you end your letters, father?'

'It depends. Your brother in Christ perhaps?'

'*Toute à toi*. I remember I used to put that phrase too. How false it sounds now.'

'You have a visitor. I've kept my word and defended you to the last ditch. I can do no more. I wouldn't have disturbed you otherwise.'

'I'm glad you came. I don't relish being alone with this. You see – the mail has caught up with me. How did anyone know I was here? Does that damned local *Journal* in Luc circulate even in Europe?'

'Mme Rycker is here, asking for you.'

'Oh well, at least it's not her husband.'

He picked up the envelope. 'Do you see, she's even got the post box number right. What patience. She must have written to the Order.'

'Who is she?'

'She was once my mistress. I left her three months ago, poor woman – and that's hypocrisy. I feel no pity. I'm sorry, father. I didn't mean to embarrass you.'

'You haven't. It's Mme Rycker who has done that. She brought us two drums of oil and she wants to speak to you.'

'Am I worth that much?'

'Her husband sent her.'

'Is that the custom here? Tell him I'm not interested.'

'She's only brought you an invitation, poor young woman. Can't you see her and thank her and say no? She seems half afraid to go back unless she can say that she has talked to you. You aren't afraid of her, are you?'

'Perhaps. In a way.'

'Forgive me for saying it, M. Querry, but you don't strike me as a man who is afraid of women.'

'Have you never come across a leper, father, who is afraid of striking his fingers because he knows they won't hurt any more?'

'I've known men rejoice when the feeling returns – even pain. But you have to give pain a chance.'

'One can have a mirage of pain. Ask the amputated. All right, father, bring her in. It's a great deal better than seeing her wretched husband anyway.'

The Superior opened the door, and there the girl was on the threshold, in the glare of sun, caught with her mouth open, like someone surprised by a camera in a night-club, looking up in the flash, with an ungainly grimace of pain. She turned sharply round and walked away to where her car was parked and they heard her inefficient attempts at starting. The Superior followed her. A line of women returning from the market delayed him. He scampered a little way after the car, the cheroot still in his mouth and his white sun-helmet tip-tilted, but she drove away under the big arch which bore the name of the leproserie, her boy watching his antics curiously through the side-window. He came limping back because he had stubbed a toe.

'Silly child,' he said, 'why didn't she stay in my room? She could have spent the night with the nuns. She'll never get to the Perrins' by dark. I only hope her boy's reliable.'

'Do you suppose she heard?'

'Of course she heard. You didn't exactly lower your voice when you spoke of Rycker. If you love a man it can't be very pleasant to hear how unwelcome . . .'

'And it's far worse, father, when you don't love him at all.'

'Of course she loves him. He's her husband.'

'Love isn't one of the commonest characteristics of marriage, father.'

'They're both Catholics.'

'Nor is it of Catholics.'

'She's a very good young woman,' the Superior said obstinately.

'Yes, father. And what a desert she must live in out there alone with that man.' He looked at the letter which lay on his desk and that phrase of immolation which everyone used and some people meant – '*toute à toi*'. It occurred to him that one could still feel the reflection of another's pain when one had ceased to feel one's own. He put the letter in his pocket: it was fair at least that he should feel the friction of the paper. 'She's been taken a long way from "Pendélé",' he said.

'What's "Pendélé"?'

'I don't know – a dance at a friend's house, a young man with a shiny simple face, going to Mass on Sunday with the family, falling asleep in a single bed perhaps.'

'People have to grow up. We are called to more complicated things than that.'

'Are we?'

'"When we are a child we think as a child".'

'I can't match quotations from the Bible with you, father, but surely there's also something about having to be as little children if we are to inherit . . . We've grown up rather badly. The complications have become too complex – we should have stopped with the amoeba – no, long before that with the silicates. If your god wanted an adult world he should have given us an adult brain.'

'We most of us make our own complications, M. Querry.'

'Why did he give us genitals then if he wanted us to think clearly? A doctor doesn't prescribe marijuana for clear thought.'

'I thought you said you had no interest in anything.'

'I haven't. I've come through to the other side, to nothing. All the same I don't like looking back,' he said and the letter crackled softly as he shifted.

'Remorse is a kind of belief.'

'Oh no, it isn't. You try to draw everything into the net of your faith, father, but you can't steal all the virtues. Gentleness isn't Christian, self-sacrifice isn't Christian, charity isn't, remorse isn't. I expect the caveman wept to see another's tears. Haven't you even seen a dog weep? In the last cooling of the world, when the emptiness of your belief is finally exposed, there'll always be some bemused fool who'll cover another's body with his own to give it warmth for an hour more of life.'

'You believe that? But once I remember you saying you were incapable of love.'

'I am. The awful thing is I know it would be my body someone would cover. Almost certainly a woman. They have a passion for the dead. Their missals are stuffed with memorial cards.'

The Superior stubbed out his cheroot and then lit another as he moved towards the door. Querry called after him, 'I've come far enough, haven't I? Keep that girl away and her bloody tears.' He struck his hand furiously on the table because it seemed to him that he had used a phrase applicable only to the stigmata.

When the Superior had gone Querry called to Deo Gratias. The man came in propped on his three toeless feet. He looked to see if the wash-basin needed emptying.

'It's not that,' Querry said. 'Sit down. I want to ask you something.'

The man put down his staff and squatted on the ground. Even the act of sitting was awkward without toes or fingers. Querry lit a cigarette and put it in the man's mouth. He said, 'Next time you try to leave here, will you take me with you?'

The man made no answer. Querry said, 'No, you needn't answer. Of course you won't. Tell me, Deo Gratias, what was the water like? Like the big river out there?'

The man shook his head.

'Like the lake at Bikoro?'

'No.'

'What was it like, Deo Gratias?'

'It fell from the sky.'

'A waterfall?' But the word had no meaning to Deo Gratias in this flat region of river and deep bush.

'You were a child in those days on your mother's back. Were there many other children?'

He shook his head.

'Tell me what happened?'

'*Nous étions heureux*,' Deo Gratias said.

PART FOUR

CHAPTER I

I

Querry and Doctor Colin sat on the steps of the hospital in the cool of the early day. Every pillar had its shadow and every shadow its crouching patient. Across the road the Superior stood at the altar saying Mass, for it was a Sunday morning. The church had open sides, except for a lattice of bricks to break the sun, so that Querry and Colin were able to watch the congregation cut into shapes like a jigsaw pattern, the nuns on chairs in the front row and behind them the lepers sitting on long benches raised a foot from the ground, built of stone because stone could be disinfected more thoroughly and quickly than wood. At this distance it was a gay scene with the broken sun spangled on the white nuns' robes and the bright mammy cloths of the women. The rings which the women wore round their thighs jingled like rosaries when they knelt to pray, and all the mutilations were healed by distance and by the brickwork which hid their feet. Beyond the doctor on the top step sat the old man with elephantiasis, his scrotum supported on the step below. They talked in a whisper, so that their voices would not disturb the Mass which went on across the way – a whisper, a tinkle, a jingle, a shuffle, private movements of which they had almost forgotten the meaning, it was so long since they had taken any part.

'Is it really impossible to operate?' Querry asked.

'Too risky. His heart mightn't stand the anaesthetic.'

'Has he got to carry that thing around then till death?'

'Yes. It doesn't weigh as much as you would think. But it seems unfair, doesn't it, to suffer all that and leprosy too.'

In the church there was a sigh and a shuffle as the congregation sat. The doctor said, 'One day I'll screw some money out of someone and have a few wheel-chairs made for the worst cases. He would need a special one, of course. Could a famous ecclesiastical architect design a chair for swollen balls?'

'I'll get you a blueprint,' Querry said.

The voice of the Superior reached them from across the road. He was preaching in a mixture of French and Creole; even a Flemish phrase crept in here and there, and a word or two that Querry assumed to be Mongo or some other tongue of the river tribes.

'And I tell you truth I was ashamed when this man he said to me, "You Klistians are all big thieves – you steal this, you steal that, you steal all the time. Oh, I know you don't steal money. You don't creep into Thomas Olo's hut and take his new radio-set, but you are thieves all the same. Worse thieves than that. You see a man who lives with one wife and doesn't beat her and looks after her when she gets a bad pain from medicines at the hospital, and you say that's Klistian love. You go to the courthouse and you hear a good judge, who say to the piccin that stole sugar from the white man's cupboard, 'You're a very sorry piccin. I not punish you, and you, you will not come here again. No more sugar palaver,' and you say that's Klistian mercy. But you are a mighty big thief when you say that – for you steal this man's love and that man's mercy. Why do you not say when you see man with knife in his back bleeding and dying, 'There's Klistian anger'?"'

'I really believe he's answering something I said to him,' Querry said with a twitch of the mouth that Colin was beginning to recognize as a rudimentary smile, 'but I didn't put it quite like that.'

'Why not say when Henry Okapa got a new bicycle and someone came and tore his brake, "There's Klistian envy?" You are like a man who steals only the good fruit and leaves the bad fruit rotting on the tree.

'All right. You tell me I'm number one thief, but I say you

make big mistake. Any man may defend himself before his judge. All of you in this church, you are my judges now, and this is my defence.'

'It's a long time since I listened to a sermon,' Doctor Colin said. 'It brings back the long tedious hours of childhood, doesn't it?'

'You pray to Yezu,' the Superior was saying. He twisted his mouth from habit as though he were dispatching a cheroot from one side to the other. 'But Yezu is not just a holy man. Yezu is God and Yezu made the world. When you make a song you are in the song, when you bake bread you are in the bread, when you make a baby you are in the baby, and because Yezu made you, he is in you. When you love it is Yezu who loves, when you are merciful it is Yezu who is merciful. But when you hate or envy it is not Yezu, for everything that Yezu made is good. Bad things are not there – they are nothing. Hate means no love. Envy means no justice. They are just empty spaces, where Yezu ought to be.'

'He begs a lot of questions,' Doctor Colin said.

'Now I tell you that when a man loves, he must be Klistian. When a man is merciful he must be Klistian. In this village do you think you are the only Klistians – you who come to church? There is a doctor who lives near the well beyond Marie Akimbu's house and he prays to Nzambe and he makes bad medicine. He worships a false God, but once when a piccin was ill and his father and mother were in the hospital he took no money; he gave bad medicine but he took no money: he made a big God palaver with Nzambe for the piccin but took no money. I tell you then he was a Klistian, a better Klistian than the man who broke Henry Okapa's bicycle. He did not believe in Yezu, but he a Klistian. I am not a thief, who steal away his charity to give to Yezu. I give back to Yezu only what Yezu made. Yezu made love, he made mercy. Everybody in the world has something that Yezu made. Everybody in the world is that much a Klistian. So how can I be a thief? There is no man so wicked he never once in his life show in his heart something that God made.'

'That would make us both Christians,' Querry said. 'Do you feel a Christian, Colin?'

'I'm not interested,' Colin said. 'I wish Christianity could reduce the price of cortisone, that's all. Let's go.'

'I hate simplifications,' Querry said, and sat on.

The Superior said, 'I do not tell you to do good things for the love of God. That is very hard. Too hard for most of us. It is much easier to show mercy because a child weeps or to love because a girl or a young man pleases your eye. That's not wrong, that's good. Only remember that the love you feel and the mercy you show were made in you by God. You must go on using them and perhaps if you pray Klistian prayers it makes it easier for you to show mercy a second time and a third time . . .'

'And to love a second and a third girl,' Querry said.

'Why not?' the doctor asked.

'Mercy . . . love . . .' Querry said. 'Hasn't he ever known people to kill with love and kill with mercy? When a priest speaks those words they sound as though they had no meaning outside the vestry and the guild-meetings.'

'I think that is the opposite of what he's trying to say.'

'Does he want us to blame God for love? I'd rather blame man. If there is a god, let him be innocent at least. Come away, Colin, before you are converted and believe yourself an unconscious Christian.'

They rose and walked past the mutter of the *Credo* towards the dispensary.

'Poor man,' Colin said. 'It's a hard life, and he doesn't get many thanks. He does his best for everybody. If he believes I'm a crypto-Christian it's convenient for me, isn't it? There are many priests who wouldn't be happy to work with an atheist for a colleague.'

'He should have learnt from you that it's possible for an intelligent man to make his life without a god.'

'My life is easier than his – I have a routine that fills my day. I know when a man is cured by the negative skin-tests. There are no skin-tests for a good action. What were your motives, Querry, when you followed your boy into the forest?'

'Curiosity. Pride. Not Klistian love, I assure you.'

Colin said, 'All the same you talk as if you'd lost something you'd loved. I haven't. I think I have always liked my fellow men. Liking is a great deal safer than love. It doesn't demand victims. Who is your victim, Querry?'

'I have none now. I'm safe. I'm cured, Colin,' he added without conviction.

II

Father Paul took a helping of what was meant to be a cheese soufflé, then poured himself out a glass of water to ease it down. He said, 'Querry is wise today to lunch with the doctor. Can't you persuade the sisters to vary the *plat du jour*? Sunday after all is a feast-day.'

'This is meant to be a treat for us,' the Superior said. 'They believe we look forward to it all through the week. I wouldn't like to disillusion the poor things. They use a lot of eggs.'

All the cooking for the priests' house was done by the nuns and the food had to be carried a quarter of a mile in the sun. It had never occurred to the nuns that this might be disastrous for soufflés and omelettes and even for after-dinner coffee.

Father Thomas said, 'I do not think Querry minds much about his food.' He was the only priest in the leproserie with whom the Superior felt ill at ease; he still seemed to carry with him the strains and anxieties of the seminary. He had left it longer ago than any of the others, but he seemed doomed to a perpetual and unhappy youth; he was ill at ease with men who had grown up and were more concerned over the problems of the electric-light plant or the quality of the brickmaking than over the pursuit of souls. Souls could wait. Souls had eternity.

'Yes, he's a good enough guest,' the Superior said, steering a little away from the course that he suspected Father Thomas wished to pursue.

'He's a remarkable man,' Father Thomas said, struggling to regain direction.

'We have enough funds now,' the Superior said at large, 'for an electric fan in the delivery-ward.'

'We'll have air-conditioning in our rooms yet,' Father Jean said, 'and a drug-store and all the latest movie magazines including pictures of Brigitte Bardot.' Father Jean was tall, pale, and concave with a beard which struggled like an unpruned hedge. He had once been a brilliant moral theologian before he joined the Order and now he carefully nurtured the character of a film-fan, as though it would help him to wipe out an ugly past.

'I'd rather have a boiled egg for Sunday lunch,' Father Paul said.

'You wouldn't like stale eggs boiled,' Father Jean said, helping himself to more soufflé; in spite of his cadaverous appearance he had a Flemish appetite.

'They wouldn't be stale,' Father Joseph said, 'if they only learnt to manage the chickens properly. I'd be quite ready to put some of my men on to building them proper houses for intensive production. It would be easy enough to carry the electric power down from their houses . . .'

Brother Philippe spoke for the first time. He was always reluctant to intrude on the conversation of men who he considered belonged to another less mundane world. 'Electric fans, chicken houses: be careful, father, or you will be overloading the dynamos before you've done.'

The Superior was aware that Father Thomas was smouldering at his elbow. He said tactfully, 'And the new classroom, father? Have you everything that's needed?'

'Everything but a catechist who knows the first thing about his faith.'

'Oh well, so long as he can teach the alphabet. First things first.'

'I should have thought the Catechism was rather more important than the alphabet.'

'Rycker was on the telephone this morning,' Father Jean said, coming to the Superior's rescue.

'What did he want?'

'Querry of course. He said he had a message – something about an Englishman, but he refused to give it. He threatened to be over one day soon, when the ferries are working again.

I asked him if he could bring me some film magazines, but he said he didn't read them. He also wants to borrow Father Garrigou-Lagrange on Predestination.'

'There are moments,' the Superior said with moderation, 'when I almost regret M. Querry's arrival.'

'Surely we should be very glad,' Father Thomas said, 'of any small inconvenience he may bring us. We don't live a very troubled life.' The helping of soufflé he had taken remained untasted on his plate. He kneaded a piece of bread into a hard pellet and washed it down like a pill. 'You can't expect people to leave us alone while he is here. It's not only that he's a famous man. He's a man of profound faith.'

'I hadn't noticed it,' Father Paul said. 'He wasn't at Mass this morning.' The Superior lit another cheroot.

'Oh yes he was. I can tell you his eyes never left the altar. He was sitting across the way with the sick. That's as good a way of attending Mass as sitting up in front with his back to the lepers, isn't it?'

Father Paul opened his mouth to reply, but the Superior stopped him with a covert wink. 'At any rate it is a charitable way of putting it,' the Superior said. He balanced his cheroot on the edge of his plate and rose to give thanks. Then he crossed himself and picked up his cheroot again. 'Father Thomas,' he said, 'can you spare me a minute?'

He led the way to his room and installed Father Thomas in the one easy chair that he kept for visitors by the filing-cabinet. Father Thomas watched him tensely, sitting bolt upright, like a cobra watching a mongoose. 'Have a cheroot, father?'

'You know I don't smoke.'

'Of course. I'm sorry. I was thinking of someone else. Is that chair uncomfortable? I'm afraid the springs may have gone. It's foolish having springs in the tropics, but it was given us with a lot of junk . . .'

'It's quite comfortable, thank you.'

'I'm sorry you don't find your catechist satisfactory. It's not so easy to find a good one now that we have three classes for boys. The nuns seem to manage better than we do.'

'Only if you consider Marie Akimbu a suitable teacher.'

'She works very hard I'm told by Mother Agnes.'

'Certainly, if you call having a baby every year by a different man hard work. I can't see that it's right allowing her to teach with her cradle in the class. She's pregnant again. What kind of an example is that?'

'Oh well, you know, *autres pays autres mœurs*. We are here to help, father, not condemn, and I don't think we can teach the sisters their business. They know the young woman better than we do. Here, you must remember, there are few people who know their own fathers. The children belong to the mother. Perhaps that's why they prefer us, and the Mother of God, to the Protestants.' The Superior searched for words. 'Let me see, father, you've been with us now – it must be over two years?'

'Two years next month.'

'You know you don't eat enough. That soufflé wasn't exactly inviting . . .'

'I have no objection to the soufflé. I happen to be fasting for a private intention.'

'Of course you have your confessor's consent?'

'It wasn't necessary for just one day, father.'

'The soufflé day was a good day to choose then, but you know this climate is very difficult for Europeans, especially at the beginning. By the time our leave comes at the end of six years we have become accustomed to it. Sometimes I almost dread going home. The first years . . . one mustn't drive oneself.'

'I am not aware of driving myself unduly, father.'

'Our first duty, you know, is to survive, even if that means taking things a little more easily. You have a great spirit of self-sacrifice, father. It's a wonderful quality, but it's not always what's required on the battlefield. The good soldier doesn't court death.'

'I am quite unaware . . .'

'We all of us have a feeling of frustration sometimes. Poor Marie Akimbu, we have to take the material we have to hand. I'm not sure that you'd find better material in some of the parishes of Liège, though sometimes I've wondered whether perhaps you might be happier there. The African mission is not for everyone. If a man feels himself ill-adapted here, there's no defeat in asking for a transfer. Do you sleep properly, father?'

'I have enough sleep.'

'Perhaps you ought to have a check-up with Doctor Colin. It's wonderful what a pill will do at the right time.'

'Father, why are you so against M. Querry?'

'I hope I'm not. I'm unaware of it.'

'What other man in his position – he's world-famous, father, even though Father Paul may never have heard of him – would bury himself here, helping with the hospital?'

'I don't look for motives, Father Thomas. I hope I accept what he does with gratitude.'

'Well, I do look for motives. I've been talking to Deo Gratias. I hope I would have done what he did, going out at night into the bush looking for a servant, but I doubt . . .'

'Are you afraid of the dark?'

'I'm not ashamed to say that I am.'

'Then it would have needed more courage in your case. I have still to find what does frighten M. Querry.'

'Well, isn't that heroic?'

'Oh no. I am disturbed by a man without fear as I would be by a man without a heart. Fear saves us from so many things. Not that I'm saying, of course, that M. Querry . . .'

'Does it show a lack of heart staying beside his boy all night, praying with him?'

'They are telling that story in the city, I know, but did he pray? It's not what Querry told the doctor.'

'I asked Deo Gratias. He said yes. I asked him what prayers – the *Ave Maria*, I asked him? He said yes.'

'Father Thomas, when you have been in Africa a little longer, you will learn not to ask an African a question which may be answered by yes. It is their form of courtesy to agree. It means nothing at all.'

'I think after two years I can tell when an African is lying.'

'Those are not lies. Father Thomas, I can well understand

why you are attracted to Querry. You are both men of extremes. But in our way of life, it is better for us not to have heroes – not live heroes, that is. The saints should be enough for us.'

'You are not suggesting there are not live saints?'

'Of course not. But don't let's recognize them before the Church does. We shall be saved a lot of disappointment that way.'

III

Father Thomas stood by his netted door staring through the wire mesh at the ill-lighted avenue of the leproserie. Behind him on his table he had prepared a candle and the flame shone palely below the bare electric globe; in five minutes all the lights would go out. This was the moment he feared; prayers were of no avail to heal the darkness. The Superior's words had reawakened his longing for Europe. Liège might be an ugly and brutal city, but there was no hour of the night when a man, lifting his curtain, could not see a light shining on the opposite wall of the street or perhaps a late passer-by going home. Here at ten o'clock, when the dynamos ceased working, it needed an act of faith to know that the forest had not come up to the threshold of the room. Sometimes it seemed to him that he could hear the leaves brushing on the mosquito wire. He looked at his watch – four minutes to go.

He had admitted to the Superior that he was afraid of the dark. But the Superior had brushed away his fear as of no account. He felt an enormous longing to confide, but it was almost impossible to confide in men of his own Order, any more than a soldier could admit his cowardice to another soldier. He couldn't say to the Superior, 'Every night I pray that I won't be summoned to attend someone dying in the hospital or in his kitchen, that I won't have to light the lamp of my bicycle and pedal through the dark.' A few weeks ago an old man had so died, but it was Father Joseph who went out to find the corpse where it sat in a rickety deck-chair with some fetish or other for Nzambi placed in its lap and a holy medal round its neck; he had given conditional absolution by the light of the bicycle-lamp because there were no candles to be found.

He believed that the Superior grudged the admiration he felt for Querry. His companions, it seemed to him, spent their lives with small concerns which they could easily discuss together – the cost of foot-baths, a fault in the dynamo, a holdup at the brick-kiln, but the things which worried him he could discuss with no one. He envied the happily married man who had a ready confidante at bed and board. Father Thomas was married to the Church and the Church responded to his confidence only in the clichés of the confessional. He remembered how even in the seminary his confessor had checked him whenever he had gone farther than the platitudes of his problem. The word 'scruple' was posted like a traffic sign in whichever direction the mind drove. 'I want to talk, I want to talk,' Father Thomas cried silently to himself as all the lights went out and the beat of the dynamos stopped. Somebody came down the veranda in the dark; the steps passed the room of Father Paul and would have passed his own if he had not called out, 'Is it you, M. Querry?'

'Yes.'

'Won't you come in for a moment?'

Querry opened the door and came into the small radiance of the candle. He said, 'I've been explaining to the Superior the difference between a bidet and a foot-bath.'

'Please won't you sit down? I can never sleep so early as this and my eyes are not good enough to read by candle-light.' Already in one sentence he had admitted more to Querry than he had ever done to his Superior, for he knew that the Superior would only too readily have given him a torch and permission to read for as long as he liked after the lights went, but that permission would have drawn attention to his weakness. Querry looked for a chair. There was only one and Father Thomas began to pull back the mosquito-net from the bed.

'Why not come to my room?' Querry asked. 'I have some whisky there.'

'Today I am fasting,' Father Thomas said. 'Please take the

chair. I will sit here.' The candle burnt straight upwards to a smoky tip like a crayon. 'I hope you are happy here,' Father Thomas said.

'Everyone has been very kind to me.'

'You are the first visitor to stay here since I came.'

'Is that so?'

Father Thomas's long narrow nose was oddly twisted at the end; it gave him the effect of smelling sideways at some elusive odour. 'Time is needed to settle in a place like this.' He laughed nervously. 'I'm not sure that I'm settled myself yet.'

'I can understand that,' Querry said mechanically for want of anything better to say, but the bromide was swallowed like wine by Father Thomas.

'Yes, you have great understanding. I sometimes think a layman has more capacity for understanding than a priest. Sometimes,' he added, 'more faith.'

'That's certainly not true in my case,' Querry said.

'I have told this to no one else,' Father Thomas said, as though he were handing over some precious object which would leave Querry for ever in his debt. 'When I finished at the seminary I sometimes thought that only by martyrdom could I save myself – if I could die before I lost everything.'

'One doesn't die,' Querry said.

'I wanted to be sent to China, but they wouldn't accept me.'

'Your work here must be just as valuable,' Querry said, dealing out his replies quickly and mechanically like cards.

'Teaching the alphabet?' Father Thomas shifted on the bed and the drape of mosquito-net fell over his face like a bride's veil or a beekeeper's. He turned it back and it fell again, as though even an inanimate object had enough consciousness to know the best moment to torment.

'Well, it's time for bed,' Querry said.

'I'm sorry. I know I'm keeping you up. I'm tiring you.'

'Not at all,' Querry said. 'Besides I sleep badly.'

'You do? It's the heat. I can't sleep for more than a few hours.'

'I could let you have some pills.'

'Oh no, no, thank you. I must learn somehow – this is the place God has sent me to.'

'Surely you volunteered?'

'Of course, but if it hadn't been His will . . .'

'Perhaps it's his will that you should take a nembutal. Let me fetch you one.'

'It does me so much more good just to talk to you for a little. You know in a community one doesn't talk – about anything important. I'm not keeping you from your work, am I?'

'I can't work by candle-light.'

'I'll release you very soon,' Father Thomas said, smiling weakly, and then fell silent again. The forest might be approaching, but for once he had a companion. Querry sat with his hands between his knees waiting. A mosquito hummed near the candle-flame. The dangerous desire to confide grew in Father Thomas's mind like the pressure of an orgasm. He said, 'You won't understand how much one needs, sometimes, to have one's faith fortified by talking to a man who believes.'

Querry said, 'You have the fathers.'

'We talk only about the dynamo and the schools.' He said, 'Sometimes I think if I stay here I'll lose my faith altogether. Can you understand that?'

'Oh yes, I can understand that. But I think it's your confessor you should talk to, not me.'

'Deo Gratias talked to you, didn't he?'

'Yes. A little.'

'You make people talk. Rycker . . .'

'God forbid.' Querry moved restlessly on the hard chair. 'What I would say to you wouldn't help you at all. You must believe that. I'm not a man of – faith.'

'You are a man of humility,' Father Thomas said. 'We've all noticed that.'

'If you knew the extent of my pride . . .'

'Pride which builds churches and hospitals is not so bad a pride.'

'You mustn't use me to buttress your faith, father. I'd be the weak spot. I don't want to say anything that could disturb you more – but I've nothing for you – nothing. I wouldn't even call myself a Catholic unless I were in the army or in a prison. I am a legal Catholic, that's all.'

'We both of us have our doubts,' Father Thomas said. 'Perhaps I have more than you. They even come to me at the altar with the Host in my hands.'

'I've long ceased to have doubts. Father, if I must speak plainly, I don't believe at all. Not at all. I've worked it out of my system – like women. I've no desire to convert others to disbelief, or even to worry them. I want to keep my mouth shut, if only you'd let me.'

'You can't think what a lot of good our conversation has done me,' Father Thomas said with excitement. 'There's not a priest here to whom I can talk as we're talking. One sometimes desperately needs a man who has experienced the same weaknesses as oneself.'

'But you've misunderstood me, father.'

'Don't you see that perhaps you've been given the grace of aridity? Perhaps even now you are walking in the footsteps of St John of the Cross, the *noche oscura*.'

'You are so very far from the truth,' Querry said, making a movement with his hands of bewilderment or rejection.

'I've watched you here,' Father Thomas said, 'I am capable of judging a man's actions.' He leant forward until his face was not very far from Querry's and Querry could smell the lotion Father Thomas used against mosquito bites. 'For the first time since I came to this place, I feel I can be of use. If you ever have the need to confess, always remember I am here.'

'The only confession I am ever likely to make,' Querry said, 'would be to an examining magistrate.'

'Ha, ha.' Father Thomas caught the joke in mid-air and confiscated it, like a schoolboy's ball, under his soutane. He said, 'Those doubts you have. I can assure you I know them too. But couldn't we perhaps go over together the philosophical arguments . . . to help us both?'

'They wouldn't help me, father. Any sixteen-year-old student could demolish them, and anyway I need no help. I don't want to be harsh, father, but I don't wish to believe. I'm cured.'

'Then why do I get more sense of faith from you than from anyone here?'

'It's in your own mind, father. You are looking for faith and so I suppose you find it. But I'm not looking. I don't want any of the things I've known and lost. If faith were a tree growing at the end of the avenue, I promise you I'd never go that way. I don't mean to say anything to hurt you, father. I would help you if I could. If you feel in pain because you doubt, it is obvious that you are feeling the pain of faith, and I wish you luck.'

'You really do understand, don't you?' Father Thomas said, and Querry could not restrain an expression of tired despair. 'Don't be irritated. Perhaps I know you better than you do yourself. I haven't found so much understanding, "not in all Israel" if you can call the community that. You have done so much good. Perhaps – another night – we could have a talk again. On our problems – yours and mine.'

'Perhaps, but –'

'And pray for me, M. Querry. I would value your prayers.'

'I don't pray.'

'I have heard differently from Deo Gratias,' Father Thomas said, fetching up a smile like a liquorice-stick, dark and sweet and prehensile. He said, 'There are interior prayers, the prayers of silence. There are even unconscious prayers when men have goodwill. A thought from you may be a prayer in the eyes of God. Think of me occasionally, M. Querry.'

'Of course.'

'I would like to be of help to you as you have been to me.' He paused as though he were waiting for some appeal, but Querry only put a hand to his face and brushed away the sticky tendrils which a spider had left dangling between him and the door. 'I shall sleep tonight,' Father Thomas said, threateningly.

CHAPTER 2

I

About twice a month the Bishop's boat was due to come in with the heavier provisions for the leproserie, but sometimes many weeks went by without a visit. They waited for it with forced patience; perhaps the captain of the Otraco boat which brought the mail would also bring news of her small rival – a snag in the river might have pierced its bottom: it might be stranded on a mud-bank; perhaps the rudder had been twisted in collision with a fallen tree-trunk; or the captain might be down with fever or have been appointed a professor of Greek by the Bishop who had not yet found a priest to take his place. It was not a very popular job among members of the Order. No knowledge of navigation was required, not even of machinery, for the African mate was in virtual charge of the engine and the bridge. Four weeks of loneliness on the river every trip, the attempt at each halt to discover some cargo which had not been pledged to Otraco, such a life compared unfavourably with employment at the cathedral in Luc or even at a seminary in the bush.

It was dusk when the inhabitants of the leproserie heard the bell of the long-overdue boat; the sound came to Colin and Querry where they sat over the first drink of the evening on the doctor's veranda. 'At last,' Colin said, finishing his whisky, 'if only they have brought the new X-ray . . .'

White flowers had opened with twilight on the long avenue; fires were being lit for the evening meal, and the mercy of darkness was falling at last over the ugly and the deformed. The wrangles of the night had not yet begun, and peace was there, something you could touch like a petal or smell like wood smoke. Querry said to Colin, 'You know I am happy here.' He closed his mouth on the phrase too late; it had escaped him on the sweet evening air like an admission. 'I remember the day you came,' Colin said. 'You were walking up this road and I asked you how long you were going to stay. You said – do you reemember? –'

But Querry was silent and Colin saw that he already regretted having spoken at all.

The white boat came slowly round the bend of the river; a lantern was alight at the bow, and the pressure-lamp was burning in the saloon. A black figure, naked except for a loincloth, was poised with a rope on the pontoon, preparing to throw it. The fathers in their white soutanes gathered on the veranda like moths round a treacle-jar, and when Colin looked behind him he could see the glow of the Superior's cheroot following them down the road.

Colin and Querry halted at the top of the steep bank above the river. An African dived in from the pontoon and swam ashore as the engines petered out. He caught the rope and made it fast around a rock and the top-heavy boat eased in. A sailor pushed a plank across for a woman who came ashore carrying two live turkeys on her head; she fussed with her mammy cloths, draping and redraping them about her waist.

'The great world comes to us,' Colin said.

'What do you mean?'

The captain waved from the window of the saloon. Along the narrow deck the door of the Bishop's cabin was closed, but a faint light shone through the mosquito netting.

'Oh, you never know what the boat may bring. After all, it brought you.'

'They seem to have a passenger,' Querry said.

The captain gesticulated to them from the window; his arm invited them to come aboard. 'Has he lost his voice?' the Superior said, joining them at the top of the bank, and cupping his hands he yelled as loudly as he could, 'Well, captain, you are late.' The sleeve of a white soutane moved in the dusk; the captain had put a finger to his lips. 'In God's name,' the Superior said, 'has he got the Bishop on board?' He led the way down the slope and across the gang-plank.

Colin said, 'After you.' He was aware of Querry's hesitation. He said, 'We'll have a glass of beer. It's the custom,' but Querry made no move. 'The captain will be glad to see you again,' he went on, his hand under Querry's elbow to help him down the bank. The Superior was picking his way among the women, the goats and the cooking-pots, which littered the pontoon, towards the iron ladder by the engine.

'What you said about the world?' Querry said. 'You don't really suppose, do you . . . ?' and he broke off with his eyes on the cabin that he had once occupied, where the candle-flame was wavering in the river-draught.

'It was a joke,' Colin said. 'I ask you – does it look like the great world?' Night which came in Africa so quickly had wiped the whole boat out, except the candle in the Bishop's cabin, the pressure-lamp in the saloon where two white figures silently greeted each other, and the hurricane-lamp at the foot of the ladder where a woman sat preparing her husband's chop.

'Let's go,' Querry said.

At the top of the ladder the captain greeted them. He said, 'So you are still here, Querry. It is a pleasure to see you again.' He spoke in a low voice; he might have been exchanging a confidence. In the saloon the beer was already uncapped and awaiting them. The captain shut the door and for the first time raised his voice. He said, 'Drink up quickly, Doctor Colin. I have a patient for you.'

'One of the crew?'

'Not one of the crew,' the captain said, raising his glass. 'A real passenger. I've only had two real passengers in two years, first there was M. Querry and now this man. A passenger who pays, not a father.'

'Who is he?'

'He comes from the great world,' the captain said, echoing Colin's phrase. 'It has been difficult for me. He speaks no Flemish and very little French, and that made it yet more complicated when he went down with fever. I am very glad to be here,' he said and seemed about to lapse into his more usual silence.

'Why has he come?' the Superior asked.

'How do I know? I tell you – he speaks no French.'

'Is he a doctor?'

'He is certainly not a doctor or he wouldn't be so frightened of a little fever.'

'Perhaps I should see him right away,' Colin said. 'What language does he speak?'

'English. I tried him in Latin,' the captain said. 'I even tried him in Greek, but it was no good.'

'I can speak English,' Querry said with reluctance.

'How is his fever?' Colin said.

'This is the worst day. Tomorrow it will be better. I said to him, "*Finitum est*," but I think he believed that I meant he was dying.'

'Where did you pick him up?'

'At Luc. He had some kind of introduction to the Bishop – from Rycker, I think. He had missed the Otraco boat.'

Colin and Querry went down the narrow deck to the Bishop's cabin. Hanging at the end of the deck was the misshapen life-belt looking like a dried eel, the steaming shower, the lavatory with the broken door, and beside it the kitchen-table and the hutch where two rabbits munched in the dark; nothing, except presumably the rabbits, had changed. Colin opened the cabin door, and there was the photograph of the church under snow, but in the rumpled bed which Querry had somehow imagined would still bear, like a hare's form, his own impression, lay the naked body of a very fat man. His neck as he lay on his back was forced into three ridges like gutters and the sweat filled them and drained round the curve of his head on to the pillow.

'I suppose we'll have to take him ashore,' Colin said. 'If there's a spare room at the fathers'.' On the table stood a Rolleiflex camera and a portable Remington, and inserted in the typewriter was a sheet of paper on which the man had begun to type. When Querry brought the candle closer he could read one sentence in English: 'The eternal forest broods along the banks unchanged since Stanley and his little band –' It petered out without punctuation. Colin lifted the man's wrist and felt his pulse. He said, 'The captain's right. He'll be up in a few days. This sleep marks the end.'

'Then why not leave him here?' Querry said.

'Do you know him?'

'I've never seen him before.'

'I thought you sounded afraid,' Colin said. 'We can hardly ship him back if he's paid his passage here.'

The man woke as Colin dropped his wrist. 'Are you the doctor?' he asked in English.

'Yes. My name is Doctor Colin.'

'I'm Parkinson,' the man said firmly as though he were the sole survivor of a whole tribe of Parkinsons. 'Am I dying?'

'He wants to know if he is dying,' Querry translated.

Colin said, 'You will be all right in a few days.'

'It's bloody hot,' Parkinson said. He looked at Querry. 'Thank God there's someone here at last who speaks English.' He turned his head towards the Remington and said, 'The white man's grave.'

'Your geography's wrong. This is not West Africa,' Querry corrected him with dry dislike.

'They won't know the bloody difference,' Parkinson said.

'And Stanley never came this way,' Querry went on, without attempting to disguise his antagonism.

'Oh yes he did. This river's the Congo, isn't it?'

'No. You left the Congo a week ago after Luc.'

The man said again ambiguously. 'They won't know the bloody difference. My head's splitting.'

'He's complaining about his head,' Querry told Colin.

'Tell him I'll give him something when we've taken him ashore. Ask him if he can walk as far as the fathers'. He would be a terrible weight to carry.'

'Walk!' Parkinson exclaimed. He twisted his head and the sweat-gutters drained on to the pillow. 'Do you want to kill me? It would be a bloody good story, wouldn't it, for everyone but me. Parkinson buried where Stanley once . . .'

'Stanley was never here,' Querry said.

'I don't care whether he was or not. Why keep bringing it

up? I'm bloody hot. There ought to be a fan. If the chap here is a doctor, why can't he take me to a proper hospital?'

'I doubt if you'd like the hospital we have,' Querry said. 'It's for lepers,'

'Then I'll stay where I am.'

'The boat returns to Luc tomorrow.'

Parkinson said, 'I can't understand what the doctor says. Is he a good doctor? Can I trust him?'

'Yes, he's a good doctor.'

'But they never tell the patient, do they?' Parkinson said. 'My old man died thinking he only had a duodenal ulcer.'

'You are not dying. You have got a touch of malaria, that's all. You are over the worst. It would be much easier for all of us if you'd walk ashore. Unless you want to return to Luc.'

'When I start a job,' Parkinson said obscurely, 'I finish a job.' He wiped his neck dry with his fingers. 'My legs are like butter,' he said. 'I must have lost a couple of stone. It's the strain on the heart I'm afraid of.'

'It's no use,' Querry told Colin. 'We'll have to have him carried.'

'I will see what can be done,' Colin said and left them. When they were alone, Parkinson said, 'Can you use a camera?'

'Of course.'

'With a flash bulb?'

'Yes.'

He said, 'Would you do me a favour and take some pictures of me carried ashore? Get as much atmosphere in as you can – you know the kind of thing, black faces gathered round looking worried and sympathetic.'

'Why should they be worried?'

'You can easily fix that,' Parkinson said. 'They'll be worried enough anyway in case they drop me – and *they* won't know the difference.'

'What do you want the picture for?'

'It's the kind of thing they like to have. You can't distrust a photograph, or so people think. Do you know, since you came into the cabin and I could talk again, I've been feeling

better? I'm not sweating so much, am I? And my head . . .'
He twisted it tentatively and gave a groan again. 'Oh well, if
I hadn't had this malaria, I daresay I'd have had to invent it.
It gives the right touch.'

'I wouldn't talk so much if I were you.'

'I'm bloody glad the boat-trip's over, I can tell you that.'

'Why have you come here?'

'Do you know a man called Querry?' Parkinson said.

The man had struggled round on to his side. The reflection from the candle shone back from the dribbles and pools
of sweat so that the face appeared like a too-travelled road
after rain. Querry knew for certain he had never seen the man
before, and yet he remembered how Doctor Colin had said
to him, 'The great world comes to us.'

'Why do you want Querry?' he asked.

'It's my job to want him,' Parkinson said. He groaned again.
'It's no bloody picnic this. You wouldn't lie to me, would you,
about the doctor? And what he said?'

'No.'

'It's my heart, as I told you. Two stone in a week. This too
too solid flesh is surely melting. Shall I tell you a secret? The
daredevil Parkinson is sometimes damned afraid of death.'

'Who are you?' Querry asked. The man turned his face
away with irritable indifference and closed his eyes. Soon he
was asleep again.

He was still asleep when they carried him off the boat
wrapped in a piece of tarpaulin like a dead body about to be
committed to the deep. It needed six men to lift him and they
got in each other's way, so that once as they struggled up the
bank, a man slipped and fell. Querry was in time to prevent
the body falling. The head rammed his chest and the smell of
hair-oil poisoned the night. He wasn't used to supporting such
a weight and he was breathless and sweating as they got the
body over the rise and came on Father Thomas standing there
holding a hurricane-lamp. Another African took Querry's
place and Querry walked behind at Father Thomas's side.
Father Thomas said, 'You shouldn't have done that – a weight
like that, in this heat – it's rash at your age. Who is he?'

'I don't know. A stranger.'

Father Thomas said, 'Perhaps a man can be judged by his rashness.' The glow of the Superior's cheroot approached them through the dark. 'You won't find much rashness here,' Father Thomas went angrily on. 'Bricks and mortar and the monthly bills – that's what we think about. Not the Samaritan on the road to Jericho.'

'Nor do I. I just took a hand for a few minutes, that's all.'

'We could all learn from you,' Father Thomas said, taking Querry's arm above the elbow as though he were an old man who needed the support of a disciple.

The Superior overtook them. He said, 'I don't know where we are going to put him. We haven't a room free.'

'Let him share mine. There's room for the two of us,' Father Thomas said, and he squeezed Querry's arm as if he wished to convey to him, 'I at least have learnt your lesson. I am not as my brothers are.'

CHAPTER 3

I

Doctor Colin had before him a card which carried the outline drawing of a man. He had made the drawing himself; the cards he had ordered in Luc because he despaired of obtaining any like them from home. The trouble was they cost too little; the invoices had fallen like fine dust through the official tray that sifted his requests for aid. There was nobody on the lower levels of the Ministry at home with authority to allow an expenditure of six hundred francs, and nobody with courage enough to worry a senior officer with such a paltry demand. Now whenever he used the charts he felt irritated by his own bad drawings. He ran his fingers over a patient's back and detected a new thickening of the skin below the left shoulder-blade. He drew the shading on his chart and called, 'Next.' Perhaps he might have forestalled that patch if the new hospital had been finished and the new apparatus installed for taking the temperature of the skin. 'It is not a case of what I have done,' he thought, 'but of what I am going to do.' This optimistic phrase had an ironic meaning for Doctor Colin.

When he first came to this country, there was an old Greek shopkeeper living in Luc – a man in his late seventies who was famous for his reticence. A few years before he had married a young African woman who could neither read nor write. People wondered what kind of contact they could have, at his age, with his reticence and her ignorance. One day he saw his African clerk bedding her down at the back of the warehouse behind some sacks of coffee. He said nothing at all, but next day he went to the bank and took out his savings. Most of the savings he put in an envelope and posted in at the door of the local orphanage which was always chock-a-block with

93

unwanted half-castes. The rest he took with him up the hill behind the courthouse to a garage which sold ancient cars, and there he bought the cheapest car they could sell him. It was so old and so cheap that even the manager, perhaps because he too was a Greek, had scruples. The car could only be trusted to start on top of a hill, but the old man said that didn't matter. It was his ambition to drive a car once before he died – his whim if you liked to call it that. So they showed him how to put it into gear and how to accelerate, and shoving behind they gave him a good running start. He rode down to the square in Luc where his store was situated and began hooting as soon as he got there. People stopped to look at the strange sight of the old man driving his first car, and as he passed the store his clerk came out to see the fun. The old man drove all round the square a second time – he couldn't have stopped the car anyway because it would not start on the flat. Round he came with his clerk waving in the doorway to encourage him, then he twisted the wheel, trod down on the accelerator and drove straight over his clerk into the store, where the car came to the final halt of all time up against the cash register. Then he got out of the car, and leaving it just as it was, he went into his parlour and waited for the police to arrive. The clerk was not dead, but both his legs were crushed and the pelvis was broken and he wouldn't be any good for a woman ever again. Presently the Commissioner of Police walked in. He was a young man and this was his first case and the Greek was highly respected in Luc. 'What have you done?' he demanded when he came into the parlour. 'It is not a case of what have I done,' the old man said, 'but of what I am going to do,' and he took a gun from under the cushion and shot himself through the head. Doctor Colin since those days had often found comfort in the careful sentence of the old Greek storekeeper.

He called again, 'Next.' It was a day of extreme heat and humidity and the patients were languid and few. It had never ceased to surprise the doctor how human beings never became acclimatized to their own country; an African suffered from the heat like any European, just as a Swede he once knew suffered from the long winter night as though she had been born in a southern land. The man who now came to stand before the doctor would not meet his eyes. On the chart he was given the name of Attention, but now any attention he had was certainly elsewhere.

'Trouble again like the other night?' the doctor asked.

The man looked over the doctor's shoulder as if someone he feared were approaching and said, 'Yes.' His eyes were heavy and bloodshot; he pushed his shoulders forward on either side of his sunken chest as though they were the corners of a book he was trying to close.

'It will be over soon,' the doctor said. 'You must be patient.'

'I am afraid,' the man said in his own tongue. 'Please when night comes let them bind my hands.'

'Is it as bad as that?'

'Yes. I am afraid for my boy. He sleeps beside me.'

The D.D.S. tablets were not a simple cure. Reactions from the drug were sometimes terrible. When it was only a question of pain in the nerves you could treat a patient with cortisone, but in a few cases a kind of madness came over the mind in the hours of darkness. The man said, 'I am afraid of killing my boy.'

The doctor said, 'This will pass. One more night, that's all. Remember you have just to hold on. Can you read the time?'

'Yes.'

'I will give you a clock that shines so that you can read it in the dark. The trouble will start at eight o'clock. At eleven o'clock you will feel worse. Don't struggle. If we tie your hands you will struggle. Just look at the clock. At one you will feel very bad, but then it will begin to pass. At three you will feel no worse than you do now, and after that less and less – the madness will go. Just look at the clock and remember what I say. Will you do that?'

'Yes.'

'Before dark I will bring you the clock.'

'My child . . .'

'Don't worry about your child. I will tell the sisters to look

95

after him till the madness has gone. You must just watch the clock. As the hands move the madness will move too. And at five the clock will ring a bell. You can sleep then. Your madness will have gone. It won't come back.'

He tried to speak with conviction, but he felt the heat blurring his intonation. When the man had gone he felt that something had been dragged out of him and thrown away. He said to the dispenser, 'I can't see anybody today.'

'There are only six more.'

'Am I the only one who must not feel the heat?' But he felt some of the shame of a deserter as he walked away from his tiny segment of the world's battlefield.

Perhaps it was shame that led his steps towards another patient. As he passed Querry's room he saw him busied at his drawing-board; he went on and came to Father Thomas's room. Father Thomas too had taken the morning off – his schools like the dispensary would have been all but emptied by the heat. Parkinson sat on the only chair, wearing the bottom of his pyjamas: the cord looked as if it were tied insecurely round an egg. Father Thomas was talking excitedly, as Colin entered, in what even the doctor recognized to be very odd English. He heard the name 'Querry'. There was hardly space to stand between the two beds.

'Well,' Colin said, 'you see, M. Parkinson, you are not dead. One doesn't die of a small fever.'

'What's he saying?' Parkinson asked Father Thomas. 'I'm tired of not understanding. What was the good of the Norman Conquest if we don't speak the same language now?'

'Why has he come here, Father Thomas? Have you found that out?'

'He is asking me a great many questions about Querry.'

'Why? What business is it of his?'

'He told me that he had come here specially to talk to him.'

'Then he would have done better to have gone back with the boat because Querry won't talk.'

'Querry, that's right, Querry,' Parkinson said. 'It's stupid of him to pretend to hide away. No one really wants to hide from Montagu Parkinson. Aren't I the end of every man's desire? Quote. Swinburne.'

'What have you told him, father?'

Father Thomas said defensively, 'I've done no more than confirm what Rycker told him.'

'Rycker! Then he's been listening to a pack of lies.'

'Is the story of Deo Gratias a lie? Is the new hospital a lie? I hope that I have been able to put the story in the right context, that's all.'

'What is the right context?'

'The Catholic context,' Father Thomas replied.

The Remington portable had been set up on Father Thomas's table beside the crucifix. On the other side of the crucifix, like the second thief, the Rolleiflex hung by its strap from a nail. Doctor Colin looked at the typewritten sheet upon the table. He could read English more easily than he could speak it. He read the heading: 'The Recluse of the Great River,' then looked accusingly at Father Thomas. 'Do you know what this is about?'

'It is the story of Querry,' Father Thomas said.

'This nonsense!'

Colin looked again at the typewritten sheet. 'That is the name which the natives have given to a strange newcomer in the heart of darkest Africa.' Colin said, '*Qui êtes-vous?*'

'Parkinson,' the man said. 'I've told you already. Montagu Parkinson.' He added with disappointment, 'Doesn't the name mean anything at all to you?'

Lower down the page Colin read,

three weeks by boat to reach this wild territory. Struck down after seven days by the bites of tsetse flies and mosquitoes I was carried ashore unconscious. Where once Stanley battled his way with Maxim guns, another fight is being waged – this time in the cause of the African – against the deadly infection of leprosy . . . woke from my fever to find myself a patient in a leper hospital. . . .

'But these are lies,' Colin said to Father Thomas.

'What's he grousing about?' Parkinson asked.

'He says that what you have written there is – not altogether true.'

'Tell him it's more than the truth,' Parkinson said. 'It's a page of modern history. Do you really believe Caesar said "*Et tu, Brute*"? It's what he ought to have said and someone on the spot – old Herodotus, no, he was the Greek, wasn't he, it must have been someone else, Suetonius perhaps, spotted what was needed. The truth is always forgotten. Pitt on his deathbed asked for Bellamy's Pork Pies, but history altered that.' Even Father Thomas could not follow the convolutions of Parkinson's thoughts. 'My articles have to be remembered like history. At least from one Sunday to another. Next Sunday's instalment. "The Saint with a Past".'

'Do you understand a word of all this, father?' Colin asked.

'Not very much,' Father Thomas admitted.

'Has he come here to make trouble?'

'No, no. Nothing like that. Apparently his paper sent him to Africa to write about some disturbances in British territory. He arrived too late, but by that time we had our own trouble in the capital, so he came on.'

'Not even knowing French?'

'He had a first-class return ticket to Nairobi. He told me that his paper could not afford two star writers in Africa, so they cabled him to move on into our territory. He was too late again, but then he heard some rumours of Querry. He said that he had to bring *something* back. When he got to Luc he happened at the Governor's to meet Rycker.'

'What does he know of Querry's past? Even we . . .'

Parkinson was watching the discussion closely; his eyes travelled from one face to another. Here and there a word must have meant something to him and he drew his rapid, agile, erroneous conclusions.

'It appears,' Father Thomas said, 'that the British newspapers have what they call a *morgue*. He has only to cable them and they will send him a précis of all that has ever been published about Querry.'

'It's like a police persecution.'

'Oh, I'm convinced they'll find nothing to his discredit.'

'Have neither of you,' Parkinson asked sorrowfully, 'heard my name Montagu Parkinson? Surely it's memorable enough.' It was impossible to tell whether he was laughing at himself.

Father Thomas began to answer him. 'To be quite truthful until you came . . .'

'My name is writ in water. Quote. Shelley,' Parkinson said.

'Does Querry know what it's all about?' Colin asked Father Thomas.

'Not yet.'

'He was beginning to be happy here.'

'You mustn't be hasty,' Father Thomas said. 'There is another side to all of this. Our leproserie may become famous – as famous as Schweitzer's hospital, and the British, one has heard, are a generous people.'

Perhaps the name Schweitzer enabled Parkinson to catch at Father Thomas's meaning. He brought quickly out, 'My articles are syndicated in the United States, France, Germany, Japan, and South America. No other living journalist . . .'

'We have managed without publicity until now, father,' Colin said.

'Publicity is only another name for propaganda. And we have a college for that in Rome.'

'Perhaps it is more fitted for Rome, father, than Central Africa.'

'Publicity can be an acid test for virtue. Personally I am convinced that Querry . . .'

'I have never enjoyed blood-sports, father. And a man-hunt least of all.'

'You exaggerate, doctor. A great deal of good can come from all of this. You know how you have always lacked money. The mission can't provide it. The State will not. Your patients deserve to be considered.'

'Perhaps Querry is also a patient,' Colin said.

'That's nonsense. I was thinking of the lepers – you have always dreamt of a school for rehabilitation, haven't you, if you could get the funds. For those poor burnt-out cases of yours.'

'Querry may be also a burnt-out case,' the doctor said. He

looked at the fat man in the chair. 'Where now will he be able to find *his* therapy? Limelight is not very good for the mutilated.'

The heat of the day and the anger they momentarily felt for each other made them careless, and it was only Parkinson who saw that the man they were discussing was already over the threshold of Father Thomas's room.

'How are you, Querry?' Parkinson said. 'I didn't recognize you when I met you on the boat.'

Querry said, 'Nor I you.'

'Thank God,' Parkinson said, 'you aren't finished like the riots were. I've caught up with one story anyway. We've got to have a talk, you and I.'

II

'So that's the new hospital,' Parkinson said. 'Of course I don't know about these things, but there seems to me nothing very original . . .' He bent over the plans and said with the obvious intention of provoking. 'It reminds me of something in one of our new satellite towns. Hemel Hempstead perhaps. Or Stevenage.'

'This is not architecture,' Querry said. 'It's a cheap building job. Nothing more. The cheaper the better, so long as it stands up to heat, rain, and humidity.'

'Do they require a man like you for that?'

'Yes. They have no builder here.'

'Are you going to stay till it's finished?'

'Longer than that.'

'Then what Rycker told me must be partly true.'

'I doubt if anything that man says could ever be true.'

'You'd need to be a kind of a saint, wouldn't you, to bury yourself here.'

'No. Not a saint.'

'Then what are you? What are your motives? I know a lot about you already. I've briefed myself,' Parkinson said. He sat his great weight down on the bed and said confidingly, 'You aren't exactly a man who loves his fellows, are you? Leaving out women, of course.' There is a strong allurement in corruption and there was no doubt of Parkinson's; he carried it on the surface of his skin like phosphorus, impossible to mistake. Virtue had died long ago within that mountain of flesh for lack of air. A priest might not be shocked by human failings, but he could be hurt or disappointed; Parkinson would welcome any kind of failing. Nothing would hurt Parkinson or disappoint him but the size of a cheque.

'You heard what the doctor called me just now – one of the burnt-out cases. They are the lepers who lose everything that can be eaten away before they are cured.'

'You are a whole man as far as one can see,' said Parkinson, looking at the fingers resting on the drawing-board.

'I've come to an end. This place, you might say, is the end. Neither the road nor the river go any further. You have been washed up here too, haven't you?'

'Oh, no, I came with a purpose.'

'I was afraid of you on the boat, but I'm afraid of you no longer.'

'I can't understand what you had to fear. I'm a man like other men.'

'No,' Querry said, 'you are a man like me. Men with vocations are different from the others. They have more to lose. Behind all of us in various ways lies a spoilt priest. You once had a vocation, admit it, if it was only a vocation to write.'

'That's not important. Most journalists begin that way.' The bed bent below Parkinson's weight as he shifted his buttocks like sacks.

'And end your way?'

'What are you driving at? Are you trying to insult me? I'm beyond insult, Mr Querry.'

'Why should I insult you? We are two of a kind. I began as an architect and I am ending as a builder. There's little pleasure in that kind of progress. Is there pleasure in *your* final stage, Parkinson?' He looked at the typewritten sheet that he had picked up in Father Thomas's room and carried in with him.

'It's a job.'

'Of course.'

'It keeps me alive,' Parkinson said.

'Yes.'

'It's no use saying I'm like you. At least I enjoy life.'

'Oh yes. The pleasures of the senses. Food, Parkinson?'

'I have to be careful.' He took the dangling corner of the mosquito-net to mop his forehead with. 'I weigh eighteen stone.'

'Women, Parkinson?'

'I don't know why you are asking me these questions. I came to interview *you*. Of course I screw a bit now and then, but there comes a time in every man's life . . .'

'You're younger than I am.'

'My heart's not all that strong.'

'You really have come to an end like me, haven't you, Parkinson, so here we find ourselves together. Two burnt-out cases. There must be many more of us in the world. We should have a masonic sign to recognize each other.'

'I'm not burnt-out. I have my work. The biggest syndication . . .' He seemed determined to prove that he was dissimilar to Querry. Like a man presenting his skin to a doctor he wanted to prove that there was no thickening, no trace of a nodule, nothing that might class him with the other lepers.

'There was a time,' Querry said, 'when you would not have written that sentence about Stanley.'

'It's a small mistake in geography, that's all. One has to dramatize. It's the first thing they teach a reporter on the *Post* – he has to make every story stand up. Anyway no one will notice.'

'Would you write the real truth about me?'

'There are laws of libel.'

'I would never bring an action. I promise you that.' He read the advance announcement aloud. 'The Past of a Saint. What a saint!'

'How do you know that Rycker's not right about you? We none of us really know ourselves.'

'We have to if we are to be cured. When we reach the farthest point, there's no mistaking it. When the fingers are

gone and the toes too and the smear-reactions are all negative, we can do no more harm. Would you write the truth,
Parkinson, even if I told it to you? I know you wouldn't. You
aren't burnt-out after all. You are still infectious.'

Parkinson looked at Querry with bruised eyes. He was like
a man who has reached the limit of the third degree, when
there is nothing else to do but admit everything. 'They would
sack me if I tried,' he said. 'It's easy enough to take risks when
you are young. To think I am farther off from heaven, etc.,
etc. Quote. Edgar Allan Poe.'

'It wasn't Poe.'

'Nobody notices things like that.'

'What is the past you have given me?'

'Well, there was the case of Anne Morel, wasn't there? It
even reached the English papers. After all you had an English
mother. And you had just completed that modern cathedral
in Bruges.'

'It wasn't Bruges. What story did they tell about that?'

'That she killed herself for love of you. At eighteen. For a
man of forty.'

'It was more than fifteen years ago. Do papers have so long
a memory?'

'No. But the *morgue* serves us instead. I shall describe in
my best Sunday-paper style how you came here in expiation
. . .'

'Papers like yours invariably make small mistakes. The
woman's name was Marie and not Anne. She was twenty-five
and not eighteen. Nor did she kill herself for love of me. She
wanted to escape me. That was all. So you see I am expiat-
ing nothing.'

'She wanted to escape the man she loved?'

'Exactly that. It must be a terrible thing for a woman to
make love nightly with an efficient instrument. I never failed
her. She tried to leave me several times, and each time I got
her to come back. You see it hurt my vanity to be left by a
woman. I always wanted to do the leaving.'

'How did you bring her back?'

'Those of us who practise one art are usually adept at

another. A painter writes. A poet makes a tune. I happened in those days to be a good actor for an amateur. Once I used tears. Another time an overdose of nembutal, but not, of course, a dangerous dose. Then I made love to a second woman to show her what she was going to miss if she left me. I even persuaded her that I couldn't do my work without her. I made her think that I would leave the Church if I hadn't her support to my faith – she was a good Catholic, even in bed. In my heart of course I had left the Church years before, but she never realized that. I believed a little of course, like so many do, at the major feasts, Christmas and Easter, when memories of childhood stir us to a kind of devotion. She always mistook it for the love of God.'

'All the same there must be some reason that you came out here among the lepers . . .'

'Not in expiation, Mr Parkinson. There were plenty of women after Marie Morel as there had been women before her. Perhaps for ten more years I managed to believe in my own emotion – "my dearest love", "*toute à toi*", and all the rest. One always tries not to repeat the same phrases, just as one tries to preserve some special position in the act of sex, but there are only thirty-two positions according to Aretine and there are less than that number of endearing words, and in the end most women reach their climax most easily in the commonest position of all and with the commonest phrase upon the tongue. It was only a question of time before I realized that I didn't love at all. I've never really loved. I'd only accepted love. And then the worst boredom settled in. Because if I had deceived myself with women I had deceived myself with work too.'

'No one has ever questioned your reputation.'

'The future will. Somewhere in a back street of Brussels now there's a boy at a drawing-board who will show me up. I wish I could see the cathedral he will build . . . No, I don't. Or I wouldn't be here. He'll be no spoilt priest. He'll pass the novice-master.'

'I don't know what you are talking about, Querry. Sometimes you talk like Rycker.'

'Do I? Perhaps he has the Masonic sign too . . .'

'If you are so bored, why not be bored in comfort? A little apartment in Brussels or a villa in Capri. After all, you are a rich man, Querry.'

'Boredom is worse in comfort. I thought perhaps out here there would be enough pain and enough fear to distract . . .' He looked at Parkinson. 'Surely *you* can understand me if anyone can.'

'I can't understand a word.'

'Am I such a monster that even you . . . ?'

'What about your work, Querry? Whatever you say, you can't be bored with that. You've been a raging success.'

'You mean money? Haven't I told you that the work wasn't good enough? What were any of my churches compared with the cathedral at Chartres? They were all signed with my name of course – nobody could mistake a Querry for a Corbusier, but which one of us knows the architect of Chartres? He didn't care. He worked with love not vanity – and with belief too, I suppose. To build a church when you don't believe in a god seems a little indecent, doesn't it? When I discovered I was doing that, I accepted a commission for a city hall, but I didn't believe in politics either. You never saw such an absurd box of concrete and glass as I landed on the poor city square. You see I discovered what seemed only to be a loose thread in my jacket – I pulled it and all the jacket began to unwind. Perhaps it's true that you can't believe in a god without loving a human being or love a human being without believing in a god. They use the phrase "make love", don't they? But which of us are creative enough to "make" love? We can only be loved – if we are lucky.'

'Why are you telling me this, Mr Querry – even if it's true?'

'Because at least you are someone who won't mind the truth, though I doubt whether you'll ever write it. Perhaps – who knows? – I might persuade you to drop altogether this absurd pious nonsense that Rycker talks about me. I am no Schweitzer. My God, he almost tempts me to seduce his wife. That at least might change his tune.'

'Could you?'

'It's an awful thing when experience and not vanity makes one say yes.'

Parkinson made an oddly humble gesture. He said, 'Let me have men about me that are fat. Quote. Shakespeare. I got that one right anyway. As for me I wouldn't even know how to begin.'

'Begin with readers of the *Post*. You are famous among your readers and fame is a potent aphrodisiac. Married women are the easiest, Parkinson. The young girl too often has her weather-eye open on security, but a married woman has already found it. The husband at the office, the children in the nursery, a condom in the bag. Say that she's been married at twenty, she's ready for a limited excursion before she's reached thirty. If her husband is young too, don't be afraid; she may have had enough of youth. With a man of my age and yours she needn't expect jealous scenes.'

'What you are talking about doesn't have much to do with love, does it? You said you'd been loved. You complained of it if I remember right, but I probably don't. As you realize well enough, I'm only a bloody journalist.'

'Love comes quickly enough with gratitude, only too quickly. The loveliest of women feels gratitude, even to an ageing man like me, if she learns to feel pleasure again. Ten years in the same bed withers the little bud, but now it blooms once more. Her husband notices the way she looks. Her children cease to be a burden. She takes an interest again in housekeeping as she used to in the old days. She confides a little in her intimate friends, because to be the mistress of a famous man increases her self-respect. The adventure is over. Romance has begun.'

'What a cold-blooded bastard you are,' Parkinson said with deep respect, as though he were talking of the *Post*'s proprietor.

'Why not write that instead of this pious nonsense you are planning?'

'I couldn't. My newspaper is for family reading. Although of course that word the Past has a certain meaning. But it means abandoned follies, doesn't it? not abandoned virtues.

We'll touch on Mlle Morel – delicately. And there was some-body else, wasn't there, called Grison?'

Querry didn't answer.

'It's no use denying things now,' Parkinson said. 'Grison is mummified in the *morgue* too.'

'Yes, I do remember him. I don't care to because I don't like farce. He was a senior employee in the Post Office. He challenged me to a duel after I had left his wife. One of those bogus modern duels where nobody fires straight. I was tempted to break the conventions and to wing him, but his wife would have mistaken it for passion. Poor man, he was quite content so long as we were together, but when I left her he had to suffer such scenes with her in public . . . She had much less mercy on him than I had.'

'It's odd that you admit all this to me,' Parkinson said. 'People are more cautious with me as a rule. Except that I remember once there was a murderer – he talked as much as you.'

'Perhaps it's the mark of a murderer, loquacity.'

'They didn't hang this chap and I pretended to be his brother and visited him twice a month. All the same I'm puzzled by your attitude. You didn't strike me when I saw you first as exactly a talking man.'

'I have been waiting for you, Parkinson, or someone like you. Not that I didn't fear you too.'

'Yes, but why?'

'You are my looking-glass. I can talk to a looking-glass, but one can be a little afraid of one too. It returns such a straight image. If I talked to Father Thomas as I've talked to you, he'd twist my words.'

'I'm grateful for your good opinion.'

'A good opinion? I dislike you as much as I dislike myself. I was nearly happy when you arrived, Parkinson, and I've only talked to you now so that you'll have no excuse to stay. The interview is over, and you've never had a better one. You don't want my opinion, do you, on Gropius? Your public hasn't heard of Gropius.'

'All the same I jotted down some questions,' Parkinson

said. 'We might get on to those now that we've cleared the way.'

'I said the interview was over.'

Parkinson leaned forward on the bed and then swayed back like a Chinese wobbling toy made in the likeness of the fat God of Prosperity. He said, 'Do you consider that the love of God or the love of humanity is your principal driving force, Querry? What in your opinion is the future of Christianity? Has the Sermon on the Mount influenced your decision to give your life to the lepers? Who is your favourite saint? Do you believe in the efficacy of prayer?' He began to laugh, the great belly rolling like a dolphin. 'Do miracles still occur? Have you yet visited Fatima?'

He got off the bed. 'We can forget the rest of the crap. "In his bare cell in the heart of the dark continent one of the greatest of modern architects and one of the most famous Catholics of his day bared his conscience to the correspondent of the *Post*. Montagu Parkinson, who was on the spot last month in South Korea, is on the spot again. He will reveal to our readers in his next instalment how remorse for the past is Querry's driving force. Querry is atoning for a reckless youth by serving others. St Francis was the gayest spark in all the gay old city of Firenze – Florence to you and me."'

Parkinson went out into the hard glare of the Congo day, but he hadn't said enough. He returned and put his face close up against the net and blew his words through it in a fine spray. '"Next Sunday's instalment: A girl dies for love." I don't like you any more than you like me, Querry, but I'm going to build you up. I'll build you up so high they'll raise a statue to you by the river. In the worst possible taste, you know the sort of thing, you won't be able to avoid it because you'll be dead and buried – you on your knees surrounded by your bloody lepers teaching them to pray to the god you don't believe in and the birds shitting on your hair. I don't mind you being a religious fake, Querry, but I'll show you that you can't use me to ease your bleeding conscience. I wouldn't be surprised if there weren't pilgrims at your shrine in twenty years, and that's how history's written, believe you me. *Exegi monumentum*. Quote. Virgil.'

Querry took from his pocket the meaningless letter with the all-inclusive phrase which might, of course, be genuine. The letter had not come to him from one of the women Parkinson had mentioned: the *morgue* of the *Post* was not big enough to hold all possible bodies. He read it through again in the mood that Parkinson had elicited. 'Do you remember?' She was one of those who would never admit that when an emotion was dead, the memory of the occasion was dead as well. He had to take her memories on trust, because she had always been a truthful woman. She reminded him of a guest who claims one particular matchbox as her own out of the debris of a broken party.

He went to his bed and lay down. The pillow gathered heat under his neck, but this noonday he couldn't face the sociabilities of lunch with the fathers. He thought: there was only one thing I could do and that is reason enough for being here. I can promise you, Marie, *toute à toi*, all of you, never again from boredom or vanity to involve another human being in my lack of love. I shall do no more harm, he thought, with the kind of happiness a leper must feel when he is freed at last by his seclusion from the fear of passing on contagion to another. For years he had not thought of Marie Morel; now he remembered the first time he had heard her name spoken. It was spoken by a young architectural student whom he had been helping with his studies. They had come back together from a day at Bruges into the neon-lighted Brussels evening and they had passed the girl accidentally outside the northern station. He had envied a little his dull undistinguished companion when he saw her face brighten under the lamps. Has anyone ever seen a man smile at a woman as a woman smiles at the man she loves, fortuitously, at a bus-stop, in a railway carriage, at some chain-store in the middle of buying groceries, a smile so naturally joyful, without premeditation and without caution? The converse, of course, is probably true also. A man can never smile quite so falsely as the girl in a brothel parlour. But the girl in the brothel, Querry thought, is imitating something true. The man has nothing to imitate.

PART FIVE

CHAPTER I

It is characteristic of Africa the way that people come and go, as though the space and emptiness of an undeveloped continent encourage drift; the high tide deposits the flotsam on the edge of the shore and sweeps it away again in its withdrawal, to leave elsewhere. No one had expected Parkinson, he had come unannounced, and a few days later he went again, carrying his Rolleiflex and Remington down to the Otraco boat bound for some spot elsewhere. Two weeks later a motor-boat came up the river in the late evening carrying a young administrator who played a game of liar-dice with the fathers, drank one glass of whisky before bed, and left behind him, as if it had been the sole intention of his voyage, a copy of an English journal, the *Architectural Review*, before departing without so much as breakfast into the grey and green immensity. (The review contained – apart from the criticism of a new arterial road – some illustrations of a hideous cathedral newly completed in a British colony. Perhaps the young man thought that it would serve as a warning to Querry.) Again a few weeks went unnoticed by – a few deaths from tuberculosis, the hospital climbing a few feet higher from its foundations – and then two policemen got off the Otraco boat to make inquiries about a Salvation Army leader who was wanted in the capital. He was said to have persuaded the people of a neighbouring tribe to sell their blankets to him because they would be too heavy to wear at the Resurrection of the Dead and then to give him the money back so that he might keep it for them in a secure place where no thieves would break in and steal. As a recompense he had given certificates insuring them against the danger of being kidnapped by the Catholic and Protestant missionaries who, he said, were exporting bodies with the help of witchcraft wholesale to Europe in sealed railway trucks where they were turned into canned food labelled Best African Tunny. The policemen could learn nothing of the fugitive at the leproserie, and they departed again on the same boat two hours later, floating away with the small islands of water-jacinth at the same speed and in the same direction, as though they were all a part of nature too.

Querry in time began to forget Parkinson. The great world had done its worst and gone, and a kind of peace descended. Rycker stayed aloof, and no echo from any newspaper article out of distant Europe came to disturb Querry. Even Father Thomas moved away for a while from the leproserie to a seminary in the bush from which he hoped to obtain a teacher for yet another new class. Querry's feet were becoming familiar with the long laterite road that stretched between his room and the hospital; in the evening, when the worst heat was over, the laterite glowed, like a night-blooming flower, in shades of rose and red.

The fathers were unconcerned with private lives. A husband, after he had been cured, left the leproserie and his wife moved into the hut of another man, but the fathers asked no questions. One of the catechists, a man who had reached the limit of mutilation, having lost nose, fingers, toes (he looked as though he had been lopped, scraped, and tidied by a knife), fathered a baby with the woman, crippled by polio, who could only crawl upon the ground dragging her dwarfed legs behind her. The man brought the baby to the Church for baptism and there it was baptized Emanuel – there were no questions and no admonitions. The fathers were too busy to bother themselves with what the Church considered sin (moral theology was the subject they were least concerned with). In Father Thomas some thwarted instinct might be seen deviously at work, but Father Thomas was no longer there to trouble the leproserie with his scruples and anxieties.

The doctor was a less easy character to understand. Unlike the fathers he had no belief in a god to support him in his hard vocation. Once when Querry made a comment on his life – a question brought to his mind by the sight of some pitiable and squalid case – the doctor looked up at him with much the same clinical eye with which he had just examined the patient. He said, 'Perhaps if I tested your skin now I would get a second negative reaction.'

'What do you mean?'

'You are showing curiosity again about another human being.'

'Who was the first?' Querry asked.

'Deo Gratias. You know I have been luckier in my vocation than you.'

Querry looked down the long row of worn-out mattresses where bandaged people lay in the awkward postures of the bed-ridden. The sweet smell of sloughed skin was in the air. 'Lucky?' he said.

'It needs a very strong man to survive an introspective and solitary vocation. I don't think you were strong enough. I know I couldn't have stood your life.'

'Why does a man choose a vocation like this?' Querry asked.

'He's chosen. Oh, I don't mean by god. By accident. There is an old Danish doctor still going the rounds who became a leprologist late in life. By accident. He was excavating an ancient cemetery and found skeletons there without finger-bones – it was an old leper-cemetery of the fourteenth century. He X-rayed the skeletons and he made discoveries in the bones, especially in the nasal area, which were quite unknown to any of us – you see most of us haven't the chance to work with skeletons. He became a leprologist after that. You will meet him at any international conference on leprosy carrying his skull with him in an airline's overnight bag. It has passed through a lot of *douaniers*' hands. It must be rather a shock, that skull, to them, but I believe they don't charge duty on it.'

'And you, Doctor Colin? What was your accident?'

'Only the accident of temperament, perhaps,' the doctor replied evasively. They came out together into the unfresh and humid air. 'Oh, don't mistake me. I had no death-wish as

Damien had. Now that we can cure leprosy, we shall have fewer of those vocations of doom, but they weren't uncommon once.' They began to cross the road to the shade of the dispensary where the lepers waited on the steps; the doctor halted in the hot centre of the laterite. 'There used to be a high suicide-rate among leprologists – I suppose they couldn't wait for that positive test they all expected some time. Bizarre suicides for a bizarre vocation. There was one man I knew quite well who injected himself with a dose of snake-venom, and another who poured petrol over his furniture and his clothes and then set himself alight. There is a common feature, you will have noticed, in both cases – unnecessary suffering. That can be a vocation too.'

'I don't understand you.'

'Wouldn't you rather suffer than feel discomfort? Discomfort irritates our ego like a mosquito-bite. We become aware of ourselves, the more uncomfortable we are, but suffering is quite a different matter. Sometimes I think that the search for suffering and the remembrance of suffering are the only means we have to put ourselves in touch with the whole human condition. With suffering we become part of the Christian myth.'

'Then I wish you'd teach me how to suffer,' Querry said. 'I only know the mosquito-bites.'

'You'll suffer enough if we stand here any longer,' Doctor Colin said and he drew Querry off the laterite into the shade. 'Today I am going to show you a few interesting eye cases.' He sat at his surgery table and Querry took the chair beside him. Only on the linen masks that children wear at Christmas had he seen such scarlet eyes, representing avarice or senility, as now confronted them. 'You only need a little patience,' Doctor Colin said. 'Suffering is not so hard to find,' and Querry tried to remember who it was that had said much the same to him months ago. He was irritated by his own failure of memory.

'Aren't you being glib about suffering?' he asked. 'That woman who died last week . . .'

'Don't be too sorry for those who die after some pain. It

makes them ready to go. Think of how a death sentence must sound when you are full of health and vigour.' Doctor Colin turned away from him to speak in her native tongue to an old woman whose palsied eyelids never once moved to shade the eyes.

That night, after taking dinner with the fathers, Querry strolled over to the doctor's house. The lepers were sitting outside their huts to make the most of the cool air which came with darkness. At a little stall, lit by a hurricane-lamp, a man was offering for five francs a handful of caterpillars he had gathered in the forest. Somebody was singing a street or two away, and by a fire Querry came upon a group of dancers gathered round his boy Deo Gratias, who squatted on the ground and used his fists like drum-sticks to beat the rhythm on an old petrol-tin. Even the bat-eared dogs lay quiet as though carved on tombs. A young woman with bare breasts kept a rendezvous where a path led away into the forest. In the moonlight the nodules on her face ceased for a while to exist, and there were no patches on her skin. She was any young girl waiting for a man.

It seemed to Querry that some persistent poison had been drained from his system after his outbreak to the Englishman. He could remember no evening peace to equal this since the night when he had given the last touches to his first architectural plans, perhaps the only ones which had completely satisfied him. The owners, of course, had spoilt the building afterwards as they spoiled everything. No building was safe from the furniture, the pictures, the human beings that it would presently contain. But first there had been this peace. *Consummatum est*: pain over and peace falling round him like a little death.

When he had drunk his second whisky he said to the doctor, 'When a smear-test is negative, does it always stay so?'

'Not always. It's too early to loose the patient on the world until the tests have been negative – oh, for six months. There are relapses even with our present drugs.'

'Do they sometimes find it hard to be loosed?'

'Very often. You see they become attached to their hut and

their patch of land, and of course for the burnt-out cases life outside isn't easy. They carry the stigma of leprosy. People are apt to think once a leper, always a leper.'

'I begin to find your vocation a little easier to understand. All the same – the fathers believe they have the Christian truth behind them, and it helps them in a place like this. You and I have no such truth. Is the Christian myth that you talked about enough for you?'

'I want to be on the side of change,' the doctor said. 'If I had been born an amoeba who could think, I would have dreamed of the day of the primates. I would have wanted anything I did to contribute to that day. Evolution, as far as we can tell, has lodged itself finally in the brains of man. The ant, the fish, even the ape has gone as far as it can go, but in our brain evolution is moving – my God – at what a speed! I forget how many hundreds of millions of years passed between the dinosaurs and the primates, but in our own life-time we have seen the change from diesel to jet, the splitting of the atom, the cure of leprosy.'

'Is change so good?'

'We can't avoid it. We are riding a great ninth evolution-ary wave. Even the Christian myth is part of the wave, and perhaps, who knows, it may be the most valuable part. Suppose love were to evolve as rapidly in our brains as tech-nical skill has done. In isolated cases it may have done, in the saints . . . in Christ, if the man really existed.'

'You can really comfort yourself with all that?' Querry asked. 'It sounds like the old song of progress.'

'The nineteenth century wasn't as far wrong as we like to believe. We have become cynical about progress because of the terrible things we have seen men do during the last forty years. All the same through trial and error the amoeba did become the ape. There were blind starts and wrong turnings even then, I suppose. Evolution today can produce Hitlers as well as St John of the Cross. I have a small hope, that's all, a very small hope, that someone they call Christ was the fertile element, looking for a crack in the wall to plant its seed. I think of Christ as an amoeba who took the right turning. I want to be on the side of the progress which survives. I'm no friend of pterodactyls.'

'But if we are incapable of love?'

'I'm not sure such a man exists. Love is planted in man now, even uselessly in some cases, like an appendix. Sometimes of course people call it hate.'

'I haven't found any trace of it in myself.'

'Perhaps you are looking for something too big and too important. Or too active.'

'What you are saying seems to me every bit as superstitious as what the fathers believe.'

'Who cares? It's the superstition I live by. There was another superstition – quite unproven – Copernicus had it – that the earth went round the sun. Without that superstition we shouldn't be in a position now to shoot rockets at the moon. One has to gamble on one's superstitions. Like Pascal gambled on his.' He drank his whisky down.

'Are you a happy man?' Querry asked.

'I suppose I am. It's not a question that I've ever asked myself. Does a happy man ever ask it? I go on from day to day.'

'Swimming on your wave,' Querry said with envy. 'Do you never need a woman?'

'The only one I ever needed,' the doctor said, 'is dead.'

'So that's why you came out here.'

'You are wrong,' Colin said. 'She's buried a hundred yards away. She was my wife.'

CHAPTER 2

In the last three months the hospital had made great progress.
It was no longer a mere ground-plan looking like the exca-
vation of a Roman villa; the walls had risen; the window-
spaces were there waiting for wire nets. It was even possible
to estimate the time when the roof would be fixed. The lepers
worked more rapidly as the end came in sight. Querry was
walking through the building with Father Joseph; they passed
through non-existent doors like revenants, into rooms that
did not yet exist, into the future operating theatre, the X-ray
room, the fire-proof room with the vats of paraffin wax for
the palsied hands, into the dispensary, into the two main
wards.

'What will you do,' Father Joseph said, 'when this is
finished?'

'What will you, father?'

'Of course it's for the Superior and the doctor to decide,
but I would like to build a place where the mutilated can
learn to work – occupational therapy, I suppose they call it
at home. The sisters do what they can with individuals, especially the mutilated. No one wants to be a special case. They
would learn much quicker in a class where they could joke a
bit.'

'And after that?'

'There's always more building to be done for the next
twenty years, if only lavatories.'

'Then there'll always be something for me to do, father.'

'An architect like you is wasted on the work we have here.
These are only builders' jobs.'

'I have become a builder.'

'Don't you ever want to see Europe again?'

'Do you, father?'

'There's a big difference between us. Europe is much the
same as this for those of our Order – a group of buildings,

very like the ones we have here, our rooms aren't any different, nor the chapel (even the Stations are the same), the same classrooms, the same food, the same clothes, the same kind of faces. But surely to you Europe means more than that – theatres, friends, restaurants, bars, books, shops, the company of your equals – the fruits of fame whatever that means.'

Querry said, 'I am content here.'

It was nearly time for the midday meal, and they walked back together towards the mission, passing the nuns' house and the doctor's and the small shabby cemetery. It was not kept well – the service of the living took up too much of the fathers' time. Only on All Souls night was the graveyard properly remembered when a lamp or a candle shone on every grave, pagan and Christian. About half the graves had crosses, and they were as simple and uniform as those of the mass dead in a war cemetery. Querry knew now which grave belonged to Mme Colin. It stood crossless and a little apart, but the only reason for the separation was to leave space for Doctor Colin to join her.

'I hope you'll find room for me there too,' Querry said. 'I won't rate a cross.'

'We shall have trouble with Father Thomas over that. He'll argue that once baptized you are always a Christian.'

'I would do well to die then before he returns.'

'Better be quick about it. He will be back sooner than we think.' Even his brother priests were happier without Father Thomas; it was impossible not to feel a grudging pity for so unattractive a man.

Father Joseph's warning proved wise too quickly. Absorbed in examining the new hospital they had failed to hear the bell of the Otraco boat. Father Thomas was already ashore with the cardboard box in which he carried all his personal belongings. He stood in the doorway of his room and greeted them as they passed. He had the curious and disquieting air of receiving them like guests.

'Well, Father Joseph, you see that I am back before my time.'

'We do see,' Father Joseph said.

'Ah, M. Querry, I have something very important to discuss with you.'

'Yes?'

'All in good time. Patience. Much has happened while I have been away.'

'Don't keep us on tenterhooks,' Father Joseph said.

'At lunch, at lunch,' Father Thomas replied, carrying his cardboard box elevated like a monstrance into his room.

As they passed the next window they could see the Superior standing by his bed. He was pushing a hair-brush, a sponge-bag, and a box of cheroots into his khaki knapsack, a relic of the last war which he carried with him across the world like a memory. He took the cross from his desk and packed it away wrapped in a couple of handkerchiefs. Father Joseph said, 'I begin to fear the worst.'

The Superior at lunch sat silent and preoccupied. Father Thomas was on his right. He crumbled his bread with the closed face of importance. Only when the meal was over did the Superior speak. He said, 'Father Thomas has brought me a letter. The Bishop wants me in Luc. I may be away some weeks or even months and I am asking Father Thomas to act for me during my absence. You are the only one, father,' he added, 'with the time to look after the accounts.' It was an apology to the other fathers and a hidden rebuke to the pride which Father Thomas was already beginning to show – he had very little in common with the doubting pitiful figure of a month ago. Perhaps even a temporary promotion could cure a failing vocation.

'You know you can trust me,' Father Thomas said.

'I can trust everyone here. My work is the least important in the place. I can't build like Father Joseph or look after the dynamos like Brother Philippe.'

'I will try not to let the school suffer,' Father Thomas said.

'I am sure you will succeed, father. You will find that my work will take up very little of your time. A superior is always replaceable.'

The more bare a life is, the more we fear change. The Superior said grace and looked around for his cheroots, but he had already packed them. He accepted a cigarette from Querry, but he wore it as awkwardly as he would have worn a suit of lay clothes. The fathers stood unhappily around unused to departures. Querry felt like a stranger present at some domestic grief.

'The hospital will be finished, perhaps, before I return,' the Superior said with a certain sadness.

'We will not put up the roof-tree till you are back,' Father Joseph replied.

'No, no, you must promise me to delay nothing. Father Thomas, those are my last instructions. The roof-tree at the earliest moment and plenty of champagne – if you can find a donor – to celebrate.'

For years in their quiet unchanging routine they had been apt to forget that they were men under obedience, but now, suddenly, they were reminded of it. Who knew what was intended for the Superior, what letters might not have passed between the Bishop and the General in Europe? He spoke of returning in a few weeks (the Bishop, he had explained, had summoned him for a consultation), but all of them were aware that he might never return. Decisions might already have been taken elsewhere. They watched him now unobtrusively, with affection, as one might watch a dying man (only Father Thomas was absent: he had already gone to move his papers into the other's room), and the Superior in turn looked at them and the bleak refectory in which he had spent his best years. It was true what Father Joseph had said. The buildings, wherever he went, would always be very much the same; the refectories would vary as little as colonial airports; but for that very reason a man became more accustomed to the minute differences. There would always be the same coloured reproduction of the Pope's portrait, but this one had a stain in the corner where the leper who made the frame had spilt the walnut colouring. The chairs too had been fashioned by lepers, who had taken as a model the regulation kind supplied to the junior grade of government officials, a kind you would find in every mission, but one of the chairs had become unique by its unreliability; they had always kept it against the wall since a visiting priest, Father Henri, had tried to imitate a circus trick by balancing on the back. Even the bookcase had an individual weakness: one shelf slanted at an angle, and there were stains upon the wall that reminded each man of something. The stains on a different wall would evoke different pictures. Wherever one went one's companions would have much the same names (there are not so many saints in common use to choose from), but the new Father Joseph would not be quite the same as the old.

From the river came the summons of the ship's bell. The Superior took the cigarette out of his mouth and looked at it as though he wondered how it had come there. Father Joseph said, 'I think we should have a glass of wine . . .' He rummaged in the cupboard for a bottle and found one which had been two-thirds finished some weeks ago on the last major feast-day. However there was a thimbleful left for all. '*Bon voyage*, father.' The ship's bell rang again. Father Thomas came to the door and said, 'I think you should be off now, father.'

'Yes. I must fetch my knapsack.'

'I have it here,' Father Thomas said.

'Well then . . .' The Superior gave one more furtive look at the room: the stained picture, the broken chair, the slanting shelf.

'A safe return,' Father Paul said. 'I will fetch Doctor Colin.'

'No, no, this is his time for a siesta. M. Querry will explain to him how it is.'

They walked down to the river bank to see the last of him and Father Thomas carried his knapsack. By the gangplank the Superior took it and slung it over his shoulder with something of a military gesture. He touched Father Thomas on the arm. 'I think you'll find the accounts in good order. Leave next month's as late as you can . . . in case I'm back.' He hesitated and said with a deprecating smile, 'Be careful of yourself, Father Thomas. Not too much enthusiasm.' Then the ship and the river took him away from them.

Father Joseph and Querry returned to the house together.

Querry said, 'Why has he chosen Father Thomas? He has been here a shorter time than any of you.'

'It is as the Superior said. We all have our proper jobs, and to tell you the truth Father Thomas is the only one who has the least notion of book-keeping.'

Querry lay down on his bed. At this hour of the day the heat made it impossible to work and almost as impossible to sleep except for superficial spells. He thought he was with the Superior on the boat going away, but in his dream the boat took the contrary direction to that of Luc. It went on down the narrowing river into the denser forest, and it was now the Bishop's boat. A corpse lay in the Bishop's cabin and the two of them were taking it to Pendélé for burial. It surprised him to think that he had been so misled as to believe that the boat had reached the farthest point of its journey into the interior when it reached the leproserie. Now he was in motion again, going deeper.

The scrape of a chair woke him. He thought it was the ship's bottom grinding across a snag in the river. He opened his eyes and saw Father Thomas sitting by his bedside.

'I had not meant to wake you,' Father Thomas said.

'I was only half asleep.'

'I have brought you messages from a friend of yours,' Father Thomas said.

'I have no friends in Africa except those I have made here.'

'You have more friends than you know. My message is from M. Rycker.'

'Rycker is no friend of mine.'

'I know he is a little impetuous, but he is a man with a great admiration for you. He feels, from something his wife has said, that he was perhaps wrong to speak of you to the English journalist.'

'His wife has more sense than he has then.'

'Luckily it has all turned out for the best,' Father Thomas said, 'and we owe it to M. Rycker.'

'The best?'

'He has written about you and all of us here in the most splendid fashion.'

'Already?'

'He telegraphed his first article from Luc. M. Rycker helped him at the post office. He made it a condition that he should read the article first – M. Rycker, of course, would never have allowed anything damaging to us to pass. He has written a real appreciation of your work. It has already been translated in *Paris Dimanche*.'

'That rag?'

'It reaches a very wide public,' Father Thomas said.

'A scandal-sheet.'

'All the more creditable then that your message should appear there.'

'I don't know what you are talking about – I have no message.' He turned impatiently away from Father Thomas's searching and insinuating gaze and lay facing the wall. He heard the rustle of paper – Father Thomas was drawing something from the pocket of his soutane. He said, 'Let me read a little bit of it to you. I assure you that it will give you great pleasure. The article is called: "An Architect of Souls. The Hermit of the Congo."'

'What nauseating rubbish. I tell you, father, nothing that man could write would interest me.'

'You are really much too harsh. I am only sorry I had no time to show it to the Superior. He makes a slight mistake about the name of the Order, but you can hardly expect anything different from an Englishman. Listen to the way he ends. "When a famous French statesman once retired into the depths of the country, to avoid the burden of office, it was said that the world made a path to his door".'

'He can get nothing right,' Querry said. 'Nothing. It was an author, not a statesman. And the author was American, not French.'

'These are trifles,' Father Thomas said rebukingly. 'Listen to this. "The whole Catholic world has been discussing the mysterious disappearance of the great architect Querry. Querry whose range of achievement extended from the latest cathedral in the United States, a palace of glass and steel, to a little white Dominican chapel on the Côte d'Azur . . ."'

'Now he's confusing me with that amateur, Matisse,' Querry said.

'Never mind small details.'

'I hope for your sake that the gospels are more accurate in small details than Parkinson.'

'"Querry has not been seen for a long while in his usual haunts. I have tracked him all the way from his favourite restaurant, l'Epaule de Mouton . . ."'

'This is absurd. Does he think I'm a gourmandizing tourist?'

'"To the heart of Africa. Near the spot where Stanley once pitched his camp among the savage tribes, I at last came on Querry . . ."' Father Thomas looked up. He said, 'It is here that he writes a great many gracious things about our work. "Selfless . . . devoted . . . in the white robes of their blameless lives." Really, you know, he does have a certain sense of style.

'"What is it that has induced the great Querry to abandon a career that brought him honour and riches to give up his life to serving the world's untouchables? I was in no position to ask him that when suddenly I found that my quest had ended. Unconscious and burning with fever, I was carried on shore from my pirogue, the frail bark in which I had penetrated what Joseph Conrad called the Heart of Darkness, by a few faithful natives who had followed me down the great river with the same fidelity their grandfathers had shown to Stanley."'

'He can't keep Stanley out of it,' Querry said. 'There have been many others in Central Africa, but I suppose the English would never have heard of them.'

'"I woke to find Querry's hand upon my pulse and Querry's eyes gazing into mine. Then I sensed the great mystery."'

'Do you really enjoy this stuff?' Querry asked. He sat up impatiently on his bed.

'I have read many lives of saints that were far worse written,' Father Thomas said. 'Style is not everything. The man's intentions are sound. Perhaps you are not the best judge. He goes on, "It was from Querry's lips that I learned the meaning of the mystery. Though Querry spoke to me as perhaps he had never spoken to another human soul, with a burning remorse for a past as colourful and cavalier as that St Francis once led in the dark alleys of the city by the Arno . . ." I wish I had been there,' Father Thomas said wistfully, 'when you spoke of that. I'm leaving out the next bit which deals mainly with the lepers. He seems to have noticed only the mutilated – a pity since it gives a rather too sombre impression of our home here.' Father Thomas, as the acting Superior, was already taking a more favourable view of the mission than he had a month before.

'Here is where he reaches what he calls the heart of the matter. "It was from Querry's most intimate friend, André Rycker, the manager of a palm-oil plantation, that I learned the secret. It is perhaps typical of Querry that what he keeps humbly hidden from the priests for whom he works he is ready to disclose to this planter – the last person you would expect to find on terms of close friendship with the great architect. 'You want to know what makes him tick?' M. Rycker said to me. 'I am sure that it is love, a completely self-less love without the barrier of colour or class. I have never known a man more deeply instructed in faith. I have sat at this very table late into the night discussing the nature of divine love with the great Querry.' So the two strange halves of Querry meet – to me Querry had spoken of the women he had loved in the world of Europe, and to his obscure friend, in his factory in the bush, he had spoken of his love of God. The world in this atomic day has need of saints. When a famous French statesman once retired into the depths of the country, to avoid the burden of office, it was said that the world made a path to his door. It is unlikely that the world which discovered the way to Schweitzer at Lambarene will fail to seek out the hermit of the Congo." I think he might have left out the reference to St Francis,' Father Thomas said, 'it might be misunderstood.'

'What lies the man does tell,' Querry exclaimed. He got up from his bed and stood near his drawing-board and the stretched sheet of blueprint. He said, 'I won't allow that man . . .'

'He is a journalist, of course,' Father Thomas said. 'These are just professional exaggerations.'

'I don't mean Parkinson. It's his job. I mean Rycker. I have never spoken to Rycker about Love or God.'

'He told me that he once had an interesting discussion with you.'

'Never. There was no discussion. All the talking, I assure you, was done by him.'

Father Thomas looked down at the newspaper cutting. He said, 'There's to be a second article, it appears, in a week's time. It says here, "Next Sunday. A Saint's Past. Redemption by Suffering. The Leper Lost in the Jungle." That will be Deo Gratias I imagine,' Father Thomas said. 'There's also a photograph of the Englishman talking to Rycker.'

'Give it to me.' Querry tore the paper into pieces and dropped them on the floor. He said, 'Is the road open?'

'It was when I left Luc. Why?'

'I'm going to take a truck then.'

'Where to?'

'To have a word with Rycker. Can't you see, father, that I must silence him? This mustn't go on. I'm fighting for my life.'

'Your life?'

'My life here. It's all I have.' He sat wearily down on the bed. He said, 'I've come a long way. There's nowhere else for me to go if I leave here.'

Father Thomas said, 'For a good man fame is always a problem.'

'But, father, I'm not a good man. Can't you believe me? Must you too twist everything like Rycker and that man? I had no good motive in coming here. I am looking after myself as I have always done, but surely even a selfish man has the right to a little happiness?'

'You have a truly wonderful quality of humility,' Father Thomas said.

PART SIX

CHAPTER I

I

Marie Rycker stopped her reading of *The Imitation of Christ* as soon as she saw that her husband was asleep, but she was afraid to move in case she might wake him, and of course there was always the possibility of a trap. She could imagine how he would reproach her, 'Could you not watch by me one hour?' for her husband was not afraid to carry imitation to great lengths. The hollow face was turned away from her so that she could not see his eyes. She thought that so long as he was ill she need not tell him her news, for one had no duty to give such unwelcome news as hers to a sick man. Through the net of the window there blew in the smell of stale margarine which she would always associate with marriage, and from where she sat she could see the corner of the engine-house, where they were feeding the ovens with the husks.

She felt ashamed of her fear and boredom and nausea. She had been bred a *colon* and she knew very well that this was not how a *colon* ought to behave. Her father had represented the same company as her husband, in a different, a roving capacity, but because his wife was delicate he had sent her home to Europe before his child's birth. Her mother had fought to stay with him, for she was a true *colon*, and in her turn the daughter of a *colon*. The word spoken in Europe so disparagingly was a badge of honour to them. Even in Europe on leave they lived in groups, went to the same restaurants and café-bars kept by former *colons* and took villas for the season at the same watering-places. Wives waited among the potted palms for their husbands to return from the land of palms; they played bridge and read aloud to each other their husbands' letters, which contained the gossip of the colony.

The letters bore bright postage stamps of beasts and birds and flowers and the postmarks of exotic places. Marie began to collect them at six, but she always preserved the envelopes and the postmarks as well, so that she had to keep them in a box instead of an album. One of the postmarks was Luc. She did not foresee that one day she would begin to know Luc better than she knew the rue de Namur.

With the tenderness that came from a sense of guilt she wiped Rycker's face with a handkerchief soaked in eau-de-Cologne, even at the risk of waking him. She knew that she was a false *colon*. It was like betraying one's country – all the worse because one's country was so remote and so maligned.

One of the labourers came out of the shed to make water against the wall. When he turned back he saw her watching him and they stared across the few yards at each other, but they were like people watching with telescopes over an immense distance. She remembered a breakfast, with the pale European sun on the water outside and bathers going in for an early dip, and her father teaching her the Mongo for 'bread' and 'coffee' and 'jam'. They were still the only three words in Mongo that she knew. But it was not enough to say coffee and bread and jam to the man outside. They had no means of communication: she couldn't even curse him, as her father or her husband could have done, in words that he under-stood. He turned and went into the shed and again she felt the loneliness of her treachery to this country of *colons*. She wanted to apologize to her old father at home; she couldn't blame him for the postmarks and the stamps. Her mother had yearned to remain with him. She had not realized how unfortunate her weakness was. Rycker opened his eyes and said, 'What time is it?'

'I think it's about three o'clock.'

He was asleep again before he could have heard her reply, and she sat on. In the yard a lorry backed towards the shed. It was piled high with nuts for the presses and the ovens; they were like dried and withered heads, the product of a savage massacre. She tried to read, but *The Imitation of Christ* could not hold her attention. Once a month she received a copy of

Marie-Chantal, but she had to read the serial in secret when Rycker was occupied, for he despised what he called women's fiction and spoke critically of daydreams. What other resources had she than dreams? They were a form of hope, but she hid them from him as a member of the Resistance used to hide his pill of cyanide. She refused to believe that this was the end, growing old in solitude with her husband and the smell of margarine and the black faces and the scrap-metal, in the heat and the humidity. She awaited day by day some radio signal which would announce the hour of libera-tion. Sometimes she thought that there were no lengths to which she would not go for the sake of liberation.

Marie-Chantal came by surface-mail; it was always two months out of date, but that hardly mattered, since the serial story, as much as any piece of literature, had eternal values. In the story she was reading now a girl in the Salle Privée at Monte Carlo had placed 12,000 francs, the last money she had in the world, upon the figure 17, but a hand had reached over her shoulder while the ball ran and shifted her tokens to 19. Then the 19 socket caught the ball and she turned to see who her benefactor could be . . . but she would have to wait another three weeks before she discovered his identity. He was approaching her now down the West African coast, by mail-boat, but even when he arrived at Matadi, there was still the long river-journey ahead of him. The dogs began bark-ing in the yard and Rycker woke.

'See who it is,' he said, 'but keep him away.' She heard a car draw up. It was probably the representative of one of the two rival breweries. Each man made the tour of the out-stations three times a year and gave a party to the local chief and the villagers with his brand of beer gratis for everyone. In some mysterious way it was supposed to aid consumption.

They were shovelling the dried heads out of the *camion* when she came into the yard. Two men sat in a small Peugeot truck. One of them was African, but she couldn't see who the other was because the sun on the windshield dazzled her, but she heard him say, 'What I have to do here should take no time at all. We will reach Luc by ten.' She came to the door of the car and saw that it was Querry. She recalled the shameful scene weeks before when she had run to her car in tears. Afterwards she had spent the night by the roadside bitten by mosquitoes rather than face another human being who might despise her husband too.

She thought gratefully, 'He has come of his own accord. What he said was just a passing mood. It was his *cafard* which spoke, not he.' She wanted to go in and see her husband and tell him, but then she remembered that he had told her, 'Keep him away.'

Querry climbed out of the truck and she saw that the boy with him was one of the *mutilés* from the leproserie. She said to Querry, 'You've come to call on us? My husband will be so glad . . .'

'I am on my way to Luc,' Querry said, 'but I want to have a word with M. Rycker first.' There was something in his expression which recalled her husband at certain moments. If *cafard* had dictated that insulting phrase the *cafard* still possessed him.

She said, 'He is ill. I'm afraid you can't see him.'

'I must. I have been three days on the road from the leproserie . . .'

'You will have to tell me.' He stood by the door of the truck. She said, 'Can't you give me your message?'

'I can hardly strike a woman,' Querry said. A sudden rictus round the mouth startled her. Perhaps he was trying to soften the phrase with a smile, but it made his face all the uglier.

'Is that your message?'

'More or less,' Querry said.

'Then you'd better come inside.' She walked slowly away without looking back. He seemed to her like an armed savage from whom she must disguise her fear. When she reached the house she would be safe. Violence in their class always happened in the open air; it was restrained by sofas and bric-à-brac. When she passed through the door she was tempted to escape to her room, leaving the sick man at Querry's mercy, but she steeled herself by the thought of what Rycker might say to her when he had gone, and with no more than a glance down the passage where safety lay she went to the veranda and heard Querry's steps following behind.

When she reached the veranda she put on the voice of a hostess as she might have done a clean frock. She said, 'Can I get you something to drink?'

'It's a little early. Is your husband really sick?'

'Of course he is. I told you. The mosquitoes are bad here. We are too close to water. He hadn't been taking his paludrin. I don't know why. You know he has moods.'

'I suppose it was here that Parkinson got his fever?'

'Parkinson?'

'The English journalist.'

'That man,' she said with distaste. 'Is he still around?'

'I don't know. You were the last people to see him. After your husband had put him on my track.'

'I'm sorry if he troubled you. I wouldn't answer any of his questions.'

Querry said, 'I had made it quite clear to your husband that I had come here to be private. He forced himself on me in Luc. He sent you out to the leproserie after me. He sent Parkinson. He has been spreading grotesque stories about me in the town. Now there's this newspaper article and another one is threatened. I have come to tell your husband that this persecution has got to stop.'

'Persecution?'

'Have you another name for it?'

'You don't understand. My husband was excited by your coming here. At finding you. There are not so many people he can talk to about what interests him. He's very alone.' She was looking across at the river and the winding-gear of the ferry and the forest on the other side. 'When he's excited by something he wants to possess it. Like a child.'

'I have never cared for children.'

'It's the only young thing about him,' she said, the words coming quickly and unintentionally out, like the spurt from a wound.

He said, 'Can't you persuade him to stop talking about me?'

'I have no influence. He doesn't listen to me. After all why should he?'

'If he loves you . . .'

'I don't know whether he does. He says sometimes that he only loves God.'

'Then I must speak to him myself. A touch of fever is not going to stop him hearing what I have to say.' He added, 'I'm not sure of his room, but there aren't many in this house. I can find it.'

'No. Please no. He'll think it's my fault. He'll be angry. I don't want him angry. I've got something to tell him. I can't if he's angry. It's ghastly enough as it is.'

'What's ghastly?'

She looked at him with an expression of despair. Tears formed in her eyes and began to drip gracelessly like sweat. She said, 'I think I have a baby on the way.'

'But I thought women usually liked . . .'

'He doesn't want one. But he wouldn't allow me to be safe.'

'Have you seen a doctor?'

'No. There's been no excuse for me to go to Luc, and we've only the one car. I didn't want him to be suspicious. He usually wants to know after a time if everything's all right.'

'Hasn't he asked you?'

'I think he's forgotten that we did anything since the time before.'

He was moved unwillingly by her humility. She was very young and surely she was pretty enough, yet it seemed never to occur to her that a man ought not to forget such an act. She said, as if that explained everything, 'It was after the Governor's cocktail party.'

'Are you sure about it?'

'I've missed twice.'

'My dear, in this climate that often happens.' He said, 'I advise you – what's your name?'

'Marie.' It was the commonest woman's name of all, but it sounded to him like a warning.

'Yes,' she said eagerly, 'you advise me . . . ?'

'Not to tell you husband yet. We must find some excuse

for you to go to Luc and see the doctor. But don't worry too much. Don't you want the child?'

'What would be the use of wanting it if *he* doesn't?'

'I would take you in with me now – if we could find you an excuse.'

'If anybody can persuade him, you can. He admires you so much.'

'I have some medicines to pick up for Doctor Colin at the hospital, and I was going to buy some surprise provisions for the fathers too, champagne for when the roof-tree goes up. But I wouldn't be able to deliver you back before tomorrow evening.'

'Oh,' she said, 'his boy can look after him far better than I can. He's been with him longer.'

'I meant that perhaps he mightn't trust me . . .'

'There hasn't been rain for days. The roads are quite good.'

'Shall I talk to him then?'

'It isn't really what you came to say, is it?'

'I'll treat him as gently as I can. You've drawn my sting.'

She said, 'It will be fun – to go to Luc alone. I mean with you.' She wiped her eyes dry with the back of her hand; she was no more ashamed of her tears than a child would have been.

'Perhaps the doctor will say you have nothing to fear. Which is his room?'

'Through the door at the end of the passage. You really won't be harsh to him?'

'No.'

Rycker was sitting up in bed when he entered. He was wearing a look of grievance like a mask, but he took it off quickly and substituted another representing welcome when he saw his visitor. 'Why, Querry? Was it you?'

'I came to see you on the way to Luc.'

'It's good of you to visit me on a bed of sickness.'

Querry said, 'I wanted to see you about that stupid article by the Englishman.'

'I gave it to Father Thomas to take to you.' Rycker's eyes were bright with fever or pleasure. 'There has never been such a sale in Luc for *Paris-Dimanche*, I can tell you that. The bookshop has sent for extra copies. They say they have ordered a hundred of the next issue.'

'Did it never occur to you how detestable it would be to me?'

'I know the paper is not a very high-class one, but the article was highly laudatory. Do you realize that it's even been reprinted in Italy? The bishop, so I'm told, has had an inquiry from Rome.'

'Will you listen to me, Rycker? I'm trying to speak gently because you are sick. But all this has to stop. I am not a Catholic, I am not even a Christian. I won't be adopted by you and your Church.'

Rycker sat under the crucifix, wearing a smile of understanding.

'I have no belief whatever in a god, Rycker. No belief in the soul, in eternity. I'm not even interested.'

'Yes. Father Thomas has told me how terribly you have been suffering from aridity.'

'Father Thomas is a pious fool, and I came out here to escape fools, Rycker. Will you promise to leave me in peace or must I go again the way I came? I was happy before this started. I found I could work. I was feeling interested, involved in something . . .'

'It's a penalty of genius to belong to the world.'

If he had to have a tormentor how gladly he would have chosen the cynical Parkinson. There were interstices in that cracked character where the truth might occasionally seed. But Rycker was like a wall so plastered over with church announcements that you couldn't even see the brickwork behind. He said, 'I'm no genius, Rycker. I am a man who had a certain talent, not a very great talent, and I have come to the end of it. There was nothing new I could do. I could only repeat myself. So I gave up. It's as simple and commonplace as that. Just as I have given up women. After all there are only thirty-two ways of driving a nail into a hole.'

'Parkinson told me of the remorse you felt . . .'

'I have never felt remorse. Never. You all dramatize too

much. We can retire from feeling just as naturally as we retire from a job. Are you sure that you still feel anything, Rycker, that you aren't pretending to feel? Would you greatly care if your factory were burnt down tomorrow in a riot?'

'My heart is not in that.'

'And your heart isn't in your wife either. You made that clear to me the first time we met. You wanted someone to save you from St Paul's threat of burning.'

'There is nothing wrong in a Christian marriage,' Rycker said. 'It's far better than a marriage of passion. But if you want to know the truth, my heart has always been in my faith.'

'I begin to think we are not so different, you and I. We don't know what love is. You pretend to love a god because you love no one else. But I won't pretend. All I have left me is a certain regard for the truth. It was the best side of the small talent I had. You are inventing all the time, Rycker, aren't you? There are men who talk about love to prostitutes – they daren't even sleep with a woman without inventing some sentiment to excuse them. You've even invented this idea of me to justify yourself. But I won't play your game, Rycker.'

'When I look at you,' Rycker said, 'I can see a man tormented.'

'Oh no you can't. I haven't felt any pain at all in twenty years. It needs something far bigger than you to cause me pain.'

'Whether you like it or not, you have set an example to all of us.'

'An example of what?'

'Unselfishness and humility,' Rycker said.

'I warn you, Rycker, that unless you stop spreading this rubbish about me . . .'

But he felt his powerlessness. He had been trapped into words. A blow would have been simpler and better, but it was too late now for blows.

Rycker said, 'Saints used to be made by popular acclaim. I'm not sure that it wasn't a better method than a trial in Rome. We have taken you up, Querry. You don't belong to yourself any more. You lost yourself when you prayed with that leper in the forest.'

'I didn't pray. I only . . .' He stopped. What was the use? Rycker had stolen the last word. Only after he had slammed the door shut did he remember that he had said nothing of Marie Rycker and of her journey to Luc.

And of course there she was waiting for him eagerly and patiently, at the other end of the passage. He wished that he had brought a bag of sweets with which to comfort her. She said excitedly, 'Did he agree?'

'I never asked him.'

'You promised.'

'I got angry, and I forgot. I'm very sorry.'

She said, 'I'll come with you to Luc all the same.'

'You'd better not.'

'Were you very angry with him?'

'Not very. I kept most of the anger to myself.'

'Then I'm coming.' She left him before he had time to protest, and a few moments later she was back with no more than a Sabena night-bag for the journey.

He said, 'You travel light.'

When they reached the truck he asked, 'Wouldn't it be better if I went back and spoke to him?'

'He might say no. Then what could I do?'

They left behind them the smell of the margarine and the cemetery of old boilers, and the shadow of the forest fell on either side. She said politely in her hostess voice, 'Is the hospital going well?'

'Yes.'

'How is the Superior?'

'He is away.'

'Did you have a heavy storm last Saturday? We did.'

He said, 'You don't have to make conversation with me.'

'My husband says that I am too silent.'

'Silence is not a bad thing.'

'It is when you are unhappy.'

'I'm sorry. I had forgotten . . .'

They drove a few more kilometres without words. Then

she asked, 'Why did you come here and not some other place?'

'Because it is a long way off.'

'Other places are a long way off. The South Pole.'

'When I was at the airport there was no plane leaving for the South Pole.' She giggled. It was easy to amuse the young, even the unhappy young. 'There was one going to Tokyo,' he added, 'but somehow this place seemed a lot farther off. And I was not interested in geishas or cherry-blossom.'

'You don't mean you really didn't know where . . . ?'

'One of the advantages of having a credit card is that you don't need to make up your mind where you are going till the last moment.'

'Haven't you any family to leave?'

'Not a family. There was someone, but she was better off without me.'

'Poor her.'

'Oh no. She's lost nothing of value. It's hard for a woman to live with a man who doesn't love her.'

'Yes.'

'There are always the times of day when one ceases to pretend.'

'Yes.' They were silent again until darkness began to fall and he switched the headlights on. They shone on a human effigy with a coconut-head, sitting on a rickety chair. She gave a gasp of fright and pressed against his shoulder. She said, 'I'm scared of things I don't understand.'

'Then you must be frightened of a great deal.'

'I am.'

He put his arm round her shoulders to reassure her. She said, 'Did you say good-bye to her?'

'No.'

'But she must have seen you packing.'

'No. I travel light too.'

'You came away without anything?'

'I had a razor and a toothbrush and a letter of credit from a bank in America.'

'Do you really mean you didn't know where you were going?'

'I had no idea. So it wasn't any good taking clothes.'

The track was rough and he needed both hands on the wheel. He had never before scrutinized his own behaviour. It had seemed to him at the time the only logical thing to do. He had eaten a larger breakfast than usual because he could not be certain of the hour of his next meal, and then he had taken a taxi. His journey began in the great all-but-empty airport built for a world-exhibition which had closed a long time ago. One could walk a mile through the corridors without seeing more than a scattering of human beings. In an immense hall people sat apart waiting for the plane to Tokyo. They looked like statues in an art gallery. He had asked for a seat to Tokyo before he noticed an indicator with African names.

He had said, 'Is there a seat on that plane too?'

'Yes, but there's no connection to Tokyo after Rome.'

'I shall go the whole way.' He gave the man his credit card.

'Where is your luggage?'

'I have no luggage.'

He supposed now that his conduct must have seemed a little odd. He said to the clerk, 'Mark my ticket with my surname only, please. On the passenger list too. I don't want to be bothered by the Press.' It was one of the few advantages which fame brought a man that he was not automatically regarded with suspicion because of unusual behaviour. Thus simply he had thought to cover his tracks, but he had not entirely succeeded or the letter signed *toute à toi* could never have reached him. Perhaps she had been to the airport herself to make inquiries. The man there must have had quite a story to tell her. Even so, at his destination, no one had known him, and at the small hotel he went to – without air-conditioning and with a shower which didn't work – no one knew his name. So it could have been no one but Rycker who had betrayed his whereabouts; the ripple of Rycker's interest had gone out across half the world like radio-waves, reaching the international Press. He said abruptly, 'How I wish I'd never met your husband.'

'So do I.'

'It's done you no harm, surely?'

'I mean – I wish I hadn't met him either.' The headlamps caught the wooden poles of a cage high in the air. She said, 'I hate this place. I want to go home.'

'We've come too far to turn back now.'

'That's not home,' she said. 'That's the factory.'

He knew very well what she expected him to say, but he refused to speak. You uttered a few words of sympathy – however false and conventional – and experience taught him what nearly always followed. Unhappiness was like a hungry animal waiting beside the track for any victim. He said, 'Have you friends in Luc to put you up?'

'We have no friends there. I'll go with you to the hotel.'

'Did you leave a note for your husband?'

'No.'

'It would have been better.'

'Did you leave a note behind before you caught the plane?'

'That was different. I was not returning.'

She said, 'Would you lend me money for a ticket home – I mean, to Europe?'

'No.'

'I was afraid you wouldn't.' As if that settled everything and there was nothing more to do about it, she fell asleep. He thought rashly: poor frightened beast – this one was too young to be a great danger. It was only when they were fully grown you couldn't trust them with your pity.

II

It was nearly eleven at night before they drove into Luc past the little river-port. The Bishop's boat was lying at her moorings. A cat stopped halfway up the gang-plank and regarded them, and Querry swerved to avoid a dead piedog stretched in their track waiting for the morning vulture. The hotel across the square from the Governor's house was decked out with the relics of gaiety. Perhaps the directors of the local brewery had been giving their annual party or some official, who thought himself lucky, had been celebrating his recall home. In the bar there were mauve and pink paper-chains hanging over the tubular steel chairs that gave the whole place the cheerless and functional look of an engine-room; shades which represented the man in the moon beamed down from the light-brackets.

There was no air-conditioning in the rooms upstairs, and the walls stopped short of the ceiling so that any privacy was impossible. Every movement was audible from the neighbouring room, and Querry could follow every stage of the girl's retirement – the zipping of the all-night bag, the clatter of a coat-hanger, the tinkle of a glass bottle on a porcelain basin. Shoes were dropped on bare boards, and water ran. He sat and wondered what he ought to do to comfort her if the doctor told her in the morning that she was pregnant. He was reminded of his long night's vigil with Deo Gratias. It had been fear then too that he had contended with. He heard the bed creak.

He took a bottle of whisky from his sack and poured himself a glass. Now it was his turn to tinkle, run water, clatter; he was like a prisoner in a cell answering by code the signals of a fellow-convict. An odd sound reached him through the wall – it sounded to him as though she were crying. He felt no pity, only irritation. She had forced herself on him and she was threatening now to spoil his night's sleep. He had not yet undressed. He took the bottle of whisky with him and knocked on her door.

He saw at once that he had been wrong. She was sitting up in bed reading a paper-back – she must have had time to stow that away too in the Sabena bag. He said, 'I'm sorry – I thought I heard you crying.'

'Oh no,' she said. 'I was laughing.' He saw that it was a popular novel dealing with the life in Paris of an English major. 'It's terribly funny.'

'I brought this along in case you needed comfort.'

'Whisky? I've never drunk it.'

'You can begin. But you probably won't like it.' He washed her toothmug out and poured her a weak drink.

'You don't like it?'

She said, 'I like the idea. Drinking whisky at midnight in a room of my own.'

'It's not midnight yet.'

'You know what I mean. And reading in bed. My husband doesn't like me reading in bed. Especially a book like this.'

'What's wrong with the book?'

'It's not serious. It's not about God. Of course,' she said, 'he has good reason. I'm not properly educated. The nuns did their best, but it simply didn't stick.'

'I'm glad you're not worrying about tomorrow.'

'There may be good news. I've got a bit of a stomach-ache at this moment. It can't be the whisky yet, can it? and it might be the curse.' The hostess-phrases had gone to limbo where the nuns' learning lay, and she had reverted to the school dormitory. It was absurd to consider that anyone so immature could be in any way a danger.

He asked, 'Were you happy when you were at school?'

'It was bliss.' She bunched her knees higher and said, 'Why don't you sit down?'

'It's quite time you were asleep.' He found it impossible not to treat her as a child. Rycker, instead of rupturing her virginity, had sealed it safely down once and for all.

She said, 'What are you going to do? When the hospital's finished, I mean?' That was the question they were all asking him, but this time he did not evade it: there was a theory that one should always tell the direct truth to the young.

He said, 'I am going to stay. I am never going back.'

'You'll have to – sometime – on leave.'

'The others perhaps, but not me.'

'You'll get sick in the end if you stay.'

'I'm very tough. Anyway what do I care? We all sooner or later get the same sickness, age. Do you see those brown marks on the backs of my hands – my mother used to call them grave-marks.'

'They are only freckles,' she said.

'Oh no, freckles come from the sunlight. These come from the darkness.'

'You are very morbid,' she said, speaking like the head of the school. 'I don't really understand you. I have to stay here, but my God if I were free like you . . .'

'I will tell you a story,' he said and poured himself out a second treble Scotch.

'That's a very large whisky. You aren't a heavy drinker, are you? My husband is.'

'I'm only a steady one. This one is to help me with the story. I'm not used to telling stories. How does one begin?' He drank slowly. 'Once upon a time.'

'Really,' she said, 'you and I are much too old for fairy stories.'

'Yes. That in a way *is* the story as you'll see. Once upon a time there was a boy who lived in the deep country.'

'Were you the boy?'

'No, you mustn't draw close parallels. They always say a novelist chooses from his general experience of life, not from special facts. I have never lived out of cities until now.'

'Go on.'

'This boy lived with his parents on a farm – not a very large farm, but it was big enough for them and two servants and six labourers, a dog, a cat, a cow . . . I suppose there was a pig. I don't know much about farms.'

'There seems to be an awful lot of characters. I shall fall asleep if I try to remember them all.'

'That's exactly what I'm trying to make you do. His parents used to tell the boy stories about the King who lived in a city a hundred miles away – about the distance of the furthest star.'

'That's nonsense. A star is billions and billions . . .'

'Yes, but the boy *thought* the star was a hundred miles away. He knew nothing about light-years. He had no idea that the star he was watching had probably been dead and dark before the world was made. They told him that, even though the King was far away, he was watching everything that went on everywhere. When a pig littered, the King knew of it, or when a moth died against a lamp. When a man and woman married, he knew that too. He was pleased by their marriage because when *they* came to litter it would increase the number of his subjects; so he rewarded them – you couldn't see the reward, for the woman frequently died in childbirth and the child was sometimes born deaf or blind, but, after all, you cannot see the air – and yet it exists according to those who know. When a servant slept with another servant in a haystack the King punished them. You couldn't always see the punishment – the man found a better job and the girl was more beautiful with her virginity gone and afterwards married the foreman, but that was only because the punishment was postponed. Sometimes it was postponed until the end of life, but that made no difference because the King was the King of the dead too and you couldn't tell what terrible things he might do to them in the grave.

'The boy grew up. He married properly and was rewarded by the King, although his only child died and he made no progress in his profession – he had always wanted to carve statues, as large and important as the Sphinx. After his child's death he quarrelled with his wife and he was punished by the King for it. Of course you couldn't have seen the punishment any more than you could the reward: you had to take both on trust. He became in time a famous jeweller, for one of the women whom he had satisfied gave him money for his training, and he made many beautiful things in honour of his mistress and of course the King. Lots of rewards began to come his way. Money too. From the King. Everyone agreed that it all came from the King. He left his wife and his mistress, he left a lot of women, but he always had a great deal of fun with them first. They called it love and so did he, he broke all the rules he could think of, and he must surely have been punished for breaking them, but you couldn't see the punishment nor could he. He grew richer and richer and he made better and better jewellery, and women were kinder and kinder to him. He had, everyone agreed, a wonderful time. The only trouble was that he became bored, more and more bored. Nobody ever seemed to say no to him. Nobody ever made him suffer – it was always other people who suffered. Sometimes just for a change he would have welcomed feeling the pain of the punishment that the King must all the time have been inflicting on him. He could travel wherever he chose and after a while it seemed to him that he had gone much further than the hundred miles that separated him from the King, further than the furthest star, but wherever he went he always came to the same place where the same things happened: articles in the papers praised his jewellery, women cheated their husbands and went to bed with him, and servants of the King acclaimed him as a loyal and faithful subject.

'Because people could only see the reward, and the punishment was invisible, he got the reputation of being a very good man. Sometimes people were a little perplexed that such a good man should have enjoyed quite so many women – it was, on the surface anyway, disloyal to the King who had made quite other rules. But they learnt in time to explain it; they said he had a great capacity for love and love had always been regarded by them as the highest of virtues. Love indeed was the greatest reward even the King could give, all the greater because it was more invisible than such little material rewards as money and success and membership of the Academy. Even the man himself began to believe that he loved a great deal better than all the so-called good people who obviously could not be so good if you knew all (you had only to look at the punishments they received – poverty, children dying, losing both legs in a railway accident, and the like). It was quite a shock to him when he discovered one day that he didn't love at all.'

'How did he discover that?'

'It was the first of several important discoveries which he made about that time. Did I tell you that he was a very clever man, much cleverer than the people around him? Even as a boy he had discovered all by himself about the King. Of course there were his parents' stories, but they proved nothing. They might have been old wives' tales. They loved the King, they said, but he went one better. He proved that the King existed by historical, logical, philosophical and etymological methods. His parents told him that was a waste of time: they knew: they had seen the King. "Where?" "In our hearts of course." He laughed at them for their simplicity and their superstition. How could the King possibly be in their hearts when he was able to prove that he had never stirred from the city a hundred miles away? His King existed objectively and there was no other King but his.'

'I don't like parables much, and I don't like your hero.'

'He doesn't like himself much, and that's why he's never spoken before – except in this way.'

'What you said about "no other king but his" reminds me a little of my husband.'

'You mustn't accuse a story-teller of introducing real characters.'

'When are you going to reach a climax? Has it a happy ending? I don't want to stay awake otherwise. Why don't you describe some of the women?'

'You are like so many critics. You want me to write your own sort of story.'

'Have you read *Manon Lescaut*?'

'Years ago.'

'We all loved it at the convent. Of course it was strictly forbidden. It was passed from hand to hand, and I pasted the cover of Lejeune's *History of the Wars of Religion* on it. I have it still.'

'You must let me finish my story.'

'Oh well,' she said with resignation, leaning back against the pillows, 'if you must.'

'I have told you about my hero's first discovery. His second came much later when he realized that he was not born to be an artist at all: only a very clever jeweller. He made one gold jewel in the shape of an ostrich egg: it was all enamel and gold and when you opened it you found inside a little gold figure sitting at a table and a little gold and enamel egg on the table, and when you opened that there was a little figure sitting at a table and a little gold and enamel egg and when you opened that . . . I needn't go on. Everyone said he was a master-technician, but he was highly praised too for the seriousness of his subject-matter because on the top of each egg there was a gold cross set with chips of precious stones in honour of the King. The trouble was that he wore himself out with the ingenuity of his design, and suddenly when he was making the contents of the final egg with an optic glass – that was what they called magnifying glasses in the old days in which this story is set, for of course it contains no reference to our time and no likeness to any living character . . .' He took another long drink of whisky; he couldn't remember how long it was since he had experienced the odd elation he was feeling now. He said, 'What am I saying? I think I am a little drunk. The whisky doesn't usually affect me in this way.'

'Something about an egg,' her sleepy voice replied from under the sheet.

'Oh yes, the second discovery.' It was, he began to think, a sad story, so that it was hard to understand this sense of freedom and release, like that of a prisoner who at last 'comes clean', admitting everything to his inquisitor. Was this the reward perhaps which came sometimes to a writer? 'I have told all: you can hang me now.' 'What did you say?'

'The last egg.'

'Oh yes, that was it. Suddenly our hero realized how bored he was – he never wanted to turn his hand any more to mounting any jewel at all. He was finished with his profession – he had come to an end of it. Nothing could ever be so ingenious as what he had done already, or more useless, and he could never hear any praise higher than what he had received. He knew what the damned fools could do with their praise.'

'So what?'

'He went to a house number 49 in a street called the rue des Remparts where his mistress had kept an apartment ever since she left her husband. Her name was Marie like yours. There was a crowd outside. He found the doctor and the police there because an hour before she had killed herself.'

'How ghastly.'

'Not for him. A long time ago he had got to the end of pleasure just as now he had got to the end of work, although it is true he went on practising pleasure as a retired dancer continues to rehearse daily at the bar, because he has spent all his mornings that way and it never occurs to him to stop. So our hero felt only relief: the bar had been broken, he wouldn't bother, he thought, to obtain another. Although, of course,

after a month or two he did. However it was too late then –
the morning-habit had been broken and he never took it up
again with quite the same zeal.'

'It's a very unpleasant fairy story,' the voice said. He could-
n't see her face because the sheet was pulled over it. He paid
no attention to her criticism.

'I tell you it isn't easy leaving a profession any more than
you would find it easy leaving a husband. In both cases people
talk a lot to you about duty. People came to him to demand
eggs with crosses (it was his duty to the King and the King's
followers). It almost seemed from the fuss they made that no
one else was capable of making eggs or crosses. To try and
discourage them and show them how his mind had changed,
he did cut a few more stones as frivolously as he knew how,
exquisite little toads for women to wear in their navels – navel-
jewels became quite a fashion for a time. He even fashioned
little soft golden coats of mail, with one hollow stone like a
knowing eye at the top, with which men might clothe their
special parts – they came to be known for some reason as
Letters of Marque and for a while they too were quite fash-
ionable as gifts. (You know how difficult it is for a woman
to find anything to give a man at Christmas.) So our hero
received yet more money and praise, but what vexed him most
was that even these trifles were now regarded as seriously as
his eggs and crosses had been. He was the King's jeweller and
nothing could alter that. People declared that he was a moral-
ist and that these were serious satires on the age – in the end
the idea rather spoilt the sale of the letters, as you can imagine. A man hardly wants to wear a moral satire in that place,
and women were chary of touching a moral satire in the way
they had liked touching a soft jewelled responsive coat.

'However the fact that his jewels ceased to be popular with
people in general only made him more popular with the connois-
seurs who distrust popular success. They began to write books
about his art; especially those who claimed to know and love
the King wrote about him. The books all said much the same
thing, and when our hero had read one he had read them all.
There was nearly always a chapter called "The Toad in the Hole:

the Art of Fallen Man", or else there was one called "From Easter Egg to Letters of Marque, the Jeweller of Original Sin".'

'Why do you keep on calling him a jeweller?' the voice said from under the sheet. 'You know very well he was an architect.'

'I warned you not to attach real characters to my story. You'll be identifying yourself with the other Marie next. Although, thank God, you're not the kind to kill yourself.'

'You'd be surprised what I could do,' she said. 'Your story isn't a bit like *Manon Lescaut*, but it's pretty miserable all the same.'

'What none of these people knew was that one day our hero had made a startling discovery – he no longer believed all those arguments historical, philosophical, logical, and etymological that he had worked out for the existence of the King. There was left only a memory of the King who had lived in his parents' heart and not in any particular place. Unfortunately his heart was not the same as the one his parents shared: it was calloused with pride and success, and it had learned to beat only with pride when a building . . .'

'You said building.'

'When a jewel was completed or when a woman cried under him, *"donne, donne, donne"*.' He looked at the whisky in the bottle: it wasn't worth preserving the little that remained; he emptied it into his glass and he didn't bother to add water.

'You know,' he said, 'he had deceived himself, just as much as he had deceived the others. He had believed quite sincerely that when he loved his work he was loving the King and that when he made love to a woman he was at least imitating in a faulty way the King's love for his people. The King after all had so loved the world that he had sent a bull and a shower of gold and a son . . .'

'You are getting it all confused,' the girl said.

'But when he discovered there was no such King as the one he had believed in, he realized too that anything that he had ever done must have been done for love of himself. How could there be any point any longer in making jewels or making love for his own solitary pleasure? Perhaps he had reached the end of his sex and the end of his vocation before he made his discovery about the King or perhaps that discovery brought about the end of everything? I wouldn't know, but I'm told that there were moments when he wondered if his unbelief were not after all a final and conclusive proof of the King's existence. This total vacancy might be his punishment for the rules he had wilfully broken. It was even possible that this was what people meant by pain. The problem was complicated to the point of absurdity, and he began to envy his parents' simple and uncomplex heart, in which they had always believed that the King lived – and not in the cold palace as big as St Peter's a hundred miles away.'

'So then?'

'I told you, didn't I, that it's just as difficult to leave a profession as to leave a husband. If you left your husband there would be acres and acres of daylight you wouldn't know how to cross, and acres of darkness as well, and of course there would always be telephone calls and the kind inquiries of friends and the chance paragraphs in the newspapers. But that part of the story has no real interest.'

'So he took a credit card . . .' she said.

The whisky was finished. He said, 'I've kept you awake.'

'I wish you'd told me a romantic story. All the same it took my mind off things.' She giggled under the sheet. 'I could almost say to him, couldn't I, that we'd spent the night together. Do you think that he'd divorce me? I suppose not. The Church won't allow divorce. The Church says, the Church orders . . .'

'Are you really so unhappy?' He got no reply. To the young sleep comes as quickly as day to the tropical town. He opened the door very quietly and went out into the passage that was still dark with one all-night globe palely burning. Some late-sleeper or early-riser closed a door five rooms away: a flush choked and swallowed in the silence. He sat on his bed. It was the hour of coolness. He thought: the King is dead, long live the King. Perhaps he had found here a country and a life.

CHAPTER 2

I

Querry was out early to do as many as he could of the doctor's errands before the day became too hot. There was no sign of Marie Rycker at breakfast, and no sound over the partition of their rooms. At the cathedral he collected the letters which had been waiting for the next boat – he was glad to find that not one of them was addressed to him. *Toute à toi* had made her one gesture towards his unknown region, and he hoped for her sake that it had been a gesture of duty and convention and not of love, for in that case his silence would do her no further hurt.

By midday he was feeling parched and finding himself not far from the wharf he went down to the river and up the gang-plank of the Bishop's boat to see whether the captain were on board. He hesitated a moment at the foot of the ladder surprised by his own action. It was the first time for a long while that he had voluntarily made a move towards companionship. He remembered how fearful he had been when he last set foot on board and the light was burning in the cabin. The crew had piled logs on the pontoons ready for another voyage, and a woman was hanging her washing between the companion-way and the boiler; he called 'Captain', as he climbed the ladder, but the priest who sat at the saloon-table going through the bills of lading was a stranger to him.

'May I come in?'

'I think I know who you are. You must be M. Querry. Shall we open a bottle of beer?'

Querry asked after the former captain. 'He has been sent to teach moral theology,' his successor said, 'at Wakanga.'

'Was he sorry to go?'

'He was delighted. The river-life did not appeal to him.'

'To you it does?'

'I don't know yet. This is my first voyage. It is a change from canon law. We start tomorrow.'

'To the leproserie?'

'We shall end there. A week. Ten days. I'm not sure yet about the cargo.'

Querry when he left the boat felt that he had aroused no curiosity. The captain had not even asked him about the new hospital. Perhaps *Paris-Dimanche* had done its worst; there was nothing more that Rycker or Parkinson could inflict on him. It was as though he were on the verge of acceptance into a new country; like a refugee he watched the consul lift his pen to fill in the final details of his visa. But the refugee remains apprehensive to the last; he has had too many experiences of the sudden afterthought, the fresh question or requirement, the strange official who comes into the room carrying another file. A man was in the hotel bar, drinking below the man in the moon and the chains of mauve paper; it was Parkinson.

Parkinson raised a glass of pink gin and said, 'Have one on me.'

'I thought you had gone away.'

'Only as far as Stanleyville for the riots. Now I've filed my story and I'm a free man again until something turns up. What's yours?'

'How long are you staying here?'

'Until I get a cable from home. Your story has gone over well. They may want a third instalment.'

'You didn't use what I gave you.'

'It wasn't family reading.'

'You can get no more from me.'

'You'd be surprised,' Parkinson said, 'what sometimes comes one's way by pure good luck.' He chinked the ice against the side of his glass. 'Quite a success that first article had. Full syndication, even the Antipodes – except of course behind the curtain. The Americans are lapping it up. Religion and an anti-colonialist angle – you couldn't have a better mixture for them. There's just one thing I do rather regret – you never took that photograph of me carried ashore with fever. I had to make do with a photograph which Mme Rycker took. But now I've got a fine one of myself in Stanleyville, beside a burnt-out car. Wasn't it you who contradicted me about Stanley? He must have been there or they wouldn't have called the place after him. Where are you going?'

'To my room.'

'Oh yes, you are number six, aren't you, in my corridor?'

'Number seven.'

Parkinson stirred the ice round with his finger. 'Oh, I see. Number seven. You aren't vexed with me, are you? I assure you those angry words the other day, they didn't mean a thing. It was just a way to get you talking. A man like me can't afford to be angry. The darts the picador sticks into the bull are not the real thing.'

'What is?'

'The next instalment. Wait till you read it.'

'I hardly expect to find the moment of truth.'

'*Touché*,' Parkinson said. 'It's a funny thing about metaphors – they never really follow through. Perhaps you won't believe me, but there was a time when I was interested in style.' He looked into his glass of gin as though into a well. 'What the hell of a long life it is, isn't it?'

'The other day you seemed afraid to lose it.'

'It's all I've got,' Parkinson said.

The door opened from the blinding street and Marie Rycker walked in. Parkinson said in a jovial voice, 'Well, fancy, look who's here.'

'I gave Mme Rycker a lift from the plantation.'

'Another gin,' Parkinson said to the barman.

'I do not drink gin,' Marie Rycker told him in her stilted phrase-book English.

'What *do* you drink? Now that I come to think of it, I don't remember ever seeing you with a glass in your hand all the time I stayed with you. Have an *orange pressée*, my child?'

'I am very fond of whisky,' Marie Rycker said with pride.

'Good for you. You are growing up fast.' He went down

the length of the bar to give the order and on his way he made a little jump, agile in so fat a man, and set the paper-chains rocking with the palm of his hand.

'Any news?' Querry asked.

'He can't tell me – not until the day after tomorrow. He thinks . . .'

'Yes.'

'He thinks I'm caught,' she said gloomily and then Parkinson was back beside them holding the glass. He said, 'I heard your old man had the fever.'

'Yes.'

'Don't I know what it feels like!' Parkinson said. 'He's lucky to have a young wife to look after him.'

'He does not need me for a nurse.'

'Are you staying here long?'

'I do not know. Two days perhaps.'

'Time for a meal with me then?'

'Oh no. No time for that,' she said without hesitation.

He grinned without mirth. '*Touché* again.'

When she had drained her whisky she said to Querry, 'We're lunching together, aren't we, you and I? Give me just a minute for a wash. I'll fetch my key.'

'Allow *me*,' Parkinson said, and before she had time to protest, he was already back at the bar, swinging her key on his little finger. 'Number six,' he said, 'so we are all three on the same floor.'

Querry said, 'I'll come up with you.'

She looked into her room and came quickly back to his. She asked, 'Can I come in? You can't think how squalid it is in mine. I got up too late and they haven't made the bed.' She wiped her face with his towel, then looked ruefully at the marks which her powder had left. 'I'm sorry. What a mess I've made. I didn't mean to.'

'It doesn't matter.'

'Women are disgusting, aren't they?'

'In a long life I haven't found them so.'

'See what I've landed you with now. Twenty-four more hours in a hole like this.'

'Can't the doctor write to you about the result?'

'I can't go back until I know. Don't you see how impossible that would be? If the answer's yes, I've got to tell him right away. It was my only excuse for coming anyway.'

'And if the answer's no?'

'I'll be so happy then I won't care about anything. Perhaps I won't even go back.' She asked him, 'What *is* a rabbit test?'

'I don't know exactly. I believe they take your urine, and cut the rabbit open . . .'

'Do they do *that*?' she asked with horror.

'They sew the rabbit up again. I think it survives for another test.'

'I wonder why we all have to know the worst so quickly. At a poor beast's expense.'

'Haven't you any wish at all for a child?'

'For a young Rycker? No.' She took the comb out of his brush and without examining it pushed it through her hair. 'I didn't trap you into lunch, did I? You weren't eating with anyone else?'

'No.'

'It's just that I can't stand that man out there.'

But it was impossible to get far away from him in Luc. There were only two restaurants in the town and they chose the same one. The three of them were the only people there; he watched them between bites from his table by the door. He had slung his Rolleiflex on the chair-back beside him much as civilians slung their revolvers in those uncertain days. At least you could say of him that he went hunting with a camera only.

Marie Rycker gave herself a second helping of potatoes. 'Don't tell me,' she said, 'that I'm eating enough for two.'

'I won't.'

'It's the stock *colon* joke, you know, for someone with worms.'

'How is your stomach-ache?'

'Alas, it's gone. The doctor seemed to think that it had no connection.'

'Hadn't you better telephone to your husband? Surely he'll be anxious if you don't come back today.'

'The lines are probably down. They usually are.'

'There hasn't been a storm.'

'The Africans are always stealing the wire.'

She finished off a horrible mauve dessert before she spoke again. 'I expect you are right. I'll telephone,' and she left him alone with his coffee. His cup and Parkinson's clinked in unison over the empty tables.

Parkinson called across, 'The mail's not in. I've been expecting a copy of my second article. I'll drop it in your room if it comes. Let me see. Is it six or seven? It wouldn't do to get the wrong room, would it?'

'You needn't bother.'

'You owe me a photograph. Perhaps you and Mme Rycker would oblige.'

'You'll get no photograph from me, Parkinson.'

Querry paid the bill and went to find the telephone. It stood on a desk where a woman with blue hair and blue spectacles was writing her accounts with an orange pen. 'It's ringing,' Marie Rycker said, 'but he doesn't answer.'

'I hope his fever's not worse.'

'He's probably gone across to the factory.' She put the telephone down and said, 'I've done my best, haven't I?'

'You could try again this evening before we have dinner.'

'You *are* stuck with me, aren't you?'

'No more than you with me.'

'Have you any more stories to tell?'

'No. I only know the one.'

She said, 'It's an awful time till tomorrow. I don't know what to do until I know.'

'Lie down awhile.'

'I can't. Would it be very stupid if I went to the cathedral and prayed?'

'Nothing is stupid that makes the time pass.'

'But if the thing is here,' she said, 'inside me, it couldn't suddenly disappear, could it, if I prayed?'

'I wouldn't think so.' He said reluctantly, 'Even the priests don't ask you to believe that. They would tell you, I suppose, to pray that God's will be done. But don't expect me to talk to you about prayer.'

'I'd want to know what his will was before I prayed anything like that,' she said. 'All the same, I think I'll go and pray. I could pray to be happy, couldn't I?'

'I suppose so.'

'That would cover almost everything.'

II

Querry too found the hours hanging heavily. Again he walked down to the river. Work had stopped upon the Bishop's boat, and there was no one on board. In the little square the shops were shuttered. It seemed as though all the world were asleep except himself and the girl who, he supposed, was still praying. But when he returned to the hotel he found that Parkinson at least was awake. He stood under the mauve-and-pink paper streamers, with his eyes upon the door. After Querry had crossed the threshold, he came tip-toeing forward and said with sly urgent importance, 'I must have a word with you quietly before you go to your room.'

'What about?'

'The general situation,' Parkinson said. 'Storm over Luc. Do you know who's up there?'

'Up where?'

'On the first floor.'

'You seem very anxious to tell me. Go ahead.'

'The husband,' Parkinson said heavily.

'What husband?'

'Rycker. He's looking for his wife.'

'I think he'll find her in the cathedral.'

'It's not as simple as all that. He knows you're with her.'

'Of course he does. I was at his house yesterday.'

'All the same I don't think he expected to find you here in adjoining rooms.'

'You think like a gossip-writer,' Querry said. 'What difference does it make whether rooms adjoin? You can sleep together from opposite ends of a passage just as easily.'

'Don't underrate the gossip-writers. They write history. From Fair Rosamund to Eva Braun.'

'I don't think history will be much concerned with the Ryckers.' He went to the desk and said, 'My bill, please. I'm leaving now.'

'Running away?' Parkinson asked.

'Why running away? I was only staying here to give her a lift back. Now I can leave her with her husband. She's his responsibility.'

'You *are* a cold-blooded devil,' Parkinson said. 'I begin to believe some of the things you told me.'

'Print them instead of your pious rubbish. It might be interesting to tell the truth for once.'

'But which truth? You aren't as simple-minded as you make out, Querry, and there weren't any lies of fact in what I wrote. Leaving out Stanley, of course.'

'And your *pirogue* and your faithful servants.'

'Anyway, what I wrote about *you* was true.'

'No.'

'You have buried yourself here, haven't you? You are working for the lepers. You did pursue that man into the forest . . . It all adds up, you know, to what people like to call goodness.'

'I know my own motives.'

'Do you? And did the saints? What about "most miserable sinner" and all that crap?'

'You talk – almost – as Father Thomas does. Not quite, of course.'

'History's just as likely to take my interpretation as your own. I told you I was going to build you up, Querry. Unless, of course, as now seems likely, I find it makes a better story if I pull you down.'

'Do you really believe you have all that power?'

'Montagu Parkinson has a very wide syndication.'

The woman with blue hair said, 'Your bill, M. Querry,' and he turned to pay. 'Isn't it worth your while,' Parkinson said, 'to ask me a favour?'

'I don't understand.'

'I've been threatened often in my time. I've had my camera smashed twice. I've spent a night in a police-cell. Three times in a restaurant somebody hit me.' For a moment he sounded like St Paul: 'Three times I was beaten with rods, once I was stoned; I have been shipwrecked three times . . .' He said, 'The strange thing is that no one has ever appealed to my better nature. It might work. It's probably there, you know, somewhere . . .' It was like a genuine grief.

Querry said gently, 'Perhaps I would, if I cared at all.'

Parkinson said, 'I can't bear that damned indifference of yours. Do you know what he found up there? But you would-n't ask a journalist for information, would you? There's a towel in your room. I showed it him myself. And a comb with long hair in it.' The misery of being Parkinson for a moment looked out of his wounded eyes. He said, 'I'm disappointed in you, Querry. I'd begun to believe my own story about you.'

'I'm sorry,' Querry said.

'A man's got to believe a bit or contract out altogether.'

Somebody stumbled at the turn of the stairs. It was Rycker coming down. He had a book of some kind in his hand in a pulpy scarlet cover. The fingers on the rail shook as he came, from the remains of fever or from nerves. He stopped and the fat-boy mask of the man in the moon grinned at him from a neighbouring light-bracket. He said, 'Querry.'

'Hello, Rycker, are you feeling better?'

'I can't understand it,' Rycker said. 'You of all men in the world . . .' He seemed to be searching desperately for clichés, the clichés from the *Marie-Chantal* serials rather than the clichés he was accustomed to from his reading in theology. 'I thought you were my friend, Querry.'

The orange pen was suspiciously busy behind the desk and the blue head was unconvincingly bent. 'I don't know what you are talking about, Rycker,' Querry said. 'You'd better come into the bar. We'll be more alone there.' Parkinson prepared to follow them, but Querry blocked the door. He said, 'No, this isn't a story for the *Post*.'

'I have nothing to hide from Mr Parkinson,' Rycker said in English.

'As you wish.' The heat of the afternoon had driven away even the barman. The paper streamers hung down like old man's beard. Querry said, 'Your wife tried to telephone to you at lunch-time, but there was no reply.'

'What do you suppose? I was on the road by six this morning.'

'I'm glad you've come. I shall be able to leave now.'

Rycker said, 'It's no good denying anything, Querry, anything at all. I've been to my wife's room, number six, and you've got the key of number seven in your pocket.'

'You needn't jump to stupid conclusions, Rycker. Even about towels and combs. What if she did wash in my room this morning? As for rooms they were the only ones prepared when we arrived.'

'Why did you take her away without so much as a word . . . ?'

'I meant to tell you, but you and I talked about other things.' He looked at Parkinson leaning on the bar. He was watching their mouths closely as though in that way he might come to understand the language they were using.

'She went off and left me ill with a high fever . . .'

'You had your boy. There were things she had to do in town.'

'What things?'

'I think that's for her to tell you, Rycker. A woman can have her secrets.'

'You seem to share them all right. Hasn't a husband got the right . . . ?'

'You are too fond of talking about rights, Rycker. She has her rights too. But I'm not going to stand and argue . . .'

'Where are you going?'

'To find my boy. I want to start for home. We can do nearly four hours before dark.'

'I've got a lot more to talk to you about.'

'What? The love of God?'

'No,' Rycker said, 'about this.' He held the book open at a page headed with a date. Querry saw that it was a diary with ruled lines and between them the kind of careful script girls learn to write at school. 'Go on,' Rycker said, 'read it.'

'I don't read other people's diaries.'

'Then I'll read it to you. "Spent night with Q."'

Querry smiled. He said, 'It's true – in a way. We sat drinking whisky and I told her a long story.'

'I don't believe a word you're saying.'

'You deserve to be a cuckold, Rycker, but I have never gone in for seducing children.'

'I can imagine what the courts would say to this.'

'Be careful, Rycker. Don't threaten me. I might change my mind.'

'I could make you pay,' Rycker said, 'pay heavily.'

'I doubt whether any court in the world would take your word against hers and mine. Good-bye, Rycker.'

'You can't walk out of here as though nothing had happened.'

'I would have liked to leave you in suspense, but it wouldn't be fair to her. Nothing has happened, Rycker. I haven't even kissed your wife. She doesn't attract me in that way.'

'What right have you to despise us as you do?'

'Be a sensible man. Put that diary back where you found it and say nothing.'

'"Spent the night with Q" and say nothing?'

Querry turned to Parkinson. 'Give your friend a drink and talk some sense into him. You owe him an article.'

'A duel would make a good story,' Parkinson said wistfully.

'It's lucky for her I'm not a violent man,' Rycker said. 'A good thrashing . . .'

'Is that a part of Christian marriage, too?'

He felt an extraordinary weariness; he had lived a lifetime in the middle of some such scene as this, he had been born to such voices, and if he were not careful, he would die with them in his ears. He walked out on the two of them, paying no attention at all to the near-scream of Rycker, 'I've got a right to demand . . .' In the cabin of the truck sitting beside Deo Gratias he was at peace again. He said, 'You've never been back, have you, into the forest, and I know you'll never take me there . . . All the same, I wish . . . Is Pendélé very far away?'

Deo Gratias sat with his head down, saying nothing.

'Never mind.'

Outside the cathedral Querry stopped the truck and got out. It would be wiser to warn her. The doors were open for ventilation, and the hideous windows through which the hard light glared in red and blue made the sun more clamorous than outside. The boots of a priest going to the sacristy squealed on the tiled floor, and a mammy chinked her beads. It was not a church for meditation; it was as hot and public as a marketplace, and in the side-chapels stood plaster stall-holders, offering a baby or a bleeding heart. Marie Rycker was sitting under a statue of Sainte Thérèse of Lisieux. It seemed a less than suitable choice. The two had nothing in common but youth.

He asked her, 'Still praying?'

'Not really. I didn't hear you come.'

'Your husband's at the hotel.'

'Oh,' she said flatly, looking up at the saint who had disappointed her.

'He's been reading a diary you left in your room. You oughtn't to have written what you did – "Spent the night with Q."'

'It was true, wasn't it? Besides I put in an exclamation mark to show.'

'Show what?'

'That it wasn't serious. The nuns never minded if you put an exclamation mark. "Mother Superior in a tearing rage!" They always called it the "exaggeration mark".'

'I don't think your husband knows the convent code.'

'So he really believes . . . ?' she asked and giggled.

'I've tried to persuade him otherwise.'

'It seems such a waste, doesn't it, if he believes that. We might just as well have really done it. Where are you going now?'

'I'm driving home.'

'I'd come with you if you liked. Only I know you don't like.'

He looked up at the plaster face with its simpering and holy smile. 'What would she say?'

'I don't consult her about everything. Only in *extremis*. Though this is pretty *extremis* now, I suppose, isn't it? What with this and that. Have I got to tell him about the baby?'

'It would be better to tell him before he finds out.'

'And I prayed to her so hard for happiness,' she said disdainfully. 'What a hope. Do you believe in prayer at all?'

'No.'

'Did you never?'

'I suppose I believed once. When I believed in giants.'

He looked around the church, at the altar, the tabernacle, the brass candles, and the European saints, pale like albinos in the dark continent. He could detect in himself a dim nostalgia for the past, but everyone always felt that, he supposed, in middle age, even for a past of pain, when pain was associated with youth. If there were a place called Pendélé, he thought, I would never bother to find my way back.

'You think I've been wasting my time, don't you, praying?'

'It was better than lying on your bed brooding.'

'You don't believe in prayer at all – or in God?'

'No.' He said gently, 'Of course, I may be wrong.'

'And Rycker does,' she said, calling him by his surname as though he were no longer her husband. 'I wish it wasn't always the wrong people who believed.'

'Surely the nuns . . .'

'Oh, they are professionals. They believe in anything. Even the Holy House of Loretto. They ask us to believe too much and then we believe less and less.' Perhaps she was talking in order to postpone the moment of return. She said, 'Once I got into trouble drawing a picture of the Holy House in full flight with jet-engines. How much did you believe – when you believed?'

'I suppose, like the boy in the story I told you, I persuaded myself to believe almost everything with arguments. You can brainwash yourself into anything you want – even into marriage or a vocation. Then the years pass and the marriage or the vocation fails and it's better to get out. It's the same with belief. People hang on to a marriage for fear of a lonely old age or to a vocation for fear of poverty. It's not a good reason. And it's not a good reason to hang on to the Church for the sake of some mumbo-jumbo when you come to die.'

'And what about the mumbo-jumbo of birth?' she asked. 'If there's a baby inside me now, I'll have to have it christened, won't I? I'm not sure that I'd be happy if it wasn't. Is that dishonest. If only it hadn't *him* for a father.'

'Of course it isn't dishonest. You mustn't think your marriage has failed yet.'

'Oh but it has.'

'I didn't mean with Rycker, I meant . . .' He said sharply, 'For God's sake, don't you start taking me for an example, too.'

CHAPTER 3

I

The rather sweet champagne was the best that Querry had been able to find in Luc, and it had not been improved by the three-day drive in the truck and a breakdown at the first ferry. The nuns provided tinned pea-soup, four lean roast chickens, and an ambiguous sweet omelette which they had made with guava jelly: the omelette had sat down halfway between their house and the fathers'. But on this day, when the ceremony of raising the roof-tree was over at last, no one felt in a mood to criticize. An awning had been set up outside the dispensary, and at long trestle tables the priests and nuns had provided a feast for the lepers who had worked on the hospital and their families, official and unofficial; beer was there for the men and fizzy fruit drinks and buns for the women and children. The nuns' own celebration had been prepared in strict privacy, but it was rumoured to consist mainly of extra strong coffee and some boxes of *petits fours* that had been kept in reserve since the previous Christmas and had probably turned musty in the interval.

Before the feast there was a service. Father Thomas traipsed round the new hospital, supported by Father Joseph and Father Paul, sprinkling the walls with holy water, and several hymns were sung in the Mongo language. There had been prayers and a sermon from Father Thomas which went on far too long – he had not yet learned enough of the native tongue to make himself properly understood. Some of the younger lepers grew impatient and wandered away, and a child was found by Brother Philippe arrosing the new walls with his own form of water.

Nobody cared that a small dissident group who had nothing

to do with the local tribe sang their own hymns apart. Only the doctor, who had once worked in the Lower Congo, recognized them for what they were, trouble-makers from the coast more than a thousand kilometres away. It was unlikely that any of the lepers could understand them, so he let them be. The only sign of their long journey by path and water and road was an unfamiliar stack of bicycles up a side-path into the bush which he had happened to take that morning.

> *'E ku Kinshasa ka bazeyi ko:*
> *E ku Luozi ka bazeyi ko. . .'*

> 'In Kinshasa they know nothing:
> In Luozi they know nothing.'

The proud song of superiority went on: superiority to their own people, to the white man, to the Christian god, to everyone beyond their own circle of six, all of them wearing the peaked caps that advertised Polo beer.

> 'In the Upper Congo they know nothing:
> In heaven they know nothing:
> Those who revile the Spirit know nothing:
> The Chiefs know nothing.
> The whites know nothing.'

Nzambi had never been humiliated as a criminal: he was an exclusive god. Only Deo Gratias moved some way towards them; he squatted on the ground between them and the hospital, and the doctor remembered that as a child he had come west from the Lower Congo too.

'Is that the future?' Querry said. He couldn't understand the words, only the aggressive slant of the Polo-beer caps.

'Yes.'

'Do you fear it?'

'Of course. But I don't want my own liberty at the expense of anyone else's.'

'They do.'

'We taught them.'

What with one delay and another it was nearly sunset before the tree was raised on to the roof and the feast began. By that time the awning outside the dispensary was no longer needed to shelter the workmen from the heat, but judging from the black clouds massing beyond the river, Father Joseph decided that it might yet serve to protect them from the rain.

Father Thomas's decision to raise the roof-tree had not been made without argument. Father Joseph wished to wait a month in the hope that the Superior would return, and Father Paul had at first supported him, but when Doctor Colin agreed with Father Thomas they had withdrawn their opposition. 'Let Father Thomas have his feast and his hymns,' the doctor said to them. 'I want the hospital.'

Doctor Colin and Querry left the group from the east and turned back to the last of the ceremony. 'We were right, but all the same,' the doctor said, 'I wish the Superior were here. He would have enjoyed the show and at least he would have talked to these people in a language they can understand.'

'More briefly too,' Querry said. The hollow African voices rose around them in another hymn.

'And yet you stay and watch,' the doctor said.

'Oh yes, I stay.'

'I wonder why.'

'Ancestral voices. Memories. Did you ever lie awake when you were a child listening to them talking down below? You couldn't understand what they were saying, but it was a noise that somehow comforted. So it is now with me. I am happy listening, saying nothing. The house is not on fire, there's no burglar lurking in the next room: I don't want to understand or believe. I would have to think if I believed. I don't want to think any more. I can build you all the rabbit-hutches you need without thought.'

Afterwards at the mission there was a great deal of raillery over the champagne. Father Paul was caught pouring himself a glass out of turn; somebody – Brother Philippe seemed an unlikely culprit – filled an empty bottle with soda-water, and the bottle had circulated half around the table before anyone noticed. Querry remembered an occasion months ago: a night at a seminary on the river when the priests cheated over their cards. He had walked out into the bush unable to bear their laughter and their infantility. How was it that he could sit here now and smile with them? He even found himself resenting the strict face of Father Thomas who sat at the end of the table unamused.

The doctor proposed the toast of Father Joseph and Father Joseph proposed the toast of the doctor. Father Paul proposed the toast of Brother Philippe, and Brother Philippe lapsed into confusion and silence. Father Jean proposed the toast of Father Thomas who did not respond. The champagne had almost reached an end, but someone disinterred from the back of the cupboard a half-finished bottle of Sandeman's port and they drank it out of liqueur glasses to make it go further. 'After all the English drink port at the end of a meal,' Father Jean said. 'An extraordinary custom, Protestant perhaps, but nevertheless . . .'

'Are you sure there's nothing against it in moral theology?' Father Paul asked.

'Only in canon law. *Lex contra Sandemanium*, but even that, of course, was interpreted by that eminent Benedictine, Dom . . .'

'Father Thomas, won't you have a glass of port?'

'No thank you, father. I have drunk enough.'

The darkness outside the open door suddenly drew back and for a moment they could see the palm trees bending in a strange yellow light the colour of old photographs. Then everything went dark again, and the wind blew in, rustling the pages of Father Jean's film magazines. Querry got up to close it against the coming storm, but on a second thought he stepped outside and shut it behind him. The northern sky lightened again, in a long band above the river. From where the lepers were celebrating came the sound of drums and the thunder answered like the reply of a relieving force. Somebody moved on the veranda. When the lightning flashed he saw that it was Deo Gratias.

'Why aren't you at the feast, Deo Gratias?' Then he remembered that the feast was only for the non-mutilated, for the masons and carpenters and bricklayers. He said, 'Well, they've done a good job on the hospital.' The man made no reply. Querry said, 'You aren't planning to run away again, are you?' and he lit a cigarette and put it between the man's lips.

'No,' Deo Gratias said.

In the darkness Querry felt himself prodded by the man's stump. He said, 'What's troubling you, Deo Gratias?'

'You will go,' Deo Gratias said, 'now that the hospital house is built.'

'Oh no, I won't. This is where I'm going to end my days. I can't go back to where I came from, Deo Gratias. I don't belong there any more.'

'Have you killed a man?'

'I have killed everything.' The thunder came nearer, and then the rain: first it was like skirmishers rustling furtively among the palm-tree fans, creeping through the grass; then it was the confident tread of a great watery host beating a way from across the river to sweep up the veranda steps. The drums of the lepers were extinguished; even the thunder could be heard only faintly behind the great charge of rain.

Deo Gratias hobbled closer. 'I want to go with you,' he said.

'I tell you I'm staying here. Why won't you believe me? For the rest of my life. I shall be buried here.'

Perhaps he had not made himself heard through the rain, for Deo Gratias repeated, 'I will go with you.' Somewhere a telephone began to ring – a trivial human sound persisting like an infant's cry through the rain.

II

After Querry had left the room Father Thomas said, 'We seem to have toasted everyone except the man to whom we owe most.'

Father Joseph said, 'He knows well enough how grateful we are. Those toasts were not very seriously meant, Father Thomas.'

'I think I ought to express the gratitude of the community, formally, when he comes back.'

'You'll only embarrass him,' Doctor Colin said. 'All he wants of any of us is to be left alone.' The rain pounded on the roof; Brother Philippe began to light candles on the dresser in case the electric current failed.

'It was a happy day for all of us when he arrived here,' Father Thomas said. 'Who could have foreseen it? The great Querry.'

'An even happier day for him,' the doctor replied. 'It's much more difficult to cure the mind than the body, and yet I think the cure is nearly complete.'

'The better the man the worse the aridity,' Father Thomas said.

Father Joseph looked guiltily at his champagne and then at his companions; Father Thomas made them all feel as though they were drinking in church. 'A man with little faith doesn't feel the temporary loss of it.' His sentiments were impeccable. Father Paul winked at Father Jean.

'Surely,' the doctor said, 'you assume too much. His case may be much simpler than that. A man can believe for half his life on insufficient reason, and then he discovers his mistake.'

'You talk, doctor, like all atheists, as though there were no such thing as grace. Belief without grace is unthinkable, and God will never rob a man of grace. Only a man himself can do that – by his own actions. We have seen Querry's actions here, and they speak for themselves.'

'I hope you won't be disappointed,' the doctor said. 'In our treatment we get burnt-out cases, too. But we don't say they are suffering from aridity. We only say the disease has run its course.'

'You are a very good doctor, but all the same I think we are better judges of a man's spiritual condition.'

'I dare say you are – if such a thing exists.'

'You can detect a patch on the skin where we see nothing at all. You must allow us to have a nose for – well . . .' Father Thomas hesitated and then said '. . . heroic virtue.' Their voices were raised a little against the storm. The telephone began to ring.

Doctor Colin said, 'That's probably the hospital. I'm expecting a death tonight.' He went to the sideboard where the telephone stood and lifted the receiver. He said, 'Who is it? Is that Sister Clare?' He said to Father Thomas, 'It must be one of your sisters. Will you take it? I can't hear what she is saying.'

'Perhaps they have got at our champagne,' Father Joseph said.

Doctor Colin surrendered the receiver to Father Thomas and came back to the table. 'She sounded agitated, whoever she was,' he said.

'Please speak more slowly,' Father Thomas said. 'Who is it? Sister Hélène? I can't hear you – the storm is too loud. Say that again. I don't understand.'

'It's lucky for us all,' Father Joseph said, 'that the sisters don't have a feast every day of the week.'

Father Thomas turned furiously from the telephone. He said, 'Be quiet, father. I can't hear if you talk. This is no joke. A terrible thing seems to have happened.'

'Is somebody ill?' the doctor asked.

'Tell Mother Agnes,' Father Thomas said, 'that I'll be over as soon as I can. I had better find him and bring him with me.' He put the receiver down and stood bent like a question-mark over the telephone.

'What is it, father?' the doctor said. 'Can I be of use?'

'Does anyone know where Querry's gone?'

'He went outside a few minutes ago.'

'How I wish the Superior were here.' They looked at Father Thomas with astonishment. He could not have given a more extreme signal of distress.

'You had better tell us what it's all about,' Father Paul said.

Father Thomas said, 'I envy you your skin-test, doctor. You were right to warn me against disappointment. The Superior too. He said much the same thing as you. I have trusted too much to appearances.'

'Has Querry done something?'

'God forbid one should condemn any man without hearing all the facts . . .'

The door opened and Querry entered. The rain splashed in behind him and he had to struggle with the door. He said, 'The gauge outside shows nearly half a centimetre already.'

Nobody spoke. Father Thomas came a little way towards him.

'M. Querry, is it true that when you went into Luc you went with Mme Rycker?'

'I drove her in. Yes.'

'Using *our* truck?'

'Of course.'

'While her husband was sick?'

'Yes.'

'What is this all about?' Father Joseph asked.

'Ask M. Querry,' Father Thomas replied.

'Ask me what?'

Father Thomas drew on his rubber boots and fetched his umbrella from the coat-rack.

'What am I supposed to have done?' Querry said and he looked first to Father Joseph and then to Father Paul. Father Paul made a gesture with his hand of non-comprehension.

'You had better tell us what is going on, father,' Doctor Colin said.

'I must ask you to come with me, M. Querry. We will discuss what has to be done next with the sisters. I had hoped against hope that there was some mistake. I even wish you had tried to lie. It would have been less brazen. I don't want you found here by Rycker if he should arrive.'

'What would Rycker want here?' Father Jean said.

'He might be expected to want his wife, mightn't he? She's with the sisters now. She arrived half an hour ago. After three days by herself on the road. She is with child,' Father Thomas said. The telephone began to ring again. 'Your child.'

Querry said, 'That's nonsense. She can't have told anyone that.'

'Poor girl. I suppose she hadn't the nerve to tell him to his face. She came from Luc to find you.'

The telephone rang again.

'It seems to be my turn to answer it,' Father Joseph said, approaching the telephone with trepidation.

'We gave you a warm welcome here, didn't we? We asked you no questions. We didn't pry into your past. And in return you present us with this – scandal. Weren't there enough women for you in Europe?' Father Thomas said. 'Did you have to make our little community here a base for your operations?' Suddenly he was again the nervy and despairing priest who couldn't sleep and was afraid of the dark. He began to weep, clinging to his umbrella as an African might cling to a totem-pole. He looked as though he had been left out all night like a scarecrow.

'Hullo, hullo,' Father Joseph called into the telephone. 'In the name of all the known saints, can't you speak up, whoever you are?'

'I'll go and see her with you right away,' Querry said.

'It's your right,' Father Thomas said. 'She's in no condition to argue, though. She's had nothing but a packet of chocolate to eat the last three days. She hadn't even a boy with her when she arrived. If only the Superior . . . Mme Rycker of all people. Such kindness to the mission. For God's sake, what is it now, Father Joseph?'

'It's only the hospital,' Father Joseph said with relief. He gave the receiver to Doctor Colin. 'It is the death I was expecting,' the doctor said. 'Thank goodness something tonight seems to be following a normal course.'

III

Father Thomas walked silently ahead below his great umbrella. The rain had stopped for a while, but the aftermath dripped from the ribs. Father Thomas was only visible at intervals when the lightning flared. He had no torch, but he knew the path by heart in the dark. Many omelettes and soufflés had come to grief along this track. The nuns' white house was suddenly close to them in a simultaneous flash and roar – the lightning had struck a tree somewhere close by and all the lights of the mission fused at once.

One of the sisters met them at the door carrying a candle. She looked at Querry over Father Thomas's shoulder as though he were the devil himself – with fear, distaste and curiosity. She said, 'Mother's sitting with Mme Rycker.'

'We'll go in,' Father Thomas said gloomily.

She led them to a white painted room, where Marie Rycker lay in a white painted bed under a crucifix, with a night-light burning beside her. Mother Agnes sat by the bed with a hand touching Marie Rycker's cheek. Querry had the impression of a daughter who had come safely home, after a long visit to a foreign land.

Father Thomas said in an altar-whisper, 'How is she?'

'She's taken no harm,' Mother Agnes said, 'not in the body, that is.'

Marie Rycker turned in the bed and looked up at them. Her eyes had the transparent honesty of a child who has prepared a cast-iron lie. She smiled at Querry and said, 'I am sorry. I had to come. I was scared.'

Mother Agnes withdrew her hand and watched Querry closely as though she feared a violent act against her charge.

Querry said gently, 'You mustn't be frightened. It was the long journey which scared you – that's all. Now you are safe among friends you will explain, won't you . . .' He hesitated.

'Oh yes,' she whispered, 'everything.'

'They haven't understood what you told them. About our visit to Luc together. And the baby. There's going to be a baby?'

'Yes.'

'Just tell them whose baby it is.'

'I have told them,' she said. 'It's yours. Mine, too, of course,' she added, as though by adding that qualification she were making everything quite clear and beyond blame.

Father Thomas said, 'You see.'

'Why are you telling them that? You know it's not true. We have never been in each other's company except in Luc.'

'That first time,' she said, 'when my husband brought you to the house.'

It would have been easier if he had felt anger, but he felt none: to lie is as natural at a certain age as to play with fire. He said, 'You know what you are saying is all nonsense. I'm certain you don't want to do me any harm.'

'Oh no,' she said, 'never. *Je t'aime, chéri. Je suis toute à toi.*'

Mother Agnes wrinkled her nose with distaste.

'That's why I've come to you,' Marie Rycker said.

'She ought to rest now,' Mother Agnes said. 'All this can be discussed in the morning.'

'You must let me talk to her alone.'

'Certainly not,' Mother Agnes said. 'That would not be right. Father Thomas, you won't permit him . . .'

'My good woman, do you think I'm going to beat her? You can come to her rescue at her first scream.'

Father Thomas said, 'We can hardly say no if Mme Rycker wishes it.'

'Of course I wish it,' she said. 'I came here only for that.' She put her hand on Querry's sleeve. Her smile of sad and fallen trust was worthy of Bernhardt's Marguerite Gauthier on her death-bed.

When they were alone she gave a happy sigh, 'That's that.'

'Why have you told them these lies?'

'They aren't all lies,' she said. 'I do love you.'

'Since when?'

'Since I spent a night with you.'

'You know very well that was nothing at all. We drank some whisky. I told you a story to send you to sleep.'

'Yes. That was when I fell in love. No, it wasn't. I'm afraid I'm lying again,' she said with unconvincing humility. 'It was when you came to the house the first time. *Un coup de foudre.*'

'The night you told them we slept together?'

'That was really a lie too. The night I slept with you properly was after the Governor's party.'

'What on earth are you talking about now?'

'I didn't want him. The only way I could manage was to shut my eyes and think it was you.'

'I suppose I ought to thank you,' Querry said, 'for the compliment.'

'It was then that my baby must have started. So you see it wasn't a lie that I told.'

'Not a lie?'

'Only half a lie. If I hadn't thought all the time of you, I'd have been all dried up and babies don't come so easily then, do they? So in a way it is your child.'

He looked at her with a kind of respect. It would have needed a theologian to appreciate properly the tortuous logic of her argument, to separate good from bad faith, and only recently he had thought of her as someone too simple and young to be a danger. She smiled up at him winningly, as though she hoped to entice him into yet another of his stories to postpone the hour of bed. He said, 'You'd better tell me exactly what happened when you saw your husband in Luc.'

She said, 'It was ghastly. Really ghastly. I thought once he was going to kill me. He wouldn't believe about the diary. He went on and on all that night until I was tired out and I said, "All right. Have it your own way then. I did sleep with him. Here and there and everywhere." Then he hit me. He would have hit me again, I think, if M. Parkinson hadn't interfered.'

'Was Parkinson there too, then?'

'He heard me cry and came along.'

'To take some photographs, I suppose.'

'I don't think he took any photographs.'

'And then what happened?'

'Well, of course, he found out about things in general. You see, he wanted to go home right away, and I said no, I had to stay in Luc until I knew. "Know?" he said. And then it all came out. I went and saw the doctor in the morning and when I knew the worst I just took off without going back to the hotel.'

'Rycker thinks the baby is mine?'

'I tried very hard to convince him it was his – because, of course, you could say in a way that it was.' She stretched herself down in the bed with a sigh of comfort and said, 'Goodness, I'm glad to be here. It was really scary driving all the way alone. I didn't wait in the house to get any food and I forgot a bed and I just slept in the car.'

'In his car?'

'Yes. But I expect M. Parkinson will have given him a lift home.'

'Is it any use asking you to tell Father Thomas the truth?'

'Well, I've rather burned my boats, haven't I?'

'You've burned the only home I have,' Querry said.

'I just had to escape,' she explained apologetically. For the first time he was confronted by an egoism as absolute as his own. The other Marie had been properly avenged: as for *toute à toi* the laugh was on her side now.

'What do you expect me to do?' Querry said. 'Love you in return?'

'It would be nice if you could, but, if you can't, they'll have to send me home, won't they?'

He went to the door and opened it. Mother Agnes was lurking at the end of the passage. He said, 'I've done all I can.'

'I suppose you've tried to persuade the poor girl to protect you.'

'Oh, she admits the lie to me, of course, but I have no tape-recorder. What a pity the Church doesn't approve of hidden microphones.'

'May I ask you, M. Querry, from now on to stay away from our house?'

'You don't need to ask me that. Be very careful yourselves of that little packet of dynamite in there.'

'She's a poor innocent young . . .'

'Oh, innocent . . . I daresay you are right. God preserve us from all innocence. At least the guilty know what they are about.'

The electric fuses had not yet been repaired, and only the feel of the path under his feet guided him towards the mission buildings. The rain had passed to the south, but the lightning flapped occasionally above the forest and the river. Before he reached the mission he had to pass the doctor's house. An oil lamp burned behind the window and the doctor stood beside it, peering out. Querry knocked on the door.

Colin asked, 'What has happened?'

'She'll stick to her lies. They are her only way of escape.'

'Escape?'

'From Rycker and Africa.'

'Father Thomas is talking to the others now. It was no concern of mine, so I came home.'

'They want me to go away, I suppose?'

'I wish to God the Superior were here. Father Thomas is not exactly a well-balanced man.'

Querry sat down at the table. The Atlas of Leprosy was open at a gaudy page of swirling colour. He said, 'What's this?'

'We call these "the fish swimming upstream". The bacilli – those coloured spots there – are swarming along the nerves.'

'I thought I had come far enough,' Querry said, 'when I reached this place.'

'It may blow over. Let them talk. You and I have more important things to do. Now that the hospital's finished we can get down to the mobile units and the new lavatories I talked to you about.'

'We are not dealing with your sick people, doctor, and your coloured fish. They are predictable. These are normal people, healthy people with unforeseeable reactions. It looks as though I shall get no nearer to Pendélé than Deo Gratias did.'

'Father Thomas has no authority over me. You can stay in my house from now on if you don't mind sleeping in the workroom.'

'Oh no. You can't risk quarrelling with them. You are too important to this place. I shall have to go away.'

'Where will you go to?'

'I don't know. It's strange, isn't it, how worried I was when I came here, because I thought I had become incapable of feeling pain. I suppose a priest I met on the river was right. He said one only had to wait. You said the same to me too.'

'I'm sorry.'

'I don't know that I am. You said once that when one suffers, one begins to feel part of the human condition, on the side of the Christian myth, do you remember? "I suffer, therefore I am." I wrote something like that once in my diary, but I can't remember what or when, and the word wasn't "suffer".'

'When a man is cured,' the doctor said, 'we can't afford to waste him.'

'Cured?'

'No further skin-tests are required in your case.'

IV

Father Joseph absent-mindedly wiped a knife with the skirt of his soutane; he said, 'We mustn't forget that it's only her word against his.'

'Why should she invent such a shocking story like that?' Father Thomas asked. 'In any case the baby is presumably real enough.'

'Querry has been of great use to us here,' Father Paul said. 'We've reason to be grateful . . .'

'Grateful? Can you really think that, father, after he's made us a laughing stock? The Hermit of the Congo. The Saint with a Past. All those stories the papers printed. What will they print now?'

'You were more pleased with the stories than he was,' Father Jean said.

'Of course I was pleased. I believed in him. I thought his motives for coming here were good. I even defended him to the Superior when he warned me . . . But I hadn't realized then what his true motives were.'

'If you know them tell us what they were,' Father Jean said. He spoke in the dry precise tones that he was accustomed to use in discussions on moral theology so as to rob of emotion any question dealing with sexual sin.

'I can only suppose he was flying from some woman-trouble in Europe.'

'Woman-trouble is not a very exact description, and aren't we all supposed to run away from it? St Augustine's wish to wait awhile is not universally recommended.'

'Querry is a very good builder,' Father Joseph said obstinately.

'What do you propose then, that he should stay here in the mission, living in sin with Mme Rycker?'

'Of course not,' Father Jean said. 'Mme Rycker must leave tomorrow. From what you have told us he has no wish to go with her.'

'The matter will not end there,' Father Thomas said. 'Rycker will want a separation. He may even sue Querry for divorce, and the newspapers will print the whole edifying story. They are interested enough as it is in Querry. Do you suppose the General will be pleased when he reads at his breakfast-table the scandal at our leproserie?'

'The roof-tree is safely up,' Father Joseph said, rubbing away at his knife, 'but a great deal still remains to be done.'

'There is no possible harm in simply waiting.' Father Paul said. 'The girl may be lying. Rycker may take no action. The newspapers may print nothing (it's not the picture of Querry they wanted to give the world). The story may not even reach the General's ears – or eyes.'

'Do you suppose the Bishop won't hear of it? It will be all over Luc by this time. In the absence of the Superior I am responsible . . .'

Brother Philippe spoke for the first time. 'There's a man outside,' he said. 'Had I better unlock the door?'

It was Parkinson, sodden and speechless. He had been walking very fast. He ran his hand back and forth over his heart as though he were trying to soothe an animal that he carried like a Spartan under his shirt.

'Give him a chair,' Father Thomas said.

'Where's Querry?' Parkinson said.

'I don't know. In his room perhaps.'

'Rycker's looking for him. He went to the sisters' house, but Querry had gone.'

'How did you know where to look?'

'She had left a note for Rycker at home. We would have caught her up, but we had car-trouble at the last ferry.'

'Where's Rycker now?'

'God knows. It's so pitch-dark out there. He may have walked into the river for all I know.'

'Did he see his wife?'

'No – an old nun pushed us both out and locked the door. That made him madder than ever, I can tell you. We haven't had six hours' sleep since Luc, and that was more than three days ago.'

He rocked backwards and forwards on the chair. 'Oh that this too too solid flesh. Quote. Shakespeare. I've got a weak heart,' he explained to Father Thomas who was finding it difficult with his inadequate English to follow the drift of Parkinson's thoughts. The others watched closely and understood little. The situation seemed to all of them to have got hopelessly out of control.

'Please give me a drink,' Parkinson said. Father Thomas found that there was a little champagne left at the bottom of one of the many bottles which still littered the table among the carcasses of the chickens and the remains of the mutilated uneaten soufflé.

'Champagne?' Parkinson exclaimed. 'I'd rather have had a spot of gin.' He looked at the glasses and the bottles: one glass still held an inch of port. He said, 'You do yourselves pretty well here.'

'It was a very special day,' Father Thomas said with some embarrassment, seeing the table for a moment with the eyes of a stranger.

'A special day – I should think it has been. I never thought we'd make the ferry, and now with this storm I suppose we may be stuck here. How I wish I'd never come to this damned dark continent. Quoth the raven nevermore. Quote. Somebody.'

Outside a voice shouted unintelligibly.

'That's him,' Parkinson said, 'roaming around. He's fighting mad. I said to him I thought Christians were supposed to forgive, but it's no use talking to him now.'

The voice came nearer. 'Querry,' they heard it cry, 'Querry. Where are you, Querry?'

'What a damned fuss about nothing. And I wouldn't be surprised if there had been no hanky-panky after all. I told him that. "They talked most of the night," I said, "I heard them. Lovers don't talk like that. There are intervals of silence."'

'Querry. Where are you, Querry?'

'I think he *wants* to believe the worst. It makes him Querry's equal, don't you see, when they fight over the same girl.' He added with a somewhat surprising insight, 'He can't bear not being important.'

The door opened yet again and a tousled, rain-soaked Rycker stood in the doorway; he looked from one father to another as though among them he expected to find Querry, perhaps in the disguise of a priest.

'M. Rycker,' Father Thomas began.

'Where's Querry?'

'Please come in and sit down and talk things . . .'

'How can I sit?' Rycker said. 'I am a man in agony.' He sat down, nonetheless, on the wrong chair – the weak back splintered. 'I'm suffering from a terrible shock, father. I opened my soul to that man, I told him my inmost thoughts, and this is my reward.'

'Let us talk quietly and sensibly . . .'

'He laughed at me and despised me,' Rycker said. 'What right had he to despise me? We are all equal in the sight of God. Even a poor plantation manager and *the* Querry. Breaking up a Christian marriage.' He smelt very strongly of whisky. He said, 'I'll be retiring in a couple of years. Does he think I'm going to keep his bastard on my pension?'

'You've been on the road for three days, Rycker. You need a night's sleep. Afterwards . . .'

'She never wanted to sleep with me. She always made her excuses, but then the first time he comes along, just because he's famous . . .'

Father Thomas said, 'We all want to avoid scandal.'

'Where's the doctor?' Rycker said sharply. 'They were as thick as thieves.'

'He's at home. He has nothing to do with this.'

Rycker made for the door. He stood there for a moment as though he were on a stage and had forgotten his exit line. 'There isn't a jury that would convict me,' he said and went out again into the dark and rain. For a moment nobody spoke and then Father Joseph asked them all, 'What did he mean by that?'

'We shall laugh at this in the morning,' Father Jean said.

'I don't see the humour of the situation,' Father Thomas replied.

'What I mean is it's a little like one of those Palais Royal farces that one has read . . . The injured husband pops in and out.'

'I don't read Palais Royal farces, father.'

'Sometimes I think God was not entirely serious when he gave man the sexual instinct.'

'If that is one of the doctrines you teach in moral theology . . .'

'Nor when he invented moral theology. After all, it was St Thomas Aquinas who said that he made the world in play.'

Brother Philippe said, 'Excuse me . . .'

'You are lucky not to have my responsibility, Father Jean. I can't treat the affair as a Palais Royal farce whatever St Thomas may have written. Where are you going, Brother Philippe?'

'He said something about a jury, father, and it occurred to me that, well, perhaps he's carrying a gun. I think I ought to warn . . .'

'This is too much,' Father Thomas said. He turned to Parkinson and asked him in English, 'Has he a gun with him?'

'I'm sure I don't know. A lot of people are carrying them nowadays, aren't they? But he wouldn't have the nerve to use it. I told you, he only wants to seem important.'

'I think, if you will excuse me, father, I had better go over to Doctor Colin's,' Brother Philippe said.

'Be careful, brother,' Father Paul said.

'Oh, I know a great deal about firearms,' Brother Philippe replied.

V

'Was that someone shouting?' Doctor Colin asked.

'I heard nothing.' Querry went to the window and looked

into the dark. He said, 'I wish Brother Philippe would get the lights back. It's time I went home, and I haven't a torch.'

'They won't start the current now. It's gone ten o'clock.'

'They'll want me to go as soon as I can, won't they? But the boat's unlikely to be here for at least a week. Perhaps someone can drive me out . . .'

'I doubt if the road will be passable now after the rain, and there's more to come.'

'Then we have a few days, haven't we, for talking about those mobile units you dream of. But I'm no engineer, doctor. Brother Philippe will be able to help you more than I could ever do.'

'This is a make-shift life we lead here,' Doctor Colin said. 'All I want is a kind of pre-fab on wheels. Something we can fit on to the chassis of a half-ton truck. What did I do with that sheet of paper? There's an idea I wanted to show you . . .' The doctor opened the drawer in his desk. Inside was the photograph of a woman. She lay there in wait, unseen by strangers, gathering no dust, always present when the drawer opened.

'I shall miss this room – wherever I am. You've never told me about your wife, doctor. How she came to die.'

'It was sleeping-sickness. She used to spend a lot of time out in the bush in the early days trying to persuade the lepers to come in for treatment. We didn't have such effective drugs for sleeping-sickness as we have now. People die too soon.'

'It was my hope to end up in the same patch of ground as you and she. We would have made an atheist corner between us.'

'I wonder if you would have qualified for that.'

'Why not?'

'You're too troubled by your lack of faith, Querry. You keep on fingering it like a sore you want to get rid of. I am content with the myth; you are not – you have to believe or disbelieve.'

Querry said, 'Somebody is calling out there. I thought for a moment it was my name . . . But one always seems to hear one's own name, whatever anyone really calls. It only needs a syllable to be the same. We are such egoists.'

'You must have had a lot of belief once to miss it the way you do.'

'I swallowed their myth whole, if you call that a belief. This is my body and this is my blood. Now when I read that passage it seems so obviously symbolic, but how can you expect a lot of poor fishermen to recognize symbols? Only in moments of superstition I remember that I gave up the sacrament before I gave up the belief and the priests would say there was a connection. Rejecting grace Rycker would say. Oh well, I suppose belief is a kind of vocation and most men haven't room in their brains or hearts for two vocations. If we really believe in something we have no choice, have we, but to go further. Otherwise life slowly whittles the belief away. My architecture stood still. One can't be a half-believer or a half-architect.'

'Are you saying that you've ceased to be even a half?'

'Perhaps I hadn't a strong enough vocation in either, and the kind of life I lived killed them both. It needs a very strong vocation to withstand success. The popular priest and the popular architect – their talents can be killed easily by disgust.'

'Disgust?'

'Disgust of praise. How it nauseates, doctor, by its stupidity. The very people who ruined my churches were loudest afterwards in their praise of what I'd built. The books they have written about my work, the pious motives they've attributed to me – they were enough to sicken me of the drawing-board. It needed more faith than I possessed to withstand all that. The praise of priests and pious people – the Ryckers of the world.'

'Most men seem to put up with success comfortably enough. But you came here.'

'I think I'm cured of pretty well everything, even disgust. I've been happy here.'

'Yes, you were learning to use your fingers pretty well, in spite of the mutilation. Only one sore seems to remain, and you rub it all the time.'

'You are wrong, doctor. Sometimes you talk like Father Thomas.'

'Querry,' a voice unmistakably called. 'Querry.'

'Rycker,' Querry said. 'He must have followed his wife here. I hope to God the sisters didn't let him in to see her. I'd better go and talk . . .'

'Let him cool off first.'

'I've got to make him see reason.'

'Then wait till morning. You can't see reason at night.'

'Querry. Querry. Where are you, Querry?'

'What a grotesque situation it is,' Querry said. 'That this should happen to me. The innocent adulterer. That's not a bad title for a comedy.' His mouth moved in the effort of a smile. 'Lend me the lamp.'

'You'd do much better to keep out of it, Querry.'

'I must do something. He's making so much noise . . . It will only add to what Father Thomas calls the scandal.'

The doctor reluctantly followed him out. The storm had come full circle and was beating up towards them again, from across the river. 'Rycker,' Querry called, holding the lamp up, 'I'm here.' Somebody came running towards them, but when he reached the area of light, they saw that it was Brother Philippe. 'Please go back into the house,' Brother Philippe said, 'and shut the door. We think that Rycker may be carrying a gun.'

'He wouldn't be mad enough to use it,' Querry said.

'All the same . . . to avoid unpleasantness. . .'

'Unpleasantness . . . you have a wonderful capacity, Brother Philippe, for understatement.'

'I don't know what you mean.'

'Never mind. I'll take your advice and hide under Doctor Colin's bed.'

He had walked a few steps back when Rycker's voice said, 'Stop. Stop where you are.' The man came unsteadily out of the dark. He said in a tone of trivial complaint, 'I've been looking everywhere for you.'

'Well, here I am.'

All three looked where Rycker's right hand was hidden in his pocket.

'I've got to talk to you, Querry.'

'Then talk, and when you've finished, I'd like a word too with you.' Silence followed. A dog barked somewhere in the leproserie. Lightning lit them all like a flash-bulb.

'I'm waiting, Rycker.'

'You – you renegade.'

'Are we here for a religious argument? I'll admit you know much more than I do about the love of God.'

Rycker's reply was partly buried under the heavy fall of the thunder. The last sentence stuck out like a pair of legs from beneath the rubble.

'. . . persuade me what she wrote meant nothing, and all the time you must have known there was a child coming.'

'Your child. Not mine.'

'Prove it. You'd better prove it.'

'It's difficult to prove a negative, Rycker. Of course, the doctor can make a test of my blood, but you'll have to wait six months for the . . .'

'How dare you laugh at me?'

'I'm not laughing at you, Rycker. Your wife has done us both an injury. I'd call her a liar if I thought she even knew what a lie was. She thinks the truth is anything that will protect her or send her home to her nursery.'

'You sleep with her and then you insult her. You're a coward, Querry.'

'Perhaps I am.'

'Perhaps. Perhaps. Nothing that I can say would ever anger *the* Querry, would it? He's so infernally important, how could he care what the mere manager of a palm-oil factory – I've got an immortal soul as much as you, Querry.'

'I don't make any claims to one. You can be God's important man, Rycker, for all I care. I'm not *the* Querry to anyone but you. Certainly not to myself.'

'Please come to the mission, M. Rycker,' Brother Philippe pleaded. 'We'll put up a bed for you there. We shall all of us feel better after a night's sleep. And a cold shower in the morning,' he added, and as though to illustrate his words, a waterfall of rain suddenly descended on them. Querry made an odd awkward sound which the doctor by now had learned to interpret as a laugh, and Rycker fired twice. The lamp fell with Querry and smashed; the burning wick flared up once under the deluge of rain, lighting an open mouth and a pair of surprised eyes, and then went out.

The doctor plumped down on his knees in the mud and felt for Querry's body. Rycker's voice said, 'He laughed at me. How dare he laugh at me?' The doctor said to Brother Philippe, 'I have his head. Can you find his legs? We've got to get him inside.' He called to Rycker, 'Put down that gun, you fool, and help!'

'Not at Rycker,' Querry said. The doctor leant down closer: he could hardly hear him. He said, 'Don't speak. We are going to lift you now. You'll be all right.'

Querry said, 'Laughing at myself.'

They carried him on to the veranda and laid him down out of the rain. Rycker fetched a cushion for his head. He said, 'He shouldn't have laughed.'

'He doesn't laugh easily,' the doctor said, and again there was a noise that resembled a distorted laugh.

'Absurd,' Querry said, 'this is absurd or else . . .' but what alternative, philosophical or psychological, he had in mind they never knew.

VI

The Superior had returned a few days after the funeral, and he visited the cemetery with Doctor Colin. They had buried Querry not far from Mme Colin's grave, but with enough space left for the doctor in due course. Under the special circumstances Father Thomas had given way in the matter of the cross – only a piece of hard wood from the forest was stuck up there, carved with Querry's name and dates. Nor had there been a Catholic ceremony, though Father Joseph had said unofficially a prayer at the grave. Someone – it was probably Deo Gratias – had put an old jam-pot beside the mound filled with twigs and plants curiously twined. It looked more like an offering to Nzambe than a funeral wreath. Father Thomas would have thrown it away, but Father Joseph dissuaded him.

'It's a very ambiguous offering,' Father Thomas protested, 'for a Christian cemetery.'

'He was an ambiguous man,' Father Joseph replied.

Parkinson had procured in Luc a formal wreath which was labelled 'From three million readers of the *Post*. Nature I loved and next to Nature Art. Robert Browning.' He had photographed it for future use, but with unexpected modesty he refused to be taken beside it.

The Superior said to Colin, 'I can't help regretting that I wasn't here. I might have been able to control Rycker.'

'Something was bound to happen sooner or later,' Colin said. 'They would never have let him alone.'

'Who do you mean by "they"?'

'The fools, the interfering fools, they exist everywhere, don't they? He had been cured of all but his success; but you can't cure success, any more than I can give my *mutilés* back their fingers and toes. I return them to the town, and people look at them in the stores and watch them in the street and draw the attention of others to them as they pass. Success is like that too – a mutilation of the natural man. Are you coming my way?'

'Where are you going?'

'To the dispensary. Surely we've wasted enough time on the dead.'

'I'll come a little way with you.' The Superior felt in the pocket of his soutane for a cheroot, but there wasn't one there.

'Did you see Rycker before you left Luc?' Colin asked.

'Of course. They've made him quite comfortable at the prison. He has been to confession and he intends to go to communion every morning. He's working very hard at Garrigou-Lagrange. And of course he's quite a hero in Luc. M. Parkinson has already telegraphed an interview with him and the metropolitan journalists will soon begin to pour in. I believe M. Parkinson's article was headed "Death of a Hermit. The Saint who Failed." Of course, the result of the trial is a foregone conclusion.'

'Acquittal?'

'Naturally. *Le crime passionnel*. Everybody will have got

what they wanted – it's really quite a happy ending, isn't it? Rycker feels he has become important both to God and man. He even spoke to me about the possibility of the Belgian College at Rome and an annulment. I didn't encourage him. Mme Rycker will soon be free to go home and she will keep the child. M. Parkinson has a much better story than he had ever hoped to find. I'm glad, by the way, that Querry never read his second article.'

'You can hardly say it was a happy ending for Querry.'

'Wasn't it? Surely he always wanted to go a bit further.' The Superior added shyly, 'Do you think there was anything between him and Mme Rycker?'

'No.'

'I wondered. Judging from Parkinson's second article he would seem to have been a man with a great capacity – well – for what they call love.'

'I'm not so sure of that. Nor was he. He told me once that all his life he had only made use of women, but I think he saw himself always in the hardest possible light. I even wondered sometimes whether he suffered from a kind of frigidity. Like a woman who changes partners constantly in the hope that one day she will experience the true orgasm. He said that he always went through the motions of love efficiently, even towards God in the days when he believed, but then he found that the love wasn't really there for anything except his work, so in the end he gave up the motions. And afterwards, when he couldn't even pretend that what he felt was love, the motives for work failed him. That was like the crisis of a sickness – when the patient has no more interest in life at all. It is then that some people sometimes kill themselves, but he was tough, very tough.'

'You spoke just now as though he had been cured.'

'I really think he was. He'd learned to serve other people, you see, and to laugh. An odd laugh, but it was a laugh all the same. I'm frightened of people who don't laugh.'

The Superior said shyly, 'I thought perhaps you meant that he was beginning to find his faith again.'

'Oh no, not that. Only a reason for living. You try too hard to make a pattern, father.'

'But if the pattern's there . . . you haven't a cheroot have you?'

'No.'

The Superior said, 'We all analyse motives too much. I said that once to Father Thomas. You remember what Pascal said, that a man who starts looking for God has already found him. The same may be true of love – when we look for it, perhaps we've already found it.'

'He was inclined – I only know what he told me himself – to confine his search to a woman's bed.'

'It's not so bad a place to look for it. There are a lot of people who only find hate there.'

'Like Rycker?'

'We don't know enough about Rycker to condemn him.'

'How persistent you are, father. You never let anyone go, do you? You'd like to claim even Querry for your own.'

'I haven't noticed that you relax much before a patient dies.'

They had reached the dispensary. The lepers sat on the hot cement steps waiting for something to happen. At the new hospital the ladders leant against the roof, and the last work was in progress. The roof-tree had been battered and bent by the storm, but it was held in place still by its strong palm-fibre thongs.

'I see from the accounts,' the Superior said, 'that you've given up using vitamin tablets. Is that a wise economy?'

'I don't believe the anaemia comes from the D.D.S. treatment. It comes from hookworm. It's cheaper to build lavatories than to buy vitamin tablets. That's our next project. I mean it was to have been. How many patients have turned up today?' he asked the dispenser.

'About sixty.'

'Your god must feel a bit disappointed,' Doctor Colin said, 'when he looks at this world of his.'

'When you were a boy they can't have taught you theology very well. God cannot feel disappointment or pain.'

'Perhaps that's why I don't care to believe in him.'

The doctor sat down at the table and drew forward a blank chart. 'Number one,' he called.

It was a child of three, quite naked, with a little pot-belly and a dangling tassel and a finger stuck in the corner of his mouth. The doctor ran his fingers over the skin on the back while the child's mother waited.

'I know that little fellow,' the Superior said. 'He always came to me for sweets.'

'He's infected all right,' Doctor Colin said. 'Feel the patches here and here. But you needn't worry,' he added in a tone of suppressed rage, 'we shall be able to cure him in a year or two, and I can promise you that there will be no mutilations.'

THE HISTORY OF VINTAGE

The famous American publisher Alfred A. Knopf (1892–1984) founded Vintage Books in the United States in 1954 as a paperback home for the authors published by his company. Vintage was launched in the United Kingdom in 1990 and works independently from the American imprint although both are part of the international publishing group, Random House.

Vintage in the United Kingdom was initially created to publish paperback editions of books acquired by the prestigious hardback imprints in the Random House Group such as Jonathan Cape, Chatto & Windus, Hutchinson and later William Heinemann, Secker & Warburg and The Harvill Press. There are many Booker and Nobel Prize-winning authors on the Vintage list and the imprint publishes a huge variety of fiction and non-fiction. Over the years Vintage has expanded and the list now includes great authors of the past – who are published under the Vintage Classics imprint – as well as many of the most influential authors of the present.

For a full list of the books Vintage publishes, please visit our website
www.vintage-books.co.uk

For book details and other information about the classic authors we publish, please visit the Vintage Classics website
www.vintage-classics.info